MY LADY LUDLOW

MRS GASKELL

MY LADY LUDLOW

ALAN SUTTON
1985

Alan Sutton Publishing Limited
30 Brunswick Road
Gloucester GL1 1JJ

Copyright © in this edition 1985
Alan Sutton Publishing Limited

British Library Cataloguing in Publication Data

Gaskell, Elizabeth
  My Lady Ludlow.
  I. Title
  823'.8[F]   PR4710.M9

  ISBN 0-86299-248-6

Cover picture: detail from The Wife's Remonstrance *by James Campbell.*
Birmingham Museum and Art Gallery

Typesetting and origination by
Alan Sutton Publishing Limited.
Photoset Bembo 9/10
Printed in Great Britain
by The Guernsey Press Company Limited,
Guernsey, Channel Islands.

BIOGRAPHICAL NOTE

MRS GASKELL (1810–65) was first and foremost a woman of her time, a lady of Victorian expansiveness. She was not a brilliant, nor a passionate novelist like George Eliot or Charlotte Brontë, but an intelligent, compassionate and enthusiastic woman, whose life centred around her family. At the same time she mixed in a variety of social circles, travelled widely in England and Europe, and wrote graphic, lively and rambling letters to her many acquaintances. Her greatest claim to fame today is perhaps her biography of Charlotte Brontë, but she also wrote several memorable novels, including *Mary Barton*, *Cranford*, *Ruth* and *Sylvia's Lovers*. The present volume provides an example of her many shorter stories, first published in serial form.

Elizabeth Cleghorn Stevenson was born on 29 September 1810, in Chelsea. She was the eighth child of William Stevenson, a Scot, and his English wife, Elizabeth Holland. Stevenson had been a Unitarian minister, an unsuccessful farmer, and finally Keeper of the Treasury Records. Mrs Stevenson, related to the Wedgwoods, the Darwins and the Turners, died thirteen months after the birth of Elizabeth, who was sent up to the Cheshire home of the Hollands to live with her Aunt, Hannah Lumb, at Knutsford. Her father remarried, but Elizabeth's home was in Cheshire, and she recalled later:

> Long ago I lived in Chelsea occasionally with my father and step-mother, and *very*, *very* unhappy I used to be; and if it had not been for the beautiful, grand river, which was an inexplicable comfort to me, and a family by the name of Kennett, I think my child's heart would have broken. (From an undated letter to Mary Howitt.)

On the whole, however, her childhood was not unhappy,

and she speaks enthusiastically of her school days in Stratford-on-Avon: 'I am unwilling to leave even in thought the haunts of such happy days as my schooldays were.' She attended Avonbank School, run by the Misses Byerley, probably from 1821–6, and received the traditional education in arts and the classics, decorum and propriety, suitable for young ladies of the day. Her aunts gave her the classics to read, and her father, himself a technical writer, with a keen interest in the literary world, encouraged her in her studies and personal writing. Her brother, John, provided an important early link with London publishers – he had hoped to become an author – and sent Elizabeth modern books to read, as well as vivid descriptions of life at sea, and in exotic countries when he travelled in India, where he tragically disappeared in 1828.

After she left school, at sixteen, Elizabeth appears to have spent time in London, with her Holland cousins, and her father, who died in 1829; in Newcastle, staying with the eminent Unitarian minister, William Turner, and in Edinburgh, where she was apparently sent during the cholera outbreak of 1831. It was at this time that her portrait was painted in miniature by the Edinburgh painter, Joseph Thomson, and a bust sculpted by David Dunbar, both works revealing a young woman of classical good looks. The attractiveness of both her appearance and her personality are borne out by a later description of her by Susanna Winkworth:

She was a noble-looking woman, with a queenly presence, and her high, broad, serene brow, and finely-cut mobile features, were lighted up by a constantly-varying play of expression as she poured forth her wonderful talk. It was like the ripple and rush of a clear deep stream in sunshine.

Later in 1831, Elizabeth, then staying with friends in Manchester, first met William Gaskell, a Unitarian minister, five years older than her. The following year they were married, and after a honeymoon in North Wales, always a favourite place, they established a home at 14 Dover Street, Manchester. There Elizabeth Gaskell became a conscientious minister's wife, and a mother. She had five children, four girls and a boy. Unfortunately the boy died at twelve months.

Literature was never totally excluded from Elizabeth's life. In 1836 she wrote of studying Crabbe, Dryden, Pope, Coleridge and Wordsworth. In 1837, she wrote *Sketches Among the Poor, No. 1* for *Blackwood's Magazine*, hoping to catch some of the 'poetry of the humble life'. But it was not until after the death of baby William, in 1845, that, with the encouragement of her husband, who, himself, taught English, she started writing seriously. Three short stories were published by William and Mary Howitt in *Howitt's Journal* in 1847–8, and *Mary Barton* was completed in 1847, and finally published on the recommendation of John Forster, friend of Dickens, by Chapman and Hall in 1849. It was a controversial novel showing a realistic picture of those experiencing first hand the effects of the industrial revolution, and it established Mrs Gaskell in the literary world. She must have possessed admirable energy and determination since from then until her death she was invariably involved in some literary work, in spite of the emotional and physical demands of a growing family and the social problems of industrial Manchester. Her output of short stories was prolific. She wrote for *The Ladies Companion*, including *Mr Harrison's Confession*, 1851; *Harper's Magazine*, including *The Doom of the Griffiths*, 1858; *The Cornhill Magazine* and other periodicals. Most of all she wrote for Dickens' magazines: *Household Words* and *All the Year Round*. She was his 'dear Scheherazade'. Stories which appeared for the first time in *Household Words* include *An Accursed Race*, *Half a Life Time Ago* and *The Poor Clare*, all in 1855, and also *Cranford*, told first in serial form between December 1851 and May 1853, and *North and South*, completed in 1855.

With her lively personality and enquiring mind, Mrs Gaskell could well have become a more active member of the literary world of her day. She visited London in 1849, meeting Dickens, Samuel Rogers, John Forster and Monckton Milnes among others. She was, however, essentially a home-loving family woman of high moral principals. Aware of her many-faceted personality, she wrote in 1850 of the effect of a new home in Plymouth Grove, to her sister-in-law:

And we've got a house. Yes! we *really* have. And if I had neither conscience nor prudence I should be delighted, for it

certainly *is* a beauty. . . . You *must* come and see us in
it . . . and try and make me see . . . that it is right to spend
so much ourselves on *so* purely selfish a thing as a house is,
while so many are wanting – that's the haunting thought to
me; at least to one of my 'Mes', for I have a great number,
and that's the plague. One of my mes is, I do believe, a true
Christian – (only people call her socialist and communist),
another of my mes is a wife and mother, and highly
delighted at the delight of everyone in the house . . . Now
that's my social self I suppose. Then again I've got another
self with a full taste for beauty and convenience who is
pleased on its own account. How am I to reconcile all these
warring members? I try to drown myself (my *first* self) by
saying it's Wm who is to decide on all these things, and his
feeling it right ought to be my rule. And so it is – only that
does not quite do.

And she concludes in another letter:

Well, I must try and make the house give as much pleasure
to others as I can and make it as little a selfish thing as I
can . . .

Plymouth Grove developed into a smallholding, with ducks,
bantams, pigs and a cow, as well as an extensive garden,
where Mrs Gaskell liked to work.

Running such a home and fulfilling her social
commitments, educating her daughters and travelling abroad
required a reasonable income, and Mrs Gaskell needed all the
money her writing earned. In 1853 *Ruth* was published,
another morally controversial work about a fallen woman,
and at the end of the year, after a holiday in Normandy, she
first visited Charlotte Brontë at Howarth. The biography of
Charlotte appeared eighteen months after her death, in March,
1857. Mrs Gaskell and her daughters were on holiday in Italy,
but they came home to a 'Hornet's nest' of bad feeling,
because Mrs Gaskell had felt obliged to disclose certain
'painful truths'. The following years were difficult ones as the
minister's wife supported her daughters through emotional
and religious traumas. As she entered her fifties she was as

ROUND THE SOFA

INTRODUCTION TO MY LADY LUDLOW

Long ago I was placed by my parents under the medical treatment of a certain Mr. Dawson, a surgeon in Edinburgh, who had obtained a reputation for the cure of a particular class of diseases. I was sent with my governess into lodgings near his house, in the Old Town. I was to combine lessons from the excellent Edinburgh masters, with the medicines and exercises needed for my indisposition. It was at first rather dreary to leave my brothers and sisters, and to give up our merry out-of-doors life with our country home, for dull lodgings, with only poor grave Miss Duncan for a companion; and to exchange our romps in the garden and rambles through the fields for stiff walks in the streets, the decorum of which obliged me to tie my bonnet-strings neatly, and put on my shawl with some regard to straightness.

The evenings were the worst. It was autumn, and of course they daily grew longer; they were long enough, I am sure, when we first settled down in those grey and drab lodgings. For, you must know, my father and mother were not rich, and there were a great many of us, and the medical expenses to be incurred by my being placed under Mr. Dawson's care were expected to be considerable; therefore, one great point in our search after lodgings was economy. My father, who was too true a gentleman to feel false shame, had named this necessity for cheapness to Mr. Dawson; and in return, Mr. Dawson had told him of those at No. 6 Cromer Street, in which we were finally settled. The house belonged to an old man, at one time a tutor to young men preparing for the University, in which capacity he had become known to Mr. Dawson. But his pupils had dropped off; and, when we went to lodge with him, I imagine that his principal support was

1

derived from a few occasional lessons which he gave, and from letting the rooms that we took, a drawing-room opening into a bedroom, out of which a smaller chamber led. His daughter was his housekeeper: a son, whom we never saw, was supposed to be leading the same life that his father had done before him, only we never saw or heard of any pupils; and there was one hard-working, honest little Scottish maiden, square, stumpy, neat, and plain, who might have been any age from eighteen to forty.

Looking back on the household now, there was perhaps much to admire in their quiet endurance of decent poverty; but, at this time, this poverty grated against many of my tastes, for I could not recognise the fact, that in a town the simple graces of fresh flowers, clean white muslin curtains, pretty bright chintzes, all cost money, which is saved by the adoption of dust-coloured moreen, and mud-coloured carpets. There was not a penny spent on mere elegance in that room; yet there was everything considered necessary to comfort: but after all, such mere pretences of comfort! a hard, slippery, black horsehair sofa, which was no place of rest; an old piano, serving as a sideboard; a grate, narrowed by an inner supplement, till it hardly held a handful of the small coal which could scarcely ever be stirred up into a genial blaze. But there were two evils worse than even this coldness and bareness of the rooms: one was that we were provided with a latch-key, which allowed us to open the front door whenever we came home from a walk, and go upstairs without meeting any face of welcome, or hearing the sound of a human voice in the apparently deserted house – Mr. Mackenzie piqued himself on the noiselessness of his establishment; and the other, which might almost seem to neutralise the first, was the danger we were always exposed to on going out, of the old man – sly, miserly, and intelligent – popping out upon us from his room, close to the left hand of the door, with some civility which we learned to distrust as a mere pretext for extorting more money, yet which it was difficult to refuse: such as the offer of any books out of his library, a great temptation, for we could see into the shelf-lined room; but, just as we were on the point of yielding, there was a hint of the 'consideration' to be expected for the loan of books of so much higher a class than any to be obtained at the circulating library, which made us suddenly draw back. Another time he came out of his den to offer us written cards, to distribute among our acquaintance, on which he undertook to teach the very things I was to learn; but I would rather have been the most ignorant woman that ever lived than tried to learn anything from that old fox in breeches. When we had declined all his proposals, he went apparently into dudgeon. Once, when we had forgotten our latch-key, we rang in vain for many times at the door, seeing our landlord standing all the time at the window to the right, looking out of it in an absent and philosophical state of mind, from which no signs and gestures of ours could arouse him.

The women of the household were far better, and more really respectable, though even on them poverty had laid her heavy left hand, instead of her blessing right. Miss Mackenzie kept us as short in our food as she decently could – we paid so much a week for our board, be it observed; and if one day we had less appetite than another our meals were docked to the smaller standard, until Miss Duncan ventured to remonstrate. The sturdy maid-of-all-work was scrupulously honest, but looked discontented, and scarcely vouchsafed us thanks, when on leaving we gave her what Mrs. Dawson had told us would be considered handsome in most lodgings. I do not believe Phenice ever received wages from the Mackenzies.

But that dear Mrs. Dawson! The mention of her comes into my mind like the bright sunshine into our dingy little drawing-room came on those days; – as a sweet scent of violets greets the sorrowful passer among the woodlands.

Mrs. Dawson was not Mr. Dawson's wife, for he was a bachelor. She was his crippled sister, an old maid, who had, what she called, taken her brevet rank.

After we had been about a fortnight in Edinburgh, Mr. Dawson said, in a sort of half-doubtful manner, to Miss Duncan –

'My sister bids me say, that every Monday evening a few friends come in to sit round her sofa for an hour or so, – some before going to gayer parties – and that if you and Miss Greatorex would like a little change, she would only be too glad to see you. Any time from seven to eight tonight; and I must add my injunctions, both for her sake, and for that of my

little patient's here, that you leave at nine o'clock. After all, I
do not know if you will care to come; but Margaret bade me
ask you;' and he glanced up suspiciously and sharply at us. If
either of us had felt the slightest reluctance, however well
disguised by manner, to accept this invitation, I am sure he
would have at once detected our feelings, and withdrawn it; so
jealous and chary was he of anything pertaining to the
appreciation of this beloved sister.

But, if it had been to spend an evening at the dentist's, I
believe I should have welcomed the invitation, so weary was I
of the monotony of the nights in our lodgings; and as for Miss
Duncan, an invitation to tea was of itself a pure and unmixed
honour, and one to be accepted with all becoming form and
gratitude: so Mr. Dawson's sharp glances over his spectacles
failed to detect anything but the truest pleasure, and he went
on.

'You'll find it very dull, I dare say. Only a few old fogies
like myself, and one or two good, sweet young women; I
never know who'll come. Margaret is obliged to lie in a
darkened room – only half-lighted, I mean – because her eyes
are weak, – oh, it will be very stupid, I dare say; don't thank
me till you've been once and tried it, and then if you like it,
your best thanks will be, to come again every Monday, from
half-past seven to nine, you know. Good-bye, good-bye.'

Hitherto I had never been out to a party of grown-up
people; and no court-ball to a London young lady could seem
more redolent of honour and pleasure than this Monday
evening to me.

Dressed out in a new stiff book-muslin, made up to my
throat – a frock which had seemed to me and my sisters the
height of earthly grandeur and finery – Alice, our old nurse,
had been making it at home, in contemplation of the possibility of such an event during my stay in Edinburgh, but which
had then appeared to me a robe too lovely and angelic to be
ever worn short of heaven – I went with Miss Duncan to Mr.
Dawson's at the appointed time. We entered through one
small lofty room – perhaps I ought to call it an antechamber,
for the house was old-fashioned, and stately and grand – the
large square drawing-room, into the centre of which Mrs.
Dawson's sofa was drawn. Behind her a little was placed a

table with a great cluster candlestick upon it, bearing seven or eight wax-lights; and that was all the light in the room, which looked to me very vast and indistinct after our pinched-up apartment at the Mackenzies'. Mrs. Dawson must have been sixty; and yet her face looked very soft and smooth and child-like. Her hair was quite grey: it would have looked white but for the snowiness of her cap, and satin ribbon. She was wrapped in a kind of dressing-gown of French grey merino; the furniture of the room was deep rose-colour, and white and gold, – the paper which covered the walls was Indian, beginning low down with a profusion of tropical leaves and birds and insects, and gradually diminishing in richness of detail, till at the top it ended in the most delicate tendrils and most filmy insects.

Mr. Dawson had acquired much riches in his profession, and his house gave one this impression. In the corners of the rooms were great jars of Eastern china, filled with flower-leaves and spices; and in the middle of all this was placed the sofa, on which poor Margaret Dawson passed whole days, and months, and years, without the power of moving by herself. By-and-by Mrs. Dawson's maid brought in tea and macaroons for us, and a little cup of milk and water and a biscuit for her. Then the door opened. We had come very early, and in came Edinburgh professors, Edinburgh beauties, and celebrities, all on their way to some other gayer and later party, but coming first to see Mrs. Dawson, and tell her their *bon-mots*, or their interests, or their plans. By each learned man, by each lovely girl, she was treated as a dear friend, who knew something more about their own individual selves, independent of their reputation and general society-character, than any one else.

It was very brilliant and very dazzling, and gave enough to think about and wonder about for many days.

Monday after Monday we went, stationary, silent; what could we find to say to any one but Mrs. Margaret herself? Winter passed, summer was coming; still I was ailing, and weary of my life; but still Mr. Dawson gave hopes of my ultimate recovery. My father and mother came and went; but they could not stay long, they had so many claims upon them. Mrs. Margaret Dawson had become my dear friend, although, perhaps, I had never exchanged as many words with her as I had with Miss Mackenzie; but then with Mrs. Dawson every word was a pearl or a diamond.

People began to drop off from Edinburgh, only a few were left, and I am not sure if our Monday evenings were not all the pleasanter.

There was Mr. Sperano, the Italian exile, banished even from France, where he had long resided, and now teaching Italian with meek diligence in the northern city; there was Mr. Preston, the Westmoreland squire, or, as he preferred to be called, statesman, whose wife had come to Edinburgh for the education of their numerous family, and who, whenever her husband had come over on one of his occasional visits, was only too glad to accompany him to Mrs. Dawson's Monday evenings, he and the invalid lady having been friends from long ago. These and ourselves kept steady visitors, and enjoyed ourselves all the more from having the more of Mrs. Dawson's society.

One evening I had brought the little stool close to her sofa, and was caressing her thin white hand, when the thought came into my head and out I spoke it.

'Tell me, dear Mrs. Dawson,' said I, 'how long you have been in Edinburgh; you do not speak Scotch, and Mr. Dawson says he is not Scotch.'

'No, I am Lancashire – Liverpool-born,' said she, smiling. 'Don't you hear it in my broad tongue?'

'I hear something different to other people, but I like it because it is just you; is that Lancashire?'

'I dare say it is; for, though I am sure Lady Ludlow took pains enough to correct me in my younger days, I never could get rightly over the accent.'

'Lady Ludlow,' said I, 'what had she to do with you? I heard you talking about her to Lady Madeline Stuart the first evening I ever came here; you and she seemed so fond of Lady Ludlow; who is she?'

'She is dead, my child; dead long ago.'

I felt sorry I had spoken about her, Mrs. Dawson looked so grave and sad. I suppose she perceived my sorrow, for she went on and said –

'My dear, I like to talk and to think of Lady Ludlow: she

was my true, kind friend and benefactress for many years; ask me what you like about her, and do not think you give me pain.'

I grew bold at this.

'Will you tell me all about her, then, please, Mrs. Dawson?'

'Nay,' said she, smiling, 'that would be too long a story. Here are Signor Sperano and Miss Duncan, and Mr. and Mrs. Preston are coming tonight, Mr. Preston told me; how would they like to hear an old-world story which, after all, would be no story at all, neither beginning, nor middle, nor end, only a bundle of recollections.'

'If you speak of me, madame,' said Signor Sperano, 'I can only say you do me one great honour by recounting in my presence anything about any person that has ever interested you.'

Miss Duncan tried to say something of the same kind. In the middle of her confused speech, Mr. and Mrs. Preston came in. I sprang up; I went to meet them.

'Oh,' said I, 'Mrs. Dawson is just going to tell us all about Lady Ludlow, and a great deal more, only she is afraid it won't interest anybody; do say you would like to hear it!'

Mrs. Dawson smiled at me, and in reply to their urgency she promised to tell us all about Lady Ludlow, on condition that each one of us should, after she had ended, narrate something interesting, which we had either heard, or which had fallen within our own experience. We all promised willingly, and then gathered round her sofa to hear what she could tell us about my Lady Ludlow.

MY LADY LUDLOW

CHAPTER I

I am an old woman now, and things are very different to what they were in my youth. Then we, who travelled, travelled in coaches, carrying six inside, and making a two day's journey out of what people now go over in a couple of hours with a whizz and a flash, and a screaming whistle, enough to deafen one. Then letters came in but three times a week; indeed, in some places in Scotland where I have stayed when I was a girl, the post came in but once a month; but letters were letters then; and we made great prizes of them, and read them and studied them like books. Now the post comes rattling in twice a day, bringing short, jerky notes, some without beginning or end, but just a little sharp sentence, which well-bred folks would think too abrupt to be spoken. Well, well! they may all be improvements – I dare say they are; but you will never meet with a Lady Ludlow in these days.

I will try and tell you about her. It is no story: it has as I said, neither beginning, middle, nor end.

My father was a poor clergyman with a large family. My mother was always said to have good blood in her veins; and when she wanted to maintain her position with the people she was thrown among – principally rich democratic manufacturers, all for liberty and the French Revolution – she would put on a pair of ruffles, trimmed with real old English point, very much darned to be sure – but which could not be bought new for love or money, as the art of making it was lost years before. These ruffles showed, as she said, that her ancestors had been Somebodies, when the grandfathers of the rich folk, who now looked down upon her, had been Nobodies – if, indeed, they had any grandfathers at all. I don't know whether any one out of our own family ever noticed these ruffles – but we were all taught as children to feel rather proud when my mother put them on, and to hold up our heads as became the descendants of the lady who had first possessed the lace. Not but what my dear father often told us that pride was a great sin; we were never allowed to be proud of anything but my mother's ruffles; and she was so innocently happy when she put them on – often, poor dear creature, to a very worn and threadbare gown – that I still think, even after all my experience of life, they were a blessing to the family. You will think that I am wandering away from my Lady Ludlow. Not at all. The lady who owned the lace, Ursula Hanbury, was a common ancestress of both my mother and my Lady Ludlow. And so it fell out, that when my poor father died, and my mother was sorely pressed to know what to do with her nine children, and looked far and wide for signs of willingness to help, Lady Ludlow sent her a letter, proffering aid and assistance. I see that letter now: a large sheet of thick yellow paper, with a straight broad margin left on the left-hand side of the delicate Italian writing – writing which contained far more in the same space of paper than all the sloping, or masculine handwritings of the present day. It was sealed with a coat of arms – a lozenge – for Lady Ludlow was a widow. My mother made us notice the motto, 'Foy et Loy', and told us where to look for the quarterings of the Hanbury arms before she opened the letter. Indeed, I think she was rather afraid of what the contents might be; for, as I have said, in her anxious love for her fatherless children, she had written to many people upon whom, to tell truly, she had but little claim; and their cold hard answers had many a time made her cry, when she thought none of us were looking. I do not even know if she had ever seen Lady Ludlow: all I knew of her was that she was a very grand lady, whose grandmother had been half-sister to my mother's great-grandmother; but of her character and circumstances I heard nothing, and doubt if my mother was acquainted with them.

I looked over my mother's shoulder to read the letter; it began 'Dear Cousin Margaret Dawson,' and I think I felt hopeful from the moment I saw those words. She went on to say – stay, I think I can remember the very words –

'Dear Cousin Margaret Dawson, – I have been much grieved to hear of the loss you have sustained in the death of so good a husband, and so excellent a clergyman as I have always heard that my late cousin Richard was esteemed to be.'

'There!' said my mother, laying her finger on the passage, 'read that aloud to the little ones. Let them hear how their father's good report travelled far and wide, and how well he is spoken of by one whom he never saw. *Cousin* Richard, how prettily her ladyship writes! Go on, Margaret!' She wiped her eyes as she spoke, and laid her fingers on her lips, to still my little sister, Cecily, who, not understanding anything about the important letter, was beginning to talk and make a noise.

'You say you are left with nine children. I too should have had nine, if mine had all lived. I have none left but Rudolph, the present Lord Ludlow. He is married, and lives for the most part in London. But I entertain six young gentlewomen at my house in Connington, who are to me as daughters – save that, perhaps, I restrict them in certain indulgences in dress and diet that might be befitting in young ladies of a higher rank, and of more probable wealth. These young persons – all of condition, though out of means – are my constant companions, and I strive to do my duty as a Christian lady towards them. One of these young gentlewomen died (at her own home, whither she had gone upon a visit) last May. Will you do me the favour to allow your eldest daughter to supply her place in my household? She is, as I make out, about sixteen years of age. She will find companions here who are but a little older than herself. I dress my young friends myself, and make each of them a small allowance for pocket-money. They have but few opportunities for matrimony, as Connington is far removed from any town. The clergyman is a deaf old widower; my agent is married; and as for the neighbouring farmers, they are, of course, below the notice of the young gentlewomen under my protection. Still, if any young woman wishes to marry, and has conducted herself to my satisfaction, I give her a wedding dinner, her clothes, and her house linen. And such as remain with me to my death will find a small competency provided for them in my will. I reserve to myself the option of paying their travelling expenses – disliking gadding women, on the one hand; on the other, not wishing by too long absence from the family home to weaken natural ties.

'If my proposal pleases you and your daughter – or rather, if it pleases you, for I trust your daughter has been too well brought up to have a will in opposition to yours – let me know, dear cousin Margaret Dawson, and I will make arrangements for meeting the young gentlewoman at Cavistock, which is the nearest point to which the coach will bring her.'

My mother dropped the letter and sat silent.

'I shall not know what to do without you Margaret.'

A moment before, like a young untried girl as I was, I had been pleased at the notion of seeing a new place, and leading a new life. But now – my mother's look of sorrow, and the children's cry of remonstrance: 'Mother, I won't go,' I said.

'Nay! but you had better,' replied she, shaking her head. 'Lady Ludlow has much power. She can help your brothers. It will not do to slight her offer.'

So we accepted it, after much consultation. We were rewarded – or so we thought – for afterwards, when I came to know Lady Ludlow, I saw that she would have done her duty by us, as helpless relations, however we might have rejected her kindness – by a presentation to Christ's Hospital for one of my brothers.

And this was how I came to know my Lady Ludlow.

I remember well the afternoon of my arrival at Hanbury Court. Her ladyship had sent to meet me at the nearest post-town at which the mail-coach stopped. There was an old groom inquiring for me, the ostler said, if my name was Dawson – from Hanbury Court, he believed. I felt it rather formidable; and first began to understand what was meant by going among strangers, when I lost sight of the guard to whom my mother had intrusted me. I was perched up in a high gig with a hood to it, such as in those days was called a chair, and my companion was driving deliberately through the most pastoral country I had ever yet seen. By-and-by we ascended a long hill, and the man got out and walked at the horse's head. I should have liked to walk, too, very much indeed; but I did not know how far I might do it; and, in fact, I dared not speak to ask to be helped down the deep steps of the gig. We were at last at the top – on a long, breezy sweeping, unenclosed piece of ground, called, as I afterwards learned, a Chase. The groom stopped, breathed, patted his horse, and then mounted again to my side.

'Are we near Hanbury Court?' I asked.

'Near! Why, Miss! we've a matter of ten mile yet to go.'

Once launched into conversation, we went on pretty glibly. I fancy he had been afraid of beginning to speak to me, just as I was to him; but he got over his shyness with me sooner than I did mine with him. I let him choose the subjects of conversation, although very often I could not understand the points of interest in them: for instance, he talked for more than a quarter of an hour of a famous race which a certain dog-fox had given him, above thirty years before; and spoke of all the covers and turns just as if I knew them as well as he did; and all the time I was wondering what kind of an animal a dog-fox might be.

After we left the Chase, the road grew worse. No one in these days, who has not seen the byroads of fifty years ago, can imagine what they were. We had to quarter, as Randal called it, nearly all the way along the deep-rutted, miry lanes; and the tremendous jolts I occasionally met with made my seat in the gig so unsteady that I could not look about me at all, I was so much occupied in holding on. The road was too muddy for me to walk without dirtying myself more than I liked to do, just before my first sight of my Lady Ludlow. But by-and-by, when we came to the fields in which the lane ended, I begged Randal to help me down, as I saw that I could pick my steps among the pasture grass without making myself unfit to be seen; and Randal, out of pity for his steaming horse, wearied with the hard struggle through the mud, thanked me kindly, and helped me down with a springing jump.

The pasture fell gradually down to the lower land, shut in on either side by rows of high elms, as if there had been a wide grand avenue here in former times. Down the grassy gorge we went, seeing the sunset sky at the end of the shadowed descent. Suddenly we came to a long flight of steps.

'If you'll run down there, Miss I'll go round and meet you; and then you'd beter mount again, for my lady will like to see you drive up to the house.'

'Are we near the house?' said I, suddenly checked by the idea.

'Down there, Miss,' replied he, pointing with his whip to certain stacks of twisted chimneys rising out of a group of trees, in deep shadow against the crimson light, and which lay just beyond a great square lawn at the base of the steep slope of a hundred yards, on the edge of which we stood.

I went down the steps quietly enough. I met Randal and the gig at the bottom; and, falling into a side road to the left, we rode sedately round, through the gateway, and into the great court in front of the house.

The road by which we had come lay right at the back.

Hanbury Court is a vast red-brick house – at least, it is cased in part with red bricks; and the gatehouse and walls about the place are of brick – with stone facings at every corner and door, and window, such as you see at Hampton Court. At the back are the gables, and arched doorways, and stone mullions, which show (so Lady Ludlow used to tell us) that it was once a priory. There was a prior's parlour, I know – only we called it Mrs. Medlicott's room; and there was a tithe-barn as big as a church, and rows of fish-ponds, all got ready for the monks' fasting-days in old time. But all this I did not see till afterwards. I hardly noticed, this first night, the great Virginian Creeper (said to have been the first planted in England by one of my lady's ancestors) that half covered the front of the house. As I had been unwilling to leave the guard of the coach, so did I now feel unwilling to leave Randal, a known friend of three hours. But there was no help for it; in I must go; past the grand-looking old gentleman holding the door open for me, on into the great hall on the right hand, into which the sun's last rays were sending glorious red light – the gentleman was now walking before me – up a step on to the dais, as I afterwards learned that it was called – then again to the left, through a series of sitting-rooms, opening one out of another, and all of them looking into a stately garden, glowing, even in the twilight, with the bloom of flowers. We went up four steps out of the last of these rooms, and then my guide lifted up a heavy silk curtain, and I was in the presence of my Lady Ludlow.

She was very small of stature and very upright. She wore a

great lace cap, nearly half her own height, I should think, that went round her head (caps which tied under the chin, and which we called 'mobs', came in later, and my lady held them in great contempt, saying people might as well come down in their nightcaps). In front of my lady's cap was a great bow of white satin ribbon; and a broad band of the same ribbon was tied tight round her head, and served to keep the cap straight. She had a fine Indian muslin shawl folded over her shoulders and across her chest, and an apron of the same; a black silk mode gown, made with short sleeves and ruffles, and with the tail thereof pulled through the placket-hole, so as to shorten it to a useful length: beneath it she wore, as I could plainly see, a quilted lavender satin petticoat. Her hair was snowy white, but I scarcely saw it, it was so covered with her cap; her skin, even at her age, was waxen in texture and tint; her eyes were large and dark blue, and must have been her great beauty when she was young, for there was nothing particular, as far as I can remember, either in mouth or nose. She had a great gold-headed stick by her chair; but I think it was more as a mark of state and dignity than for use; for she had as light and brisk a step when she chose as any girl of fifteen, and, in her private early walk of meditation in the mornings, would go as swiftly from garden alley to garden alley as any one of us.

She was standing up when I went in. I dropped my curtsey at the door, which my mother had always taught me as a part of good manners, and went up instinctively to my lady. She did not put out her hand, but raised herself a little on tiptoe, and kissed me on both cheeks.

'You are cold my child. You shall have a dish of tea with me.' She rang a little hand-bell on the table by her, and her waiting-maid came in from a small anteroom; and as if all had been prepared, and was awaiting my arrival, brought with her a small china service with tea ready made, and a plate of delicately cut bread and butter, every morsel of which I could have eaten, and been none the better for it, so hungry was I after my long ride. The waiting-maid took off my cloak, and I sat down, sorely alarmed at the silence, the hushed footfalls of the subdued maiden over the thick carpet, and the soft voice and clear pronunciation of my Lady Ludlow. My teaspoon fell against my cup with a sharp noise, that seemed so out of place

and season that I blushed deeply. My lady caught my eye with
hers – both keen and sweet were those dark-blue eyes of her
ladyship's.

'Your hands are very cold, my dear; take off those gloves' (I
wore thick serviceable doeskin, and had been too shy to take
them off unbidden), 'and let me try and warm them – the
evenings are very chilly.' And she held my great red hands in
hers – soft, warm, white, ring-laden. Looking at last a little
wistfully into my face, she said – 'Poor child! And you're the
eldest of nine! I had a daughter who would have been just your
age; but I cannot fancy her the eldest of nine.' Then came a
pause of silence; and then she rang her bell, and desired her
waiting-maid, Adams, to show me to my room.

It was so small that I think it must have been a cell. The
walls were whitewashed stone; the bed was of white dimity.
There was a small piece of red stair-carpet on each side of the
bed, and two chairs. In a closet adjoining were my washstand
and toilet-table. There was a text of Scripture painted on a
wall right opposite to my bed; and below hung a print,
common enough in those days, of King George and Queen
Charlotte, with all their numerous children, down to the little
Princess Amelia in a go-cart. On each side hung a small
portrait, also engraved: on the left, it was Louis the Sixteenth;
on the other, Marie Antoinette. On the chimney-piece there
was a tinder-box and a Prayer-book. I do not remember
anything else in the room. Indeed, in those days people did not
dream of writing-tables and inkstands, and portfolios, and
easy-chairs, and what not. We were taught to go into our
bedrooms for the purposes of dressing, and sleeping, and
praying.

Presently I was summoned to supper. I followed the young
lady who had been sent to call me, down the wide shallow
stairs, into the great hall, through which I had first passed on
my way to my Lady Ludlow's room. There were four other
young gentlewomen, all standing, and all silent, who curtsied
to me when I first came in. They were dressed in a kind of
uniform: muslin caps bound round their heads with blue
ribbons, plain muslin handkerchiefs, lawn aprons, and drab-
coloured stuff gowns. They were all gathered together at a
little distance from the table, on which were placed a couple of

cold chickens, a salad, and a fruit tart. On the dais there was a smaller round table, on which stood a silver jug filled with milk, and a small roll. Near that was set a carved chair, with a countess's coronet surmounting the back of it. I thought that some one might have spoken to me; but they were shy and I was shy; or else there was some other reason; but, indeed, almost the minute after I had come into the hall by the door at the lower hand, her ladyship entered by the door opening upon the dais; whereupon we all curtsied very low; I, because I saw the others do it. She stood and looked at us for a moment.

'Young gentlewomen,' said she, 'make Margaret Dawson welcome among you;' and they treated me with the kind politeness due to a stranger, but still without any talking beyond what was required for the purposes of the meal. After it was over, and grace was said by one of the party, my lady rang her hand-bell, and the servants came in and cleared away the supper things; then they brought in a portable reading-desk, which was placed on the dais, and, the whole household trooping in, my lady called to one of my companions to come up and read the Psalms and Lessons for the day. I remember thinking how afraid I should have been had I been in her place. There were no prayers. My lady thought it schismatic to have any prayers excepting those in the Prayer-book; and would as soon have preached a sermon herself in the parish church, as have allowed any one not a deacon at the least to read prayers in a private dwelling-house. I am not sure that even then she would have approved of his reading them in an unconsecrated place.

She had been maid of honour to Queen Charlotte; a Hanbury of that old stock that flourished in the days of the Plantagenets, and heiress of all the land that remained to the family, of the great estates which had once stretched into four separate counties. Hanbury Court was hers by right. She had married Lord Ludlow, and had lived for many years at his various seats, and away from her ancestral home. She had lost all her children but one, and most of them had died at these houses of Lord Ludlow's; and, I dare say that gave my lady a distaste to the places, and a longing to come back to Hanbury Court, where she had been so happy as a girl. I imagine her girlhood had been the happiest time of her life; for, now I think of it, most of her opinions, when I knew her in later life, were singular enough then, but had been universally prevalent fifty years before. For instance, while I lived at Hanbury Court, the cry for education was beginning to come up: Mr. Raikes had set up his Sunday-schools; and some clergymen were all for teaching writing and arithmetic, as well as reading. My lady would have none of this; it was levelling and revolutionary, she said. When a young woman came to be hired, my lady would have her in, and see if she liked her looks and her dress, and question her about her family. Her ladyship laid great stress upon this latter point, saying that a girl who did not warm up when any interest or curiosity was expressed about her mother, or 'the baby' (if there was one), was not likely to make a good servant. Then she would make her put out her feet, to see if they were well and neatly shod. Then she would bid her say the Lord's Prayer and the Creed. Then she inquired if she could write. If she could, and she liked all that had gone before, her face sank – it was a great disappointment, for it was an all but inviolable rule with her never to engage a servant who could write. But I have known her ladyship break through it, although in both cases in which she did so she put the girl's principles to a further and unusual test in asking her to repeat the Ten Commandments. One pert young woman – and yet I was sorry for her too, only she afterwards married a rich draper in Shrewsbury – who had got through her trials pretty tolerably, considering she could write, spoilt all, by saying glibly, at the end of the last Commandment, 'An't please your ladyship, I can cast accounts.'

'Go away, wench,' said my lady in a hurry, 'you're only fit for trade; you will not suit me for a servant.' The girl went away crestfallen; in a minute, however, my lady sent me after her to see that she had something to eat before leaving the house; and, indeed, she sent for her once again, but it was only to give her a Bible, and to bid her beware of French principles, which had led the French to cut off their king's and queen's heads.

The poor, blubbering girl said, 'Indeed, my lady, I wouldn't hurt a fly, much less a king, and I cannot abide the French, nor frogs neither, for that matter.'

But my lady was inexorable, and took a girl who could neither read nor write, to make up for her alarm about the progress of education towards addition and subtraction; and afterwards, when the clergyman who was at Hanbury parish when I came there, had died, and the bishop had appointed another, and a younger man, in his stead, this was one of the points on which he and my lady did not agree. While good old deaf Mr. Mountford lived, it was my lady's custom, when indisposed for a sermon, to stand up at the door of her large square pew – just opposite the reading-desk – and to say (at that part of the morning service where it is decreed that, in choirs and places where they sing, here followeth the anthem): 'Mr. Mountford, I will not trouble you for a discourse this morning.' And we all knelt down to the Litany with great satisfaction; for Mr. Mountford, though he could not hear, had always his eyes about this part of the service, for any of my lady's movements. But the new clergyman, Mr. Gray, was of a different stamp. He was very zealous in all his parish work; and my lady, who was just as good as she could be to the poor, was often crying him up as a godsend to the parish, and he never could send amiss to the Court when he wanted broth, or wine, or jelly, or sago for a sick person. But he needs must take up the new hobby of education; and I could see that this put my lady sadly about one Sunday, when she suspected, I know not how, that there was something to be said in his sermon about a Sunday-school which he was planning. She stood up, as she had not done since Mr. Mountford's death, two years and better before this time, and said –

'Mr. Gray, I will not trouble you for a discourse this morning.'

But her voice was not well-assured and steady; and we knelt down with more of curiosity than satisfaction in our minds. Mr. Gray preached a very rousing sermon, on the necessity of establishing a Sabbath-school in the village. My lady shut her eyes, and seemed to go to sleep; but I don't believe she lost a word of it, though she said nothing about it that I heard until the next Saturday, when two of us, as was the custom, were riding out with her in her carriage, and we went to see a poor bedridden woman, who lived some miles away at the other

end of the estate and of the parish; and as we came out of the
cottage we met Mr. Gray walking up to it, in a great heat, and
looking very tired. My lady beckoned him to her, and told
him she would wait and take him home with her, adding that
she wondered to see him there, so far from his home, for that
it was beyond a Sabbath-day's journey, and, from what she
had gathered from his sermon the last Sunday, he was all for
Judaism against Christianity. He looked as if he did not
understand what she meant; but the truth was that, besides the
way in which he had spoken up for schools and schooling, he
had kept calling Sunday the Sabbath; and as her ladyship said
'The Sabbath is the Sabbath, and that's one thing – it is
Saturday; and, if I keep it, I'm a Jew, which I'm not. And
Sunday is Sunday; and that's another thing; and, if I keep it,
I'm a Christian, which I humbly trust I am.'

But when Mr. Gray got an inkling of her meaning in talking
about a Sabbath-day's journey, he only took notice of a part of
it; he smiled and bowed, and said no one knew better than her
ladyship what were the duties that abrogated all inferior laws
regarding the Sabbath; and that he must go in and read to old
Betty Brown, so that he would not detain her ladyship.

'But I shall wait for you, Mr. Gray,' said she. 'Or I will take
a drive round by Oakfield, and be back in an hour's time.' For,
you see, she would not have him feel hurried or troubled with
a thought that he was keeping her waiting, while he ought to
be comforting and praying with old Betty.

'A very pretty young man, my dears,' said she, as we drove
away. 'But I shall have my pew glazed all the same.'

We did not know what she meant at the time; but the next
Sunday but one we did. She had the curtains all round the
grand old Hanbury family pew taken down, and, instead of
them, there was glass up to the height of six or seven feet. We
entered by a door, with a window in it that drew up and down
just like what you see in carriages. This window was generally
down, and then we could hear perfectly; but if Mr. Gray used
the word 'Sabbath', or spoke in favour of schooling or
education, my lady stepped out of her corner, and drew up the
window with a decided clang and clash.

I must tell you something more about Mr. Gray. The
presentation to the living of Hanbury was vested in two

trustees, of whom Lady Ludlow was one: Lord Ludlow had exercised this right in the appointment of Mr. Mountford, who had won his lordship's favour by his excellent horsemanship. Nor was Mr. Mountford a bad clergyman; as clergyman went in those days. He did not drink, though he liked good eating as much as any one. And if any poor person was ill, and he heard of it, he would send them plates from his own dinner of what he himself liked best; sometimes of dishes which was almost as bad a poison to sick people. He meant kindly to everybody except dissenters, whom Lady Ludlow and he united in trying to drive out of the parish; and among dissenters he particularly abhorred Methodists – some one said, because John Wesley had objected to his hunting. But that must have been long ago, for when I knew him he was far too stout and too heavy to hunt; besides, the bishop of the diocese disapproved of hunting, and had intimated his disapprobation to the clergy. For my own part, I think a good run would not have come amiss, even from a moral point of view, to Mr. Mountford. He ate so much, and took so little exercise, that we young women often heard of his being in terrible passions with his servants, and the sexton and clerk. But they none of them minded him much, for he soon came to himself, and was sure to make them some present or other – some said in proportion to his anger; so that the sexton, who was a bit of a wag (as all sextons are, I think), said that the vicar's saying, 'The Devil take you,' was worth a shilling any day, whereas 'The Deuce' was a shabby sixpence speech, only fit for a curate.

There was a great deal of good in Mr. Mountford, too. He could not bear to see pain, or sorrow, or misery of any kind; and, if it came under his notice, he was never easy till he had relieved it, for the time, at any rate. But he was afraid of being made uncomfortable; so, if he possibly could, he would avoid seeing any one who was ill or unhappy; and he did not thank any one for telling him about them.

'What would your ladyship have me to do?' he once said to my Lady Ludlow, when she wished him to go and see a poor man who had broken his leg. 'I cannot piece the leg as a doctor can; I cannot nurse him as well as his wife does; I may talk to him, but he no more understands me than I do the language of the alchemists. My coming puts him out; he stiffens himself into an uncomfortable posture, out of respect for the cloth, and dare not take the comfort of kicking, and swearing, and scolding his wife, while I am there. I hear him, with my figurative ears, my lady, heave a sigh of relief when my back is turned, and the sermon that he thinks I ought to have kept for the pulpit, and have delivered to his neighbours (whose case, as he fancies, it would just have fitted, as it seemed to him to be addressed to the sinful) is all ended, and done, for the day. I judge others as myself; I do to them as I would be done to. That's Christianity, at any rate. I should hate – saving your ladyship's presence – to have my Lord Ludlow coming and seeing me, if I were ill. 'Twould be a great honour, no doubt; but I should have to put on a clean nightcap for the occasion, and sham patience, in order to be polite, and not weary his lordship with my complaints. I should be twice as thankful to him if he would send me game, or a good fat haunch, to bring me up to that pitch of health and strength one ought to be in, to appreciate the honour of a visit from a nobleman. So I shall send Jerry Butler a good dinner every day till he is strong again; and spare the poor old fellow my presence and advice.'

My lady would be puzzled by this, and by many other of Mr. Mountford's speeches. But he had been appointed by my lord, and she could not question her dead husband's wisdom; and she knew that the dinners were always sent and often a guinea or two to help pay the doctor's bills; and Mr. Mountford was true blue, as we call it, to the backbone; hated the dissenters and the French; and could hardly drink a dish of tea without giving out the toast of 'Church and King, and down with the Rump.' Moreover he had the honour of preaching before the King and Queen, and two of the Princesses, at Weymouth; and the King had applauded his sermon audibly with – 'Very good; very good;' and that was a seal put upon his merit in my lady's eyes.

Besides, in the long winter Sunday evenings, he would come up to the Court, and read a sermon to us girls, and play a game of piquet with my lady afterwards; which served to shorten the tedium of the time. My lady would, on those occasions, invite him to sup with her on the dais; but, as her meal was invariably bread and milk only, Mr. Mountford preferred sitting down amongst us, and made a joke about its being wicked and heterodox to eat meagre on Sunday, a festival of the Church. We smiled at this joke just as much the twentieth time we heard it as we did at the first; for we knew it was coming, because he always coughed a little nervously before he made a joke, for fear my lady should not approve; and neither she nor he seemed to remember that he had ever hit upon the idea before.

Mr. Mountford died quite suddenly at last. We were all very sorry to lose him. He left some of his property (for he had a private estate) to the poor of the parish, to furnish them with an annual Christmas dinner of roast beef and plum-pudding, for which he wrote out a very good receipt in the codicil to his will.

Moreover, he desired his executors to see that the vault in which the vicars of Hanbury were interred was well aired, before his coffin was taken in; for, all his life long, he had had a dread of damp, and latterly he kept his rooms to such a pitch of warmth that some thought it hastened his end.

Then the other trustee, as I have said, presented the living to Mr. Gray, Fellow of Lincoln College, Oxford. It was quite natural for us all, as belonging in some sort to the Hanbury family, to disapprove of the other trustee's choice. But when some ill-natured person circulated the report that Mr. Gray was a Moravian Methodist, I remember my lady said, 'She could not believe anything so bad, without a great deal of evidence.'

CHAPTER II

Before I tell you about Mr. Gray, I think I ought to make you understand something more of what we did all day long at Hanbury Court. There were five of us at the time of which I am speaking, all young women of good descent, and allied (however distantly) to people of rank. When we were not with my lady, Mrs. Medlicott looked after us: a gentle little woman, who had been companion to my lady for many years, and was indeed, I have been told, some kind of relation to her. Mrs. Medlicott's parents had lived in Germany, and the consequence was, she spoke English with a very foreign accent. Another consequence was, that she excelled in all manner of needlework, such as is not known even by name in these days. She could darn either lace, table-linen, India muslin, or stockings, so that no one could tell where the hole or rent had been. Though a good Protestant, and never missing Guy Faux day at church, she was as skilful at fine work as any nun in a Papist convent. She would take a piece of French cambric, and by drawing out some threads, and working in others, it became delicate lace within a very few hours. She did the same by Hollands cloth, and made coarse strong lace, with which all my lady's napkins and table-linen were trimmed. We worked under her during a great part of the day, either in the still-room, or at our sewing in a chamber that opened out of the great hall. My lady despised every kind of work that would now be called Fancy-work. She considered that the use of coloured threads or worsted was only fit to amuse children; but that grown women ought not to be taken with mere blues and reds, but to restrict their pleasure in sewing to making small and delicate stitches. She would speak of the old tapestry in the hall as the work of her ancestresses, who lived before the Reformation, and were consequently unacquainted with pure and simple tastes in work, as well as in

24

religion. Nor would my lady sanction the fashion of the day, which, at the beginning of this century, made all the fine ladies take to making shoes. She said that such work was a consequence of the French Revolution, which had done much to annihilate all distinctions of rank and class, and hence it was that she saw young ladies of birth and breeding handling lasts, and awls, and dirty cobblers'-wax, like shoe-makers' daughters.

Very frequently one of us would be summoned to my lady to read aloud to her, as she sat in her small withdrawing-room, some improving boook. It was generally Mr. Addison's *Spectator*; but one year I remember, we had to read *Sturms Reflections*, translated from a German book Mrs. Medlicott recommended. Mr. Sturm told us what to think about for every day in the year; and very dull it was; but I believe Queen Charlotte had liked the book very much, and the thought of her royal approbation kept my lady awake during the reading. *Mrs. Chapone's Letters* and *Dr Gregory's Advice to Young Ladies* composed the rest of our library for week-day reading. I, for one, was glad to leave my fine sewing, and even my reading aloud (though this last did keep me with my dear lady) to go to the still-room and potter about among the preserves and the medicated waters. There was no doctor for many miles round, and with Mrs. Medlicott to direct us, and Dr Buchan to go by for recipes, we sent out many a bottle of physic, which, I dare say, was as good as what comes out of the druggist's shop. At any rate, I do not think we did much harm; for, if any of our physics tasted stronger than usual, Mrs. Medlicott would bid us let it down with cochineal and water, to make all safe as she said. So our bottles of medicine had very little real physic in them at last; but we were careful in putting labels on them, which looked very mysterious to those who could not read, and helped the medicine to do its work. I have sent off many a bottle of salt and water coloured red; and, whenever we had nothing else to do in the still-room, Mrs. Medlicott would set us to making bread-pills, by way of practice; and, as far as I can say, they were very efficacious, as before we gave out a box Mrs. Medlicott always told the patient what sympton to expect; and I hardly ever inquired without hearing that they had produced their effect. There was one old man who took six pills a-night, of any kind we liked to give him, to make him sleep; and if, by any chance, his daughter had forgotten to let us know that he was out of his medicine, he was so restless and miserable that, as he said, he thought he was like to die. I think ours was what would be called homœopathic practice now-a-days. Then we learnt to make all the cakes and dishes of the season in the still-room. We had plum-porridge and mince-pies at Christmas, fritters and pancakes on Shrove Tuesday, furmenty on Mothering Sunday, violet-cakes in Passion Week, tansy-pudding on Easter Sunday, three-cornered cakes on Trinity Sunday, and so on through the year: all made from good old Church receipts, handed down from one of my lady's earliest Protestant ancestresses. Every one of us passed a portion of the day with Lady Ludlow; and now and then we rode out with her in her coach and four. She did not like to go out with a pair of horses, cosidering this rather beneath her rank; and, indeed, four horses were very often needed to pull her heavy coach through the stiff mud. But it was rather a cumbersome equipage through the narrow Warwickshire lanes; and I used often to think it was well that countesses were not plentiful, or else we might have met another lady of quality in another coach and four, where there would have been no possibility of turning, or passing each other and very little chance of backing. Once, when the idea of this danger of meeting another countess in a narrow, deep-rutted lane was very prominent in my mind, I ventured to ask Mrs. Medlicott what would have to be done on such an occasion; and she told me that 'de latest creation must back, for sure', which puzzled me a good deal at the time, although I understand it now. I began to find out the use of the *Peerage*, a book which had seemed to me rather dull before; but, as I was always a coward in a coach, I made myself well acquainted with the dates of creation of our three Warwickshire earls, and was happy to find that Earl Ludlow ranked second, the oldest earl being a hunting widower, and not likely to drive out in a carriage.

All this time I have wandered from Mr. Gray. Of course, we first saw him in church when he read himself in. He was very red-faced, the kind of redness which goes with light hair and a blushing complexion; he looked slight and short, and his bright light frizzy hair had hardly a dash of powder in it. I remember my lady making this observation, and sighing over it; for, though since the famine of seventeen hundred and ninety-nine and eighteen hundred there had been a tax on hair-powder, yet it was reckoned very revolutionary and Jacobin not to wear a good deal of it. My lady hardly liked the opinions of any man who wore his own hair; but this she would say was rather a prejudice; only, in her youth none but the mob had gone wigless, and she could not get over the association of wigs with birth and breeding; a man's own hair with that class of people who had formed the rioters in seventeen hundred and eighty, when Lord George Gordon, had been one of the bugbears of my lady's life. Her husband and his brothers, she told us, had been put into breeches, and had their heads shaved on their seventh birthday, each of them, a handsome little wig of the newest fashion forming the old Lady Ludlow's invariable birthday present to her sons as they each arrived at that age; and afterwards, to the day of their death, they never saw their own hair. To be without powder, as some underbred people were talking of being now, was in fact to insult the proprieties of life by being undressed. It was English sans-culottism. But Mr. Gray did wear a little powder – enough to save him in my lady's good opinion, but not enough to make her approve of him decidedly.

The next time I saw him was in the great hall. Mary Mason and I were going to drive out with my lady in her coach; and, when we went downstairs with our best hats and cloaks on, we found Mr. Gray awaiting my lady's coming. I believe he had paid his respects to her before, but we had never seen him; and he had declined her invitation to spend Sunday evening at the Court (as Mr. Mountford used to do pretty regularly – and play a game at picquet too), which, Mrs. Medlicott told us, had caused my lady to be not over well pleased with him.

He blushed redder than ever at the sight of us, as we entered the hall and dropped him our curtsies. He coughed two or three times, as if he would have liked to speak to us, if he could but have found something to say; and every time he coughed he became hotter-looking than ever. I am ashamed to say, we were nearly laughing at him; half because we, too, were so shy that we understood what his awkwardness meant.

My lady came in, with her quick active step – she always walked quickly when she did not bethink herself of her cane – as if she was sorry to have kept us waiting – and, as she entered, she gave us all round one of those graceful sweeping curtsies, of which I think the art must have died out with her, it implied so much courtesy; – this time it said, as well as words could do, 'I am sorry to have kept you all waiting – forgive me.'

She went up to the mantelpiece, near which Mr. Gray had been standing until her entrance, curtseying afresh to him, and pretty deeply this time, because of his cloth, and her being hostess, and he, a new guest. She asked him if he would not prefer speaking to her in her own private parlour, and looked as though she would have conducted him there. But he burst out with his errand, of which he was full even to choking, and which sent the glistening tears into his large blue eyes, which stood farther and farther out with his excitement.

'My lady, I want to speak to you, and to persuade you to exert your kind interest with Mr. Lathom – Justice Lathom, of Hathaway Manor –'

'Harry Lathom?' inquired my lady, – as Mr. Gray stopped to take the breath he had lost in his hurry – 'I did not know he was in the commission.'

'He is only just appointed; he took the oaths not a month ago – more's the pity!'

'I do not understand why you should regret it. The Lathoms have held Hathaway since Edward the First, and Mr. Lathom bears a good character, although his temper is hasty –'

'My lady! he has committed Job Gregson for stealing – a fault of which he is as innocent as I – and all the evidence goes to prove it, now that the case is brought before the Bench; only the Squires hang so together that they can't be brought to see justice, and are all for sending Job to gaol, out of compliment to Mr. Lathom, saying it is his first committal, and it won't be civil to tell him there is no evidence against this man. For God's sake, my lady, speak to the gentlemen; they will attend to you, while they only tell me to mind my own business.'

Now my lady was always inclined to stand by her order and

the Lathoms of Hathaway Court were cousins to the Hanburys. Besides, it was rather a point of honour in those days to
encourage a young magistrate, by passing a pretty sharp
sentence on his first committals; and Job Gregson was the
father of a girl who had been lately turned away from her place
as scullery-maid for sauciness to Mrs. Adams, her ladyship's
own maid; and Mr. Gray had not said a word of the reasons
why he believed the man innocent – for he was in such a
hurry, I believe he would have had my lady drive off to the
Henley Court-house then and there; – so there seemed a good
deal against the man, and nothing but Mr. Gray's bare word
for him; and my lady drew herself a little up, and said –

'Mr. Gray! I do not see what reason either you or I have to
interfere. Mr. Harry Lathom is a sensible kind of young man,
well capable of ascertaining the truth without our help –'

'But more evidence has come out since,' broke in Mr. Gray.
My lady went a little stiffer, and spoke a little more coldly –

'I suppose this additional evidence is before the justices: men
of good family, and of honour and credit, well known in the
county. They naturally feel that the opinion of one of themselves must have more weight than the words of a man like
Job Gregson, who bears a very indifferent character – has been
strongly suspected of poaching, coming from no one knows
where, squatting on Hareman's Common – which by the
way, is extra-parochial, I believe; consequently you, as a
clergyman, are not responsible for what goes on there: and,
although impolitic, there might be some truth in what the
magistrates said, in advising you to mind your own business,'
said her ladyship, smiling, 'and they might be tempted to bid
me mind mine, if I interfered, Mr. Gray; might they not?'

He looked extremely uncomfortable; half angry. Once or
twice he began to speak, but choked himself, as if his words
would not not have been wise or prudent. At last he said –

'It may seem presumptuous in me – a stranger of only a few
weeks' standing – to set up my judgment as to men's character
against that of residents' – Lady Ludlow gave a little bow of
acquiescence, which was, I think, involuntary on her part, and
which I don't think he perceived – 'but I am convinced that the
man is innocent of this offence – and besides, the justices
themselves allege this ridiculous custom of paying a compli-

ment to a newly-appointed magistrate as their only reason.'

That unlucky word 'ridiculous!' It undid all the good his modest beginning had done him with my lady. I knew as well as words could have told me, that she was affronted at the expression used by the man inferior in rank to those whose actions he applied it to – and, truly, it was a great want of tact, considering to whom he was speaking.

Lady Ludlow spoke very gently and slowly; she always did so when she was annoyed; it was a certain sign, the meaning of which we had all learnt.

'I think, Mr. Gray, we will drop the subject. It is one on which we are not likely to agree.'

Mr. Gray's ruddy colour grew purple, and then faded away, and his face became pale. I think both my lady and he had forgotten our presence; and we were beginning to feel too awkward to wish to remind them of it. And yet we could not help watching and listening with the greatest interest.

Mr. Gray drew himself up to his full height, with an unconscious feeling of dignity. Little as was his stature, and awkward and embarrassed as he had been only a few minutes before, I remember thinking he looked almost as grand as my lady when he spoke.

'Your ladyship must remember that it may be my duty to speak to my parishioners on many subjects on which they do not agree with me. I am not at liberty to be silent, because they differ in opinion from me.'

Lady Ludlow's great blue eyes dilated with surprise, and – I do think – anger, at being thus spoken to. I am not sure whether it was very wise in Mr. Gray. He himself looked afraid of the consequences, but as if he was determined to bear them without flinching. For a minute there was silence. Then my lady replied –

'Mr. Gray, I respect your plain speaking, although I may wonder whether a young man of your age and position has any right to assume that he is a better judge than one with the experience which I have naturally gained at my time of life, and in the station I hold.'

'If I, madam, as the clergyman of this parish, am not to shrink from telling what I believe to be the truth to the poor and lowly, no more am I to hold my peace in the presence of

the rich and titled.' Mr. Gray's face showed that he was in that
state of excitement which in a child would have ended in a
good fit of crying. He looked as if he had nerved himself up to
doing and saying things, which he disliked above everything,
and which nothing short of serious duty could have compelled
him to do and say. And at such times every minute circumstance which could add to pain comes vividly before one. I saw
that he became aware of our presence, and that it added to his
discomfiture.

My lady flushed up. 'Are you aware, sir,' asked she, 'that
·you have gone far astray from the original subject of conversation? But, as you talk of your parish, allow me to remind you
that Hareman's Common is beyond the bounds, and that you
are really not responsible for the characters and lives of the
squatters on that unlucky piece of ground.'

'Madam, I see I have only done harm in speaking to you
about the affair at all. I beg your pardon and take my leave.'

He bowed, and looked very sad. Lady Ludlow caught the
expression of his face.

'Good morning!' she cried, in rather a louder and quicker
way than that in which she had been speaking. 'Remember,
Job Gregson is a notorious poacher and evil-doer, and you
really are not responsible for what goes on at Hareman's
Common.'

He was near the hall-door, and said something – half to
himself, which we heard (being nearer to him), but my lady
did not; although she saw that he spoke. 'What did he say?' she
asked in a somewhat hurried manner, as soon as the door was
closed. – 'I did not hear.' We looked at each other, and then I
spoke –

'He said, my lady, that "God help him! he was responsible
for all the evil he did not strive to overcome."'

My lady turned sharp round away from us, and Mary
Mason said afterwards she thought her ladyship was much
vexed with both of us for having been present, and with me
for having repeated what Mr. Gray had said. But it was not
our fault that we were in the hall; and when my lady asked
what Mr. Gray had said, I thought it right to tell her.

In a few minutes she bade us accompany her in her ride in
the coach.

Lady Ludlow always sat forwards by herself, and we girls backwards. Somehow this was a rule, which we never thought of questioning. It was true that riding backwards made some of us feel very uncomfortable and faint; and to remedy this my lady always drove with both windows open, which occasionally gave her the rheumatism; but we always went on in the old way. This day she did not pay any great attention to the road by which we were going, and Coachman took his own way. We were very silent, as my lady did not speak, and looked very serious. Or else, in general, she made these rides very pleasant (to those who were not qualmish with riding backwards), by talking to us in a very agreeable manner, and telling us of the different things which had happened to her at various places – at Paris and Versailles, where she had been in her youth – at Windsor and Kew and Weymouth, where she had been with the Queen, when maid-of-honour – and so on. But this day she did not talk at all. All at once she put her head out of the window.

'John Footman,' said she, 'where are we? Surely this is Hareman's Common.'

'Yes, an't please my lady,' said John Footman, and waited for further speech or orders. My lady thought a while, and then said she would have the steps put down and get out.

As soon as she was gone, we looked at each other, and then without a word began to gaze after her. We saw her pick her dainty way, in the little high-heeled shoes she always wore (because they had been in fashion in her youth), among the yellow pools of stagnant water that had gathered in the clayey soil. John Footman followed, stately, after; afraid too, for all his stateliness, of splashing his pure white stockings. Suddenly my lady turned round and said something to him, and he returned to the carriage with a half-pleased, half-puzzled air.

My lady went on to a cluster of rude mud houses at the higher end of the Common: cottages built, as they were occasionally at that day, of wattles and clay, and thatched with sods. As far as we could make out from dumb show, Lady Ludlow saw enough of the interiors of these places to make her hesitate before entering, or even speaking to any of the children who were playing about in the puddles. After a pause, she disappeared into one of the cottages. It seemed to us a long time before she came out; but I dare say it was not more than eight or ten minutes. She came back with her head hanging down, as if to choose her way – but we saw it was more in thought and bewilderment than for any such purpose.

She had not made up her mind where we should drive to when she got into the carriage again. John Footman stood, bare-headed, waiting for orders.

'To Hathaway. My dears, if you are tired, or if you have anything to do for Mrs. Medlicott, I can drop you at Barford Corner, and it is but a quarter of an hour's brisk walk home.'

But luckily we could safely say that Mrs. Medlicott did not want us; and as we had whispered to each other, as we sat alone in the coach, that surely my lady must have gone to Job Gregson's, we were far too anxious to know the end of it all to say that we were tired. So we all set off to Hathaway. Mr. Harry Lathom was a bachelor squire, thirty or thirty-five years of age, more at home in the field than in the drawing-room, and with sporting men than with ladies.

My lady did not alight of course; it was Mr. Lathom's place to wait upon her, and she bade the butler – who had a smack of the gamekeeper in him, very unlike our own powdered venerable fine gentleman at Hanbury – tell his master, with her compliments, that she wished to speak to him. You may think how pleased we were to find that we should hear all that was said; though, I think, afterwards we were half sorry when we saw how our presence confused the squire, who would have found it bad enough to answer my lady's questions, even without two eager girls for audience.

'Pray Mr. Lathom,' began my lady, something abruptly for her – for she was very full of her subject – 'what is this I hear about Job Gregson?'

Mr. Lathom looked annoyed and vexed, but dared not show it in his words.

'I gave out a warrant against him, my lady, for theft – that is all. You are doubtless aware of his character: a man who sets nets and springs in long cover, and fishes wherever he takes a fancy. It is but a short step from poaching to thieving.'

'That is quite true,' replied Lady Ludlow (who had a horror of poaching for this very reason): 'but I imagine you do not send a man to gaol on account of his bad character.'

'Rogues and vagabonds,' said Mr. Lathom. 'A man may be sent to prison for being a vagabond; for no specific act, but for his general mode of life.'

He had the better of her ladyship for one moment: but then she answered –

'But in this case, the charge on which you committed him is for theft; now his wife tells me he can prove he was some miles distant from Holmwood, where the robbery took place, all that afternoon; she says you had the evidence before you.'

Mr. Lathom here interrupted my lady, by saying in a somewhat sulky manner –

'No such evidence was brought before me when I gave the warrant. I am not answerable for the other magistrates' decision when they had more evidence before them. It was they who committed him to gaol. I am not responsible for that.'

My lady did not often show signs of impatience: but we knew she was feeling irritated, by the little perpetual tapping of her high-heeled shoe against the bottom of the carriage. About the same time we, sitting backwards, caught a glimpse of Mr. Gray through the open door, standing in the shadow of the hall. Doubtless Lady Ludlow's arrival had interrupted a conversation between Mr. Lathom and Mr. Gray. The latter must have heard every word of what she was saying; but of this she was not aware, and caught at Mr. Lathom's disclaimer of responsibility with pretty much the same argument which she had heard (through our repetition) that Mr. Gray had used not two hours before.

'And do you mean to say, Mr. Lathom, that you don't consider yourself responsible for all injustice or wrong-doing that you might have prevented, and have not? Nay, in this case the first germ of injustice was your own mistake. I wish you had been with me a little while ago, and seen the misery in that poor fellow's cottage.' She spoke lower, and Mr. Gray drew near, in a sort of involuntary manner, as if to hear all she was saying. We saw him, and doubtless Mr. Lathom heard his footstep, and knew who it was that was listening behind him, and approving of every word that was said. He grew yet more sullen in manner; but still my lady was my lady, and he dared not speak out before her, as he would have done to Mr. Gray.

Lady Ludlow, however caught the look of stubbornness in his face, and it roused her as I had never seen her roused.

'I am sure you will not refuse, sir, to accept my bail. I offer to bail the fellow out, and to be responsible for his appearance at the sessions. What say you to that, Mr. Lathom?'

'The offence of theft is not bailable, my lady.'

'Not in ordinary cases, I dare say. But I imagine this is an extraordinary case. The man is sent to prison out of compliment to you, and against all evidence, as far as I can learn. He will have to rot in gaol for two months, and his wife and children to starve. I, Lady Ludlow, offer to bail him out, and pledge myself for his appearance at next quarter-sessions.'

'It is against the law, my lady.'

'Bah! Bah! Bah! Who makes laws? Such as I, in the House of Lords such as you, in the House of Commons. We, who make the laws in St. Stephen's may break the mere forms of them, when we have right on our sides, on our own land, and amongst our own people.'

'The lord-lieutenant may take away my commission, if he heard of it.'

'And a very good thing for the county, Harry Lathom, and for you too, if he did if you don't go on more wisely than you have begun. A pretty set you and your brother magistrates are to administer justice through the land! I always said a good despotism was the best form of government; and I am twice as much in favour of it now I see what a quorum is! My dears!' suddenly turning round to us, 'if it would not tire you to walk home, I would beg Mr. Lathom to take a seat in my coach, and we would drive to Henley Gaol, and have the poor man out at once.'

'A walk over the fields at this time of day is hardly fitting for young ladies to take alone,' said Mr. Lathom, anxious no doubt to escape from his *tête-à-tête* drive with my lady, and possibly not quite prepared to go to the illegal length of prompt measures, which she had in contemplation.

But Mr. Gray now stepped forward, too anxious for the release of the prisoner to allow any obstacle to intervene which he could do away with. To see Lady Ludlow's face when she first perceived whom she had had for auditor and spectator of her interview with Mr. Lathom, was as good as a play. She

had been doing and saying the very things she had been so
much annoyed at Mr. Gray's saying and proposing only an
hour or two ago. She had been setting down Mr. Lathom
pretty smartly, in the presence of the very man to whom she
had spoken of that gentleman as so sensible, and of such a
standing in the county, that it was presumption to question his
doings. But before Mr. Gray had finished his offer of escort-
ing us back to Hanbury Court, my lady had recovered herself.
There was neither surprise nor displeasure in her manner, as
she answered –

'I thank you, Mr. Gray. I was not aware that you were here,
but I think I can understand on what errand you came. And
seeing you here recalls me to a duty I owe Mr. Lathom. Mr.
Lathom, I have spoken to you pretty plainly – forgetting until
I saw Mr. Gray that only this very afternoon I differed from
him on this very question; taking completely, at that time, the
same view of the whole subject which you have done;
thinking that the county would be well rid of such a man as
Job Gregson, whether he had committed this theft or not. Mr.
Gray and I did not part quite friends,' she continued, bowing
towards him; 'but it so happened that I saw Job Gregson's wife
and home – I felt that Mr. Gray had been right and I had been
wrong; so, with the famous inconsistency of my sex, I came
hither to scold you,' smiling towards Mr. Lathom, who
looked half-sulky yet, and did not relax a bit of his gravity at
her smile, 'for holding the same opinion that I had done an
hour before. Mr. Gray' (again bowing towards him) 'these
young ladies will be very much obliged to you for your escort,
and so shall I. Mr. Lathom, may I beg of you to accompany
me to Henley?'

Mr. Gray bowed very low, and went very red; Mr. Lathom
said something which we none of us heard, but which was, I
think, some remonstrance against the course he was, as it
were, compelled to take. Lady Ludlow, however, took no
notice of his murmur, but sat in an attitude of polite expectan-
cy: and, as we turned off on our walk, I saw Mr. Lathom
getting into the coach with the air of a whipped hound. I must
say, considering my lady's feeling, I did not envy him his ride
– though, I believe, he was quite in the right as to the object of
the ride being illegal.

Our walk home was very dull. We had no fears; and would far rather have been without the awkward, blushing, young man, into which Mr. Gray had sunk. At every stile he hesitated — sometimes he half got over it, thinking that he could assist us better in that way; then he would turn back, unwilling to go before ladies. He had no ease of manner, as my lady once said of him, though on any occasion of duty, he had an immense deal of dignity.

CHAPTER III

As far as I can remember it was very soon after this that I first began to have the pain in my hip which has ended in making me a cripple for life. I hardly recollect more than one walk after our return under Mr. Gray's escort from Mr. Lathom's. Indeed, at the time, I was not without suspicions (which I never named) that the beginning of my mischief was a great jump I had taken from the top of one of the stiles on that very occasion.

Well, it is a long while ago, and God disposes of us all, and I am not going to tire you out with telling you how I thought and felt, and how, when I saw what my life was to be, I could hardly bring myself to be patient, but rather wished to die at once. You can every one of you think for yourselves what becoming all at once useless and unable to move, and by-and-by growing hopeless of cure, and feeling that one must be a burden to some one all one's life long, would be to an active, wilful, strong girl of seventeen, anxious to get on in the world, so as, if possible, to help her brothers and sisters. So I shall only say, that one among the blessings which arose out of what seemed at the time a great, black sorrow was, that Lady Ludlow for many years took me, as it were, into her own special charge; and now, as I lie still and alone in my old age, it is such a pleasure to think of her!

Mrs. Medlicott was great as a nurse, and I am sure I can never be grateful enough to her memory for all her kindness. But she was puzzled to know how to manage me in other ways. I used to have long, hard fits of crying; thinking I ought to go home – and yet what could they do with me there? – and a hundred and fifty other anxious thoughts, some of which I could tell to Mrs. Medlicott, and others I could not. Her way of comforting me was hurrying off for some kind of tempting

or strengthening food – a basin of melted calves'-foot jelly
was, I am sure she thought, a cure for every woe.

'There! take it, dear, take it!' she would say; 'and don't go
on fretting for what can't be helped.'

But, I think, she got puzzled at length at the non-efficacy of
good things to eat; and one day, after I had limped down to see
the doctor, in Mrs. Medlicott's sitting-room – a room lined
with cupboards, containing preserves and dainties of all kinds,
which she perpetually made, and never touched herself – when
I was returning to my bedroom to cry away the afternoon,
under pretence of arranging my clothes, John Footman
brought me a message from my lady (with whom the doctor
had been having a conversation), to bid me go to her in that
private sitting-room at the end of the suite of apartments
about which I spoke in describing the day of my first arrival at
Hanbury. I had hardly been in it since; as, when we read to my
lady, she generally sat in the small withdrawing-room out of
which this private room of hers opened. I suppose great
people do not require what we small people value so much – I
mean privacy. I do not think that there was a room which my
lady occupied that had not two doors, and some of them had
three or four. Then my lady had always Adams waiting upon
her in her bed-chamber; and it was Mrs. Medlicott's duty to
sit within call, as it were, in a sort of ante-room that led out of
my lady's own sitting room, on the opposite side to the
drawing-room door. To fancy the house, you must take a
great square, and halve it by a line; at one end of this line was
the hall-door, or public entrance; at the opposite the private
entrance from a terrace, which was terminated at one end by a
sort of postern door in an old grey stone wall, beyond which
lay the farm buildings and offices; so that people could come
in this way to my lady on business, while, if she were going
into the garden from her own room, she had nothing to do but
to pass through Mrs. Medlicott's apartment, out into the
lesser hall; and then, turning to the right as she passed on to
the terrace, she could go down the flight of broad, shallow
steps at the corner of the house into the lovely garden, with
stretching, sweeping lawns, and gay flower-beds, and beautiful, bossy laurels, and other blooming or massy shrubs, with
full-grown beeches, or larches feathering down to the ground

a little farther off. The whole was set in a frame, as it were, by the more distant woodlands. The house had been modernised in the days of Queen Anne, I think; but the money had fallen short that was requisite to carry out all the improvements, so it was only the suite of withdrawing-rooms and the terrace-rooms, as far as the private entrance, that had the new, long, high windows put in; and these were old enough by this time to be draped with roses, and honeysuckles and pyracanthus, winter and summer long.

Well, to go back to that day when I limped into my lady's sitting-room, trying hard to look as if I had not been crying, and not to walk as if I was in much pain. I do not know whether my lady saw how near the tears were to my eyes, but she told me she had sent for me, because she wanted some help in arranging the drawers of her bureau, and asked me – just as if it was a favour I was to do for her – if I could sit down in the easy-chair near the window – (all quietly arranged before I came in with a footstool and a table quite near) – and assist her. You will wonder, perhaps why I was not bidden to sit or lie on the sofa; but (although I found one there a morning or two afterwards, when I came down) the fact was, that there was none in the room at the time. I have even fancied that the easy-chair was brought in on purpose for me; for it was not the chair in which I remember my lady sitting the first time I saw her. That chair was very much carved and gilded, with a countess's coronet at the top. I tried it one day, some time afterwards, when my lady was out of the room, and I had a fancy for seeing how I could move about; and very uncomfortable it was. Now my chair (as I learnt to call it and to think it) was soft and luxurious, and seemed somehow to give one's body rest just in that part where one most needed it.

I was not at my ease that first day, nor indeed for many days afterwards, notwithstanding my chair was so comfortable. Yet I forgot my sad pain in silently wondering over the meaning of many of the things we turned out of those curious old drawers. I was puzzled to know why some were kept at all: a scrap of writing may be, with only half-a-dozen commonplace words written on it, or a bit of broken riding-whip, and here and there a stone, of which I thought I could have picked up twenty just as good in the first walk I took. But it

seems that was just my ignorance; for my lady told me they
were pieces of valuable marble, used to make the floors of the
great Roman emperors' palaces long ago; and that when she
had been a girl, and made the grand tour long ago, her cousin,
Sir Horace Mann, the ambassador or envoy at Florence, had
told her to be sure to go into the fields inside the walls of
ancient Rome, when the farms were preparing the ground for
the onion-sowing, and had to make the soil fine, and pick up
what bits of marble she could find. She had done so, and
meant to have had them made into a table; but somehow that
plan fell through, and there they were with all the dirt out of
the onion-field upon them; but once when I thought of
cleaning them with soap and water, at any rate, she bade me
not to do so, for it was Roman dirt – earth, I think, she called
it – but it was dirt all the same.

Then in this bureau, were many other things, the value of
which I could understand – locks of hair carefully ticketed,
which my lady looked at very sadly; and lockets and bracelets
with miniatures in them, – very small pictures to what they
make now-a-days, and called miniatures; some of them had
even to be looked at through a microscope before you could
see the individual expression of the faces, or how beautifully
they were painted. I don't think that looking at these made my
lady seem so melancholy, as the seeing and touching of the
hair did. But, to be sure, the hair was, as it were, a part of
some beloved body which she might never touch and caress
again, but which lay beneath the turf, all faded and disfigured,
except perhaps the very hair from which the lock she held had
been dissevered; whereas the pictures were but pictures after
all – likenesses, but not the very things themselves. This is
only my own conjecture, mind. My lady rarely spoke out her
feelings. For, to begin with, she was of rank: and I have heard
her say that people of rank do not talk about their feelings
except to their equals, and even to them they conceal them,
except upon rare occasions. Secondly – and this is my own
reflection – she was an only child and an heiress, and as such
was more apt to think than to talk, as all well-brought-up
heiresses must be, I think. Thirdly, she had long been a
widow, without any companion of her own age with whom it
would have been natural for her to refer to old associations,

past pleasures, or mutual sorrows. Mrs. Medlicott came
nearest to her as a companion of that sort; and her ladyship
talked more to Mrs. Medlicott, in a kind of familiar way, than
she did to all the rest of the household put together. But Mrs.
Medlicott was silent by nature, and did not reply at any great
length. Adams, indeed, was the only one who spoke much to
Lady Ludlow.

After we had worked away about an hour at the bureau, her
ladyship said we had done enough for one day; and, as the
time was come for her afternoon ride, she left me, with a
volume of engravings from Mr. Hogarth's pictures on one
side of me (I don't like to write down the names of them
though my lady thought nothing of it, I am sure), and upon a
stand her great Prayer-book open at the evening psalms for the
day, on the other. But, as soon as she was gone I troubled
myself little with either, but amused myself with looking
round the room at my leisure. The side on which the fireplace
stood was all panelled – part of the old ornaments of the
house, for there was an Indian paper with birds and beasts and
insects on it, on all the other sides. There were coats of arms,
of the various families with whom the Hanburys had inter-
married, all over these panels, and up and down the ceiling as
well. There was very little looking-glass in the room, though
one of the great drawing-rooms was called the Mirror
Room, because it was lined with glass, which my lady's
great-grandfather had brought from Venice when he was
ambassador there. There were china jars of all shapes and sizes
round and about the room, and some china monsters, or idols,
of which I could never bear the sight, they were so ugly,
though I think my lady valued them more than all. There was
a thick carpet on the middle of the floor, which was made of
small pieces of rare wool fitted into a pattern; the doors were
opposite to each other, and were composed of two heavy tall
wings, and opened in the middle, moving on brass grooves
inserted into the floor – they would not have opened over a
carpet. There were two windows reaching up nearly to the
ceiling, but very narrow, and with deep window-seats in the
thickness of the wall. The room was full of scent, partly from
the flowers outside, and partly from the great jars of pot-
pourri inside. The choice of odours was what my lady piqued

herself upon, saying nothing showed birth like a keen suscep-
tibility of smell. We never named musk in her presence, her
antipathy to it was so well understood through the household:
her opinion on the subject was believed to be, that no scent
derived from an animal could ever be of a sufficiently pure
nature to give pleasure to any person of good family, where,
of course, the delicate perception of the senses had been
cultivated for generations. She would instance the way in
which sportsmen preserve the breed of dogs who have shown
keen scent; and how such gifts descend for generations
amongst animals, who cannot be supposed to have anything
of ancestral pride, or hereditary fancies about them. Musk,
then, was never mentioned at Hanbury Court. No more were
bergamot or southernwood, although vegetable in their nature. She considered these two latter as betraying a vulgar taste
in the person who chose to gather or wear them. She was
sorry to notice sprigs of them in the button-hole of any young
man in whom she took an interest, either because he was
engaged to a servant of hers or otherwise, as he came out of
church on a Sunday afternoon. She was afraid that he liked
coarse pleasures; and I am not sure if she did not think that his
preference for these coarse sweetnesses did not imply a
probability that he would take to drinking. But she distinguished between vulgar and common. Violets, pinks, and
sweetbriar were common enough; roses and mignonette, for
those who had gardens, honeysuckle for those who walked
along the bowery lanes; but wearing them betrayed no
vulgarity of taste: the queen upon her throne might be glad to
smell at a nosegay of the flowers. A beau-pot (as we called it)
of pinks and roses freshly gathered was placed every morning
that they were in bloom on my lady's own particular table. For
lasting vegetable odours she preferred lavender and sweet-
woodroof to any extract whatever. Lavender reminded her of
old customs, she said, and of homely cottage-gardens, and
many a cottager made his offering to her of a bundle of
lavender. Sweet-woodroof, again, grew in wild, woodland
places, where the soil was fine and the air delicate: the poor
children used to go and gather it for her up in the woods on
the higher lands; and for this service she always rewarded
them with bright new pennies, of which my lord, her son,

used to send her down a bagful fresh from the Mint in London every February.

Attar of roses, again, she disliked. She said it reminded her of the city and of the merchants' wives, over-rich, over-heavy in its perfume. And lilies of the valley somehow fell under the same condemnation. They were most graceful and elegant to look at (my lady was quite candid about this), flower, leaf, colour – everything was refined about them but the smell. That was too strong. But the great hereditary faculty on which my lady piqued herself, and with reason, for I never met with any person who possessed it, was the power she had of perceiving the delicious odour arising from a bed of strawberries in the late autumn, when the leaves were all fading and dying. *Bacon's Essays* was one of the few books that lay about in my lady's room; and, if you took it up and opened it carelessly, it was sure to fall apart at his 'Essay on Gardens.' 'Listen', her ladyship would say, 'to what that great philospher and statesman says. "Next to that" – he is speaking of violets, my dear – "is the musk-rose" – of which you remember the great bush, at the corner of the south wall just by the Blue Drawing-room windows; that is the old musk-rose, Shakespeare's musk-rose, which is dying out through the kingdom now. But to return to my Lord Bacon: "Then the strawberry leaves, dying with a most excellent cordial smell." Now the Hanburys can always smell this excellent cordial odour, and very delicious and refreshing it is. You see, in Lord Bacon's time, there had not been so many intermarriages between the court and the city as there have been since the needy days of his Majesty Charles the Second; and altogether, in the time of Queen Elizabeth, the great, old families of England were a distinct race, just as a cart-horse is one creature, and very useful in its place, and Childers or Eclipse is another creature, though both are of the same species. So the old families have gifts and powers of a different and higher class to what the other orders have. My dear, remember that you try if you can smell the scent of dying strawberry-leaves in this next autumn. You have some of Ursula Hanbury's blood in you, and that gives you a chance.'

But when October came, I sniffed and sniffed, and all to no purpose; and my lady – who had watched the little experiment rather anxiously – had to give me up as a hybrid. I was mortified, I confess, and thought that it was in some ostentation of her own powers tht she ordered the gardener to plant a border of strawberries on that side of the terrace that lay under her windows.

I have wandered away from time and place. I tell you all the remembrances I have of those years just as they come up, and I hope that, in my old age, I am not getting too like a certain Mrs. Nickleby, whose speeches were once read out aloud to me.

I came by degrees to be all day long in this room which I have been describing; sometimes sitting in the easy-chair, doing some little pieces of dainty work for my lady, or sometimes arranging flowers, or sorting letters according to their handwriting, so that she could arrange them afterwards, and destroy or keep, as she planned, looking ever onward to her death. Then, after the sofa was brought in, she would watch my face, and if she saw my colour change, she would bid me lie down and rest. And I used to try to walk upon the terrace every day for a short time; it hurt me very much, it is true, but the doctor had ordered it, and I knew her ladyship wished me to obey.

Before I had seen the background of a great lady's life, I had thought it all play and fine doings. But whatever other grand people are, my lady was never idle. For one thing, she had to superintend the agent for the large Hanbury estate. I believe it was mortgaged for a sum of money which had gone to improve the late lord's Scotch lands; but she was anxious to pay off this before her death, and so to leave her own inheritance free of incumbrance to her son, the present Earl; whom, I secretly think, she considered a greater person, as being the heir of the Hanburys (though through a female line), than as being my Lord Ludlow with half-a-dozen other minor titles.

With this wish of releasing her property from the mortgage, skilful care was much needed in the management of it; and as far as my lady could go, she took every pain. She had a great book, in which every page was ruled into three divisions; on the first column was written the date and the name of the tenant who addressed any letter on business to her; on the

second was briefly stated the subject of the letter, which
generally contained a request of some kind. This request
would be surrounded and enveloped in so many words, and
often inserted amidst so many odd reasons and excuses, that
Mr. Horner (the steward) would sometimes say it was like
hunting through a bushel of chaff to find a grain of wheat.
Now, in the second column of this book, the grain of meaning
was placed, clean and dry, before her ladyship every morning.
She sometimes would ask to see the original letter; sometimes
she simply answered the request by a 'Yes,' or a 'No'; and
often she would send for leases and papers, and examine them
well, with Mr. Horner at her elbow, to see if such petitions, as
to be allowed to plough up pasture fields, &c., were provided
for in the terms of the original agreement. On every Thursday
she made herself at liberty to see her tenants, from four to six
in the afternoon. Mornings would have suited my lady better,
as far as convenience went, and I believe the old custom had
been to have these levées (as her ladyship used to call them)
held before twelve. But, as she said to Mr. Horner, when he
urged returning to the former hours, it spoilt a whole day for a
farmer, if he had to dress himself in his best and leave his work
in the forenoon (and my lady liked to see her tenants come in
their Sunday clothes; she would not say a word, may be, but
she would take her spectacles slowly out, and put them on
with silent gravity, and look at a dirty or raggedly-dressed
man so solemnly and earnestly, that his nerves must have been
pretty strong if he did not wince, and resolve that, however
poor he might be, soap and water, and needle and thread,
should be used before he again appeared in her ladyship's
ante-room). The outlying tenants had always a supper provided for them in the servants' hall on Thursdays, to which,
indeed, all comers were welcome to sit down. For my lady
said, though there were not many hours left of a working-
man's day when their business with her was ended, yet that
they needed food and rest, and that she should be ashamed if
they sought either at the Fighting Lion (called at this day the
Hanbury Arms). They had as much beer as they could drink
while they were eating; and, when the food was cleared away,
they had a cup apiece of good ale, in which the oldest tenant
present, standing up, gave Madam's health; and after that was

drunk, they were expected to set off homewards; at any rate, no more liquor was given them. The tenants one and all called her 'Madam'; for they recognised in her the married heiress of the Hanburys, not the widow of a Lord Ludlow, of whom they and their forefathers knew nothing; and against whose memory, indeed, there rankled a dim unspoken grudge, the cause of which was accurately known to the very few who understood the nature of a mortgage, and were therefore aware that Madam's money had been taken to enrich my lord's poor land in Scotland. I am sure – for you can understand I was behind the scenes, as it were, and had many an opportunity of seeing and hearing, as I lay or sat motionless in my lady's room with the double doors open between it and the ante-room beyond, where Lady Ludlow saw her steward, and gave audience to her tenants – I am certain, I say, that Mr. Horner was silently as much annoyed at the money that was swallowed up by this mortgage as any one; and some time or other he had probably spoken his mind out to my lady; for there was a sort of offended reference on her part, and respectful submission to blame on his, while every now and then there was an implied protest – whenever the payments of the interest became due, or whenever my lady stinted herself of any personal expense, such as Mr. Horner thought was only decorous and becoming in the heiress of the Hanburys. Her carriages were old and cumbrous, wanting all the improvements which had been adopted by those of her rank throughout the county. Mr. Horner would fain have had the ordering of a new coach. The carriage-horses, too, were getting past their work; yet all the promising colts bred on the estate were sold for ready money, and so on. My lord, her son, was ambassador at some foreign place, and very proud we all were of his glory and dignity; but I fancy it cost money, and my lady would have lived on bread and water sooner than have called upon him to help her in paying off the mortgage, although he was the one who was to benefit by it in the end.

Mr. Horner was a very faithful steward, and very respectful to my lady; although sometimes, I thought, she was sharper to him than to any one else; perhaps because she knew that, although he never said anything, he disapproved of the

Hanburys being made to pay for the Earl Ludlow's estates and
state.

The late lord had been a sailor, and had been as extravagant
in his habits as most sailors are, I am told – for I never was at
sea; and yet he had a long sight to his own interests; but
whatever he was, my lady loved him and his memory, with
about as fond and proud a love as ever wife gave husband, I
should think.

For a part of his life Mr. Horner, who was born on the
Hanbury property, had been a clerk to an attorney in Birmingham; and these few years had given him a kind of worldly
wisdom, which, though always exerted for her benefit, was
antipathetic to her ladyship, who thought that some of her
steward's maxims savoured of trade and commerce. I fancy
that if it had been possible, she would have preferred a return
to the primitive system, of living on the produce of the land,
and exchanging the surplus for such articles as were needed,
without the intervention of money.

But Mr. Horner was bitten with new-fangled notions, as
she would say, though his new-fangled notions were what
folk at the present day would think sadly behindhand; and
some of Mr. Gray's ideas fell on Mr. Horner's mind like
sparks on tow, though they started from two different points.
Mr. Horner wanted to make every man useful and active in
this world, and to direct as much activity and usefulness as
possible to the improvement of the Hanbury estates, and the
aggrandisement of the Hanbury family, and therefore he fell
into the new cry for education.

Mr. Gray did not care much – Mr. Horner thought not
enough – for this world, and where any man or family stood
in their earthly position; but he would have every one
prepared for the world to come, and capable of understanding
and receiving certain doctrines, for which latter purpose, it
stands to reason, he must have heard of these doctrines; and
therefore Mr. Gray wanted education. The answer in the
Catechism that Mr. Horner was most fond of calling upon a
child to repeat, was that to, 'What is thy duty towards thy
neighbour?' The answer Mr. Gray liked best to hear repeated
with unction was that to the question, 'What is the inward and
spiritual grace?' The reply to which Lady Ludlow bent her

head the lowest, as we said our Catechism to her on Sundays, was to, 'What is thy duty towards God?' But neither Mr. Horner nor Mr. Gray had heard many answers to the Catechism as yet.

Up to this time there was no Sunday-school in Hanbury. Mr. Gray's desires were bounded by that object. Mr. Horner looked farther on: he hoped for a day-school at some future time, to train up intelligent labourers for working on the estate. My lady would hear of neither the one nor the other; indeed, not the boldest man whom she ever saw would have dared to name the project of a day-school within her hearing.

So Mr. Horner contented himself with quietly teaching a sharp, clever lad to read and write, with a view to making use of him as a kind of foreman in process of time. He had his pick of the farm-lads for this purpose; and, as the brightest and sharpest, although by far the raggedest and dirtiest, singled out Job Gregson's son. But all this – as my lady never listened to gossip, or, indeed, was spoken to unless she spoke first – was quite unknown to her, until the unlucky incident took place which I am going to relate

CHAPTER IV

I think my lady was not aware of Mr. Horner's views on education (as making men into more useful members of society), or the practice to which he was putting his precepts in taking Harry Gregson as pupil and protégé – if, indeed, she were aware of Harry's distinct existence at all – until the following unfortunate occasion. The ante-room, which was a kind of business-place for my lady to receive her steward and tenants in, was surrounded by shelves. I cannot call them bookshelves, though there were many books on them; but the contents of the volumes were principally manuscript, and relating to details connected with the Hanbury property. There were also one or two dictionaries, gazetteers, works of reference on the management of property; all of a very old date (the dictionary was Bailey's, I remember; we had a great Johnson in my lady's room, but, where lexicographers differed, she generally preferred Bailey).

In this ante-chamber a footman generally sat, awaiting orders from my lady; for she clung to the grand old customs, and despised any bells, except her own little hand-bell, as modern inventions; she would have her people always within summons of this silvery bell, or her scarce less silvery voice. This man had not the sinecure you might imagine. He had to reply to the private entrance: what we should call the back door in a smaller house. As none came to the front door but my lady, and those of the county whom she honoured by visiting, and her nearest acquaintance of this kind lived eight miles (of bad road) off, the majority of comers knocked at the nail-studded terrace door; not to have it opened (for open it stood, by my lady's orders, winter and summer, so that the snow often drifted into the back hall, and lay there in heaps when the weather was severe), but to summon someone to receive their message, or carry their request to be allowed to speak to my lady. I remember it was long before Mr. Gray could be made to understand that the great door was only open on state occasions, and even to the last he would as soon come in by that as the terrace entrance. I had been received there on my first setting foot over my lady's threshold; every stranger was led in by that way the first time they came; but after that (with the exceptions I have named) they went round by the terrace, as it were by instinct. It was an assistance to this instinct to be aware that, from time immemorial, the magnificent and fierce Hanbury wolf-hounds, which were extinct in every other part of the island, had been and still were kept chained in the front quadrangle, where they bayed through a great part of the day and night, and were always ready with their deep, savage growl at the sight of every person and thing, excepting the man who fed them, my lady's carriage and four, and my lady herself. It was pretty to see her small figure go up to the great, crouching brutes, thumping the flags with their heavy, wagging tails, and slobbering in an ecstasy of delight, at her light approach and soft caress. She had no fear of them; but she was a Hanbury born, and the tale went, that they and their kind knew all Hanburys instantly, and acknowledged their supremacy, ever since the ancestors of the breed had been brought from the East by the great Sir Urian Hanbury, who lay with his legs crossed on the altar tomb in the church. Moreover, it was reported that, not fifty years before, one of these dogs had eaten up a child, which had inadvertently strayed within reach of its chain. So you may imagine how most people preferred the terrace door. Mr. Gray did not seem to care for the dogs. It might be absence of mind, for I have heard of his starting away from their sudden spring when he had unwittingly walked within reach of their chains; but it could hardly have been absence of mind, when one day he went right up to one of them, and patted him in the most friendly manner, the dog meanwhile looking pleased, and affably wagging his tail, just as if Mr. Gray had been a Hanbury. We were all very much puzzled by this, and to this day I have not been able to account for it.

But now let us go back to the terrace-door, and the footman sitting in the ante-chamber.

One morning we heard a parleying, which rose to such a

vehemence, and lasted for so long, that my lady had to ring her hand-bell twice before the footman heard it.

'What is the matter, John?' asked she, when he entered.

'A little boy, my lady, who says he comes from Mr. Horner, and must see your ladyship. Impudent little lad!' (This last to himself.)

'What does he want?'

'That's just what I have asked him, my lady; but he won't tell me, please your ladyship.'

'It is, probably, some message from Mr. Horner,' said Lady Ludlow, with just a shade of annoyance in her manner; for it was against all etiquette to send a message to her, and by such a messenger too!

'No! please your ladyship, I asked him if he had any message, and he said no, he had none; but he must see your ladyship for all that.'

'You had better show him in then, without more words,' said her ladyship quietly, but still, as I have said, rather annoyed.

As if in mockery of the humble visitor, the footman threw open both battants of the door, and in the opening there stood a lithe, wiry lad, with a thick head of hair, standing out in every direction, as if stirred by some electrical current, a short, brown face, red now from affright and excitement, wide, resolute mouth, and bright, deep-set eyes, which glanced keenly and rapidly round the room, as if taking in everything (and all that was new and strange), to be thought and puzzled over at some future time. He knew enough of manners not to speak first to one above him in rank, or else he was afraid.

'What do you want with me?' asked my lady, in so gentle a tone that it seemed to surprise and stun him.

'An't please your ladyship?' said he, as if he had been deaf.

'You come from Mr. Horner's: why do you want to see me?' again asked she, a little more loudly.

'An't please your ladyship, Mr. Horner was sent for all on a sudden to Warwick this morning.'

His face began to work; but he felt it, and closed his lips into a resolute form.

'Well?'

'And he went off all on a sudden like.'

'Well?'

'And he left a note for your ladyship with me, your ladyship.'

'Is that all? You might have given it to the footman.'

'Please your ladyship, I've clean gone and lost it.'

He never took his eyes off her face. If he had not kept his look fixed, he would have burst out crying.

'That was very careless,' said my lady gently. 'But I am sure you are very sorry for it. You had better try and find it; it may have been of consequence.'

'Please mum – please your ladyship – I can say it off by heart.'

'You! What do you mean?' I was really afraid now. My lady's blue eyes absolutely gave out light, she was so much displeased, and, moreover, perplexed. The more reason he had for affright, the more his courage rose. He must have seen – so sharp a lad must have perceived – her displeasure; but he went on quickly and steadily.

'Mr. Horner, my lady, has taught me to read, write, and cast accounts, my lady. And he was in a hurry, and he folded his paper up but he did not seal it; and I read it, my lady; and now, my lady, it seems like as if I had got it off by heart;' and he went on with a high-pitched voice, saying out very loud what, I have no doubt, were the identical words of the letter, date, signature and all: it was merely something about a deed, which required my lady's signature.

When he had done, he stood almost as if he expected commendation for his accurate memory.

My lady's eyes contracted till the pupils were as needle-points; it was a way she had when much disturbed. She looked at me, and said –

'Margaret Dawson, what will this world come to?' and then she was silent.

The lad, beginning to perceive he had given deep offence, stood stock still – as if his brave will had brought him into this presence, and impelled him to confession, and the best amends he could make, but had now deserted him, or was extinct, and left his body motionless, until some one else with word or deed made him quit the room. My lady looked again at him, and saw the frowning dumb-foundering terror at his misdeed, and the manner in which his confession had been received.

'My poor lad!' said she, the angry look leaving her face, 'Into whose hands have you fallen?'

The boy's lips began to quiver.

'Don't you know what tree we read of in Genesis? – No! I hope you have not got to read so easily as that.' A pause. 'Who has taught you to read and write?'

'Please, my lady, I meant no harm, my lady.' He was fairly blubbering, overcome by her evident feeling of dismay and regret, the soft repression of which was more frightening to him than any strong or violent words would have been.

'Who taught you I ask?'

'It were Mr. Horner's clerk who learned me, my lady.'

'And did Mr. Horner know of it?'

'Yes, my lady. And I am sure I thought for to please him.'

'Well? perhaps you were not to blame for that. But I wonder at Mr. Horner. However, my boy, as you have got possession of edge-tools, you must have some rules how to use them. Did you never hear that you were not to open letters?'

'Please, my lady, it were open. Mr. Horner forgot to seal it, in his hurry to be off.'

'But you must not read letters that are not intended for you. You must never try to read any letters that are not directed to you, even if they be open before you.'

'Please, my lady, I thought it were good for practice, all as one as a book.'

My lady looked bewildered as to what way she could farther explain to him the laws of honour as regarded letters.

'You would not listen, I am sure,' said she, 'to anything you were not intended to hear.'

He hesitated for a moment, partly because he did not fully comprehend the question. My lady repeated it. The light of intelligence came into his eager eyes, and I could see that he was not certain if he would tell the truth.

'Please, my lady, I always hearken when I hear folk talking secrets; but I mean no harm.'

My poor lady sighed: she was not prepared to begin a long way off in morals. Honour was, to her, second nature, and she had never tried to find out on what principle its laws were based. So, telling the lad that she wished to see Mr. Horner when he returned from Warwick, she dismissed him with a despondent look; he, meanwhile, right glad to be out of the awful gentleness of her presence.

'What is to be done?' said she, half to herself and half to me. I could not answer, for I was puzzled myself.

'It was a right word,' she continued, 'that I used, when I called reading and writing "edge-tools." If our lower orders have these edge-tools given to them, we shall have the terrible scenes of the French Revolution acted over again in England. When I was a little girl, one never heard of the rights of men, one only heard of the duties. Now, here was Mr. Gray, only last night, talking of the right every child has to instruction. I could hardly keep my patience with him, and at length we fairly came to words; and I told him I would have no such thing as a Sunday-school (or a Sabbath-school, as he calls it, just like a Jew) in my village.'

'And what did he say, my lady?' I asked; for the struggle that seemed now to have come to a crisis had been going on for some time in a quiet way.

'Why, he gave way to temper, and said, he was bound to remember he was under the bishop's authority, not under mine; and implied that he should persevere in his designs, notwithstanding my expressed opinion.'

'And your ladyship' – I half inquired.

'I could only rise and curtsey, and civilly dismiss him. When two persons have arrived at a certain point of expression on a subject, about which they differ as materially as I do from Mr. Gray, the wisest course, if they wish to remain friends, is to drop the conversation entirely and suddenly. It is one of the few cases where abruptness is desirable.'

I was sorry for Mr. Gray. He had been to see me several times, and had helped me to bear my illness in a better spirit than I should have done without his good advice and prayers. And I had gathered, from little things he said, how much his heart was set upon this new scheme. I liked him so much, and I loved and respected my lady so well, that I could not bear them to be on the cool terms to which they were constantly getting. Yet I could do nothing but keep silence.

I suppose my lady understood something of what was

passing in my mind; for, after a minute or two, she went on –

'If Mr. Gray knew all I knew – if he had my experience, he would not be so ready to speak of setting up his new plans in opposition to my judgment. Indeed,' she continued, lashing herself up with her own recollections, 'times are changed when the parson of a village comes to beard the liege lady in her own house. Why, in my grandfather's days, the parson was family chaplain too, and dined at the Hall every Sunday. He was helped last, and expected to have done first. I remember seeing him take up his plate and knife and fork, and say, with his mouth full all the time he was speaking; "If you please, Sir Urian, and my lady, I'll follow the beef into the housekeeper's room"; for, you see, unless he did so, he stood no chance of a second helping. A greedy man, that parson was, to be sure! I recollect his once eating up the whole of some little bird at dinner, and, by way of diverting attention from his greediness, he told how he had heard that a rook soaked in vinegar and then dressed in a particular way, could not be distinguished from the bird he was then eating. I saw by the grim look on my grandfather's face that the parson's doing and saying displeased him; and, child as I was, I had some notion of what was coming, when, as I was riding out on my little white pony by my grandfather's side the next Friday, he stopped one of the gamekeepers, and bade him shoot one of the oldest rooks he could find. I knew no more about it till Sunday, when a dish was set right before the parson, and Sir Urian said: "Now Parson Hemming, I have had a rook shot, and soaked in vinegar, and dressed as you described last Sunday. Fall to, man, and eat it with as good an appetite as you had last Sunday. Pick the bones clean, or by – , no more Sunday dinners shall you eat at my table!" I gave one look at poor Mr. Hemming's face, as he tried to swallow the first morsel, and make believe as though he thought it very good, but I could not look again for shame, although my grandfather laughed, and kept asking us all round if we knew what could have become of the parson's appetite.'

'And did he finish it?' I asked.

'Oh yes my dear. What my grandfather said was to be done, was done always. He was a terrible man in his anger! But to think of the difference between Parson Hemming and Mr.

Gray! Or even of poor Mr. Mountford and Mr. Gray. Mr. Mountford would never have withstood me as Mr. Gray did!'

'And your ladyship really thinks that it would not be right to have a Sunday-school?' I asked, feeling very timid as I put the question.

'Certainly not. As I told Mr. Gray, I consider a knowledge of the Creed, and of the Lord's Prayer, as essential to salvation; and that any child may have, whose parents bring it regularly to church. Then there are the Ten Commandments, which teach simple duties in the plainest language. Of course, if a lad is taught to read and write (as that unfortunate boy has been who was here this morning) his duties become complicated, and his temptations much greater, while, at the same time, he has no hereditary principles and honourable training to serve as safeguards. I might take up my old simile of the race-horse and cart-horse, I am distressed,' continued she, with a break in her ideas, 'about that boy. The whole thing reminds me so much of a story of what happened to a friend of mine – Clément de Créquy. Did I ever tell you about him?'

'No, your ladyship,' I replied.

'Poor Clément! More than twenty years ago, Lord Ludlow and I spent a winter in Paris. He had many friends there; perhaps not very good or very wise men, but he was so kind that he liked every one, and every one liked him. We had an apartment, as they call it there, in the Rue de Lille; we had the first-floor of a grand hôtel, with the basement for our servants. On the floor above us the owner of the house lived, a Marquise de Créquy, a widow. They tell me that the Créquy coat-of-arms is still emblazoned, after all these terrible years, on a shield above the arched *porte-cochére,* just as it was then, though the family is quite extinct. Madam de Créquy had only one son, Clément, who was just the same age as my Urian – you may see his portrait in the great hall – Urian's, I mean.' I knew that Master Urian had been drowned at sea; and often had I looked at the presentment of his bonny hopeful face, in his sailor's dress, with right hand outstretched to a ship on the sea in the distance, as if he had just said, 'Look at her! all her sails are set, and I'm just off.' Poor Master Urian! he went down in this very ship not a year after the picture was taken. But now I will go back to my lady's story. 'I can see those two

boys playing now,' continued she softly, shutting her eyes, as
if the better to call up the vision, 'as they used to do
five-and-twenty years ago in those old-fashioned French
gardens behind our hôtel. Many a time I have watched them
from my windows. It was, perhaps, a better play-place than
an English garden would have been, for there were but few
flower-beds, and no lawn at all to speak about; but instead,
terraces and balustrades and vases and flights of stone steps
more in the Italian style; and there were *jets-d'eau*, and little
fountains that could be set playing by turning water-cocks that
were hidden here and there. How Clément delighted in
turning the water on to surprise Urian, and how gracefully he
did the honours, as it were, to my dear, rough, sailor lad!
Urian was as dark as a gipsy boy, and cared little for his
appearance, and resisted all my efforts at setting off his black
eyes and tangled curls; but Clément, without ever showing
that he thought about himself and his dress, was always dainty
and elegant, even though his clothes were sometimes but
threadbare. He used to be dressed in a kind of hunter's green
suit, open at the neck and half-way down the chest to beautiful
old lace frills; his long golden curls fell behind just like a girl's,
and his hair in front was cut over his straight dark eyebrows in
a line almost as straight. Urian learnt more of a gentleman's
carefulness and propriety of appearance from that lad in two
months than he had done in years from all my lectures. I
recollect one day, when the two boys were in full romp – and,
my window being open, I could hear them perfectly – and
Urian was daring Clément to some scrambling or climbing,
which Clément refused to undertake, but in a hesitating way,
as though he longed to do it if some reason had not stood in
the way; and at times Urian, who was hasty and thoughtless,
poor fellow, told Clément that he was afraid. "Fear!" said the
French boy, drawing himself up; "You do not know what you
say. If you will be here at six tomorrow morning, when it is
only just light, I will take that starling's nest on the top of
yonder chimney." "But why not now, Clément?" said Urian,
putting his arm round Clément's neck. "Why then, and not
now, just when we are in the humour for it?" "Because we De
Créquys are poor, and my mother cannot afford me another
suit of clothes this year, and yonder stone carving is all jagged,

and would tear my coat and breeches. Now, tomorrow morning I could go up with nothing on but an old shirt."

"'But you would tear your legs."

"'My race do not care for pain," said the boy, drawing himself from Urian's arm, and walking a few steps away, with a becoming pride and reserve; for he was hurt at being spoken to as if he was afraid, and annoyed at having to confess the true reason for declining the feat. But Urian was not to be thus baffled. He went up to Clément, and put his arm once more about his neck, and I could see the two lads as they walked down the terrace away from the hôtel windows: first Urian spoke eagerly, looking with imploring fondness into Clément's face, which sought the ground till at last the French boy spoke, and by-and-by his arm was round Urian too, and they paced backwards and forwards in deep talk, but gravely, as became men, rather than boys.

'All at once, from the little chapel at the corner of the large garden belonging to the Missions Étrangères, I heard the tinkle of the little bell, announcing the elevation of the host. Down on his knees went Clément, hands crossed, eyes bent down: while Urian stood looking on in respectful thought.

'What a friendship that might have been! I never dream of Urian without seeing Clément too – Urian speaks to me, or does something but Clément only flits round Urian, and never seems to see any one else!

'But I must not forget to tell you, that the next morning, before he was out of his room, a footman of Madame de Créquy's brought Urian the starling's nest.

'Well! we came back to England, and the boys were to correspond; and Madame de Créquy and I exchanged civilities; and Urian went to sea.

'After that, all seemed to drop away. I cannot tell you all. However, to confine myself to the De Créquys. I had a letter from Clément; I knew he felt his friend's death deeply; but I should never have learnt it from the letter he sent. It was formal, and seemed like chaff to my hungering heart. Poor fellow! I dare say he had found it hard to write. What could he – or any one – say to a mother who has lost her child? The world does not think so, and, in general, one must conform to the customs of the world; but judging from my own experience, I should say that reverent silence at such times is the tenderest balm. Madame de Créquy wrote too. But I knew she could not feel my loss so much as Clément, and therefore her letter was not such a disappointment. She and I went on being civil and polite in the way of commissions, and occasionally introducing friends to each other, for a year or two, and then we ceased to have any intercourse. Then the terrible Revolution came. No one who did not live at those times can imagine the daily expectation of news – the hourly terror of rumours affecting the fortunes and lives of those whom most of us had known as pleasant hosts, receiving us with peaceful welcome in their magnificent houses. Of course, there was sin enough and suffering enough behind the scenes; but we English visitors to Paris had seen little or nothing of that – and I had sometimes thought, indeed, how even Death seemed loth to choose his victims out of that brilliant throng whom I had known. Madame de Créquy's one boy lived; while three out of my six were gone since we had met! I do not think all lots are equal, even now that I know the end of her hopes; but I do say that whatever our individual lot is, it is our duty to accept it, without comparing it with that of others.

'The times were thick with gloom and terror. "What next?" was the question we asked of every one who brought us news from Paris. Where were these demons hidden when, so few years ago, we danced and feasted, and enjoyed the brilliant salons and the charming friendships of Paris?

'One evening, I was sitting alone in Saint James's Square; my lord off at the club with Mr. Fox and others: he had left me, thinking that I should go to one of the many places to which I had been invited for that evening; but I had no heart to go anywhere, for it was poor Urian's birthday, and I had not even rung for lights, though the day was fast closing in, but was thinking over all his pretty ways, and on his warm affectionate nature, and how often I had been too hasty in speaking to him for all I loved him so dearly; and how I seemed to have neglected and dropped his dear friend Clément, who might even now be in need of help in that cruel, bloody Paris. I say I was thinking reproachfully of all this, and particularly of Clément de Créquy in connection with Urian, when Fenwick brought me a note, sealed with a coat of arms I knew well, though I could not remember at the moment where I had seen it. I puzzled over it as one does sometimes, for a minute or more, before I opened the letter. In a moment I saw it was from Clément de Créquy. "My mother is here," he said: "she is very ill, and I am bewildered in this strange country. May I entreat you to receive me for a few minutes?" The bearer of the note was the woman of the house where they lodged. I had her brought up into the ante-room, and questioned her myself, while my carriage was being brought round. They had arrived in London a fortnight or so before; she had not known their quality, judging them (according to her kind) by their dress and their luggage: poor enough, no doubt. The lady had never left her bedroom since her arrival; the young man waited upon her, did everything for her, never left her, in fact; only she (the messenger) had promised to stay within call, as soon as she returned, while he went out somewhere. She could hardly understand him, he spoke English, so badly. He had never spoken it, I dare say, since he had talked to my Urian.

CHAPTER V

'In the hurry of the moment I scarce knew what I did. I bade the housekeeper put up every delicacy she had, in order to tempt the invalid, whom yet I hoped to bring back with me to our house. When the carriage was ready I took the good woman with me to show us the exact way, which my coachman professed not to know; for, indeed, they were staying at but a poor kind of place at the back of Leicester Square, of which they had heard, as Clément told me afterwards, from one of the fishermen who had carried them across from the Dutch coast in their disguises as a Friesland peasant and his mother. They had some jewels of value concealed round their persons; but their ready money was all spent before I saw them; and Clément had been unwilling to leave his mother, even for the time necessary to ascertain the best mode of disposing of the diamonds. For, overcome with distress of mind and bodily fatigue, she had reached London only to take to her bed in a sort of low, nervous fever, in which her chief and only idea seemed to be that Clément was about to be taken from her to some prison or other; and if he were out of her sight, though but for a minute, she cried like a child, and could not be pacified or comforted. The landlady was a kind, good woman, and though she had half understood the case, she was truly sorry for them, as foreigners, and the mother sick in a strange land.

'I sent her forwards to request permission for my entrance. In a moment I saw Clément – a tall, elegant young man, in a curious dress of coarse cloth, standing at the open door of a room, and evidently – even before he accosted me – striving to soothe the terrors of his mother inside. I went towards him, and would have taken his hand, but he bent down and kissed mine.

'"May I come in, madame?" I asked, looking at the poor

sick lady, lying in the dark, dingy bed, her head propped up on coarse, and dirty pillows, and gazing with affrighted eyes at all that was going on.

'"Clément! Clément! come to me!" she cried; and when he went to the bedside she turned on one side, and took his hand in both of hers, and began stroking it and looking up in his face. I could scarce keep back my tears.

'He stood there quite still, except that from time to time he spoke to her in a low tone. At last I advanced into the room, so that I could talk to him, without renewing her alarm. I asked for the doctor's address; for I had heard that they had called in some one, at their landlady's recommendation; but I could hardly understand Clément's broken English, and mispronunciation of our proper names, and was obliged to apply to the woman herself. I could not say much to Clément, for his attention was perpetually needed by his mother, who never seemed to perceive that I was there. But I told him not to fear, however long I might be away, for that I would return before night; and bidding the woman take charge of all the heterogeneous things the housekeeper had put up, and leaving one of my men in the house, who could understand a few words of French, with directions that he was to hold himself at Madame de Créquy's orders until I sent or gave him fresh commands, I drove off to the doctor's. What I wanted was his permission to remove Madame de Créquy to my own house, and to learn how it best could be done; for I saw that every movement in the room, every sound except Clément's voice, brought on a fresh access of trembling and nervous agitation.

'The doctor was, I should think, a clever man; but he had that kind of abrupt manner which people get who have much to do with the lower orders.

'I told him the story of his patient, the interest I had in her, and the wish I entertained of removing her to my own house.

'"It can't be done," said he. "Any change will kill her."

'"But it must be done, " I replied. "And it shall not kill her."

'"Then I have nothing more to say," said he, turning away from the carriage door, and making as though he would go back into the house.

'"Stop a moment. You must help me; and if you do, you shall have reason to be glad, for I will give you fifty pounds down with pleasure. If you won't do it, another shall."

'He looked at me, then (furtively) at the carriage, hesitated, and then said – "You do not mind expense apparently. I suppose you are a rich lady of quality. Such folks will not stick at such times as the life or death of a sick woman to get their own way. I suppose I must e'en help you, for if I don't another will."

'I did not mind what he said, so that he would assist me. I was pretty sure that she was in a state to require opiates; and I had not forgotten Christopher Sly, you may be sure; so I told him what I had in my head. That in the dead of night – the quiet time in the streets – she should be carried in a hospital litter, softly and warmly covered over, from the Leicester Square lodging-house to rooms that I would have in perfect readiness for her. As I planned, so it was done. I let Clément know, by a note, of my design. I had all prepared at home, and we walked about my house as though shod with velvet, while the porter watched at the open door. At last, through the darkness, I saw the lanterns carried by my men, who were leading the little procession. The litter looked like a hearse; on one side walked the doctor, on the other Clément; they came softly and swiftly along. I could not try any farther experi-ment; we dared not change her clothes; she was laid in the bed in the landlady's coarse night-gear, and covered over warmly, and left in the shaded, scented room, with a nurse and the doctor watching by her, while I led Clément to the dressing-room adjoining, in which I had a bed placed for him. Farther than that he would not go; and there I had refreshments brought. Meanwhile, he had shown his gratitude by every possible action (for we none of us dared to speak): he had kneeled at my feet, and kissed my hand, and left it wet with his tears. He had thrown up his arms to heaven, and prayed earnestly, as I could see by the movement of his lips. I allowed him to relieve himself by these dumb expressions, if I may so call them – and then I left him, and went to my own rooms to sit up for my lord, and tell him what I had done.

'Of course, it was all right, and neither my lord nor I could sleep for wondering how Madame de Créquy would bear her awakening. I had engaged the doctor, to whose face and voice she was accustomed, to remain with her all night; the nurse was experienced, and Clément was within call. But it was with the greatest relief that I heard from my own woman, when she brought me my chocolate, that Madame de Créquy (Monsieur had said) had awakened more tranquil than she had been for many days. To be sure, the whole aspect of that bed-chamber must have been more familiar to her than the miserable place where I had found her, and she must have intuitively felt herself among friends.

'My lord was scandalised at Clément's dress, which after the first moment of seeing him, I had forgotten, in thinking of other things, and for which I had not prepared Lord Ludlow. He sent for his own tailor, and bade him bring patterns of stuffs, and engage his men to work night and day till Clément could appear as became his rank. In short, in a few days so much of the traces of their flight were removed, that we had almost forgotten the terrible causes of it, and rather felt as if they had come on a visit to us than that they had been compelled to fly their country. Their diamonds, too, were sold well by my lord's agents, though the London shops were stocked with jewellery, and, such portable values, some of rare and curious fashion, which were sold for half their real value by emigrants who could not afford to wait. Madame de Créquy was recovering her health, although her strength was sadly gone, and she would never be equal to such another flight as the perilous one which she had gone through, and to which she could not bear the slightest reference. For some time things continued in this state; – the De Créquys still our honoured visitors – many houses besides our own, even among our own friends, open to receive the poor flying nobility of France, driven from their country by the brutal republicans, and every freshly-arrived emigrant bringing new tales of horror, as if these revolutionists were drunk with blood, and mad to devise new atrocities. One day, Clément – I should tell you he had been presented to our good King George and the sweet Queen, and they had accosted him most graciously, and his beauty and elegance, and some of the circumstances attendant on his flight, made him be received in the world quite like a hero of romance; he might have been on intimate terms in many a distinguished house, had he cared to visit much; but he accompanied my lord and me with an air of indifference and languor, which I sometimes fancied made him all the more sought after; Monkshaven (that was the title my eldest son bore) tried in vain to interest him in all young men's sports. But no! it was the same through all. His mother took far more interest in the *on-dits* of the London world, into which she was far too great an invalid to venture, than he did in the absolute events themselves, in which he might have been an actor. One day, as I was saying, an old Frenchman of a humble class presented himself to our servants, several of whom understood French; and through Medlicott, I learnt that he was in some way connected with the De Créquys; not with their Paris life, but I fancy he had been intendant of their estates in the country – estates which were more useful as hunting-grounds than as adding to their income. However there was the old man; and with him, wrapped round his person, he had brought the long parchment rolls, and deeds relating to their property. These he would deliver up to none but Monsieur de Créquy, the rightful owner; and Clément was out with Monkshaven, so the old man waited; and when Clément came in, I told him of the steward's arrival, and how he had been cared for by my people. Clément went directly to see him. He was a long time away, and I was waiting for him to drive out with me, for some purpose or other, I scarce know what, but I remember I was tired of waiting and was just in the act of ringing the bell to desire that he might be reminded of his engagement with me, when he came in, his face as white as the powder in his hair, his beautiful eyes dilated with horror. I saw that he had heard something that touched him even more closely than the usual tales which every fresh emigrant brought.

'"What is it, Clément?" I asked.

'He clasped his hands, and looked as though he tried to speak, but could not bring out the words.

'"They have guillotined my uncle!" said he at last. Now, I knew that there was a Count de Créquy; but I had always understood that the elder branch held very little communication with him; in fact, that he was a vaurien of some kind, and rather a disgrace than otherwise to the family. So, perhaps, I was hard-hearted; but I was a little surprised at this excess of emotion, till I saw that peculiar look in his eyes that many people have when there is more terror in their hearts than they dare put into words. He wanted me to understand something without his saying it; but how could I? I had never heard of a Mademoiselle de Créquy.

"'Virginie!" at last he uttered. In an instant I understood it all, and remembered that, if Urian had lived, he too might have been in love.

"'Your uncle's daughter?" I inquired.

"'My cousin", he replied.

'I did not say, "your betrothed", but I had no doubt of it. I was mistaken, however.

"'Oh, madame!" he continued, "her mother died long ago – her father now – and she is in daily fear – alone, deserted."

"'Is she in the Abbaye?" asked I.

"'No! she is in hiding with the widow of her father's old concierge. Any day they may search the house for aristocrats. They are seeking them everywhere. Then, not her life alone, but that of the old woman, her hostess, is sacrificed. The old woman knows this, and trembles with fear. Even if she is brave enough to be faithful, her fears would betray her, should the house be searched. Yet, there is no one to help Virginie to escape. She is alone in Paris."

'I saw what was in his mind. He was fretting and chafing to go to his cousin's assistance; but the thought of his mother restrained him. I would not have kept back Urian from such an errand at such a time. How should I restrain him? And yet, perhaps, I did wrong in not urging the chances of danger more. Still, if it was danger to him, was it not the same or even greater danger to her? – for the French spared neither age nor sex in those wicked days of terror. So I rather fell in with his wish, and encouraged him to think how best and most prudently it might be fulfilled; never doubting, as I have said, that he and his cousin were troth-plighted.

'But when I went to Madame de Créquy – after he had imparted his, or rather our plan to her – I found out my mistake. She, who was in general too feeble to walk across the room save slowly, and with a stick, was going from end to end with quick, tottering steps; and, if now and then she sank upon a chair, it seemed as if she could not rest, for she was up again in a moment, pacing along, wringing her hands and speaking rapidly to herself. When she saw me, she stopped: "Madame," she said, "you have lost your own boy. You might have left me mine."

'I was so astonished I hardly knew what to say. I had spoken to Clément as if his mother's consent were secure (as I felt my own would have been if Urian had been alive to ask it). Of course, both he and I knew that his mother's consent must be asked and obtained, before he could leave her to go on such an undertaking; but, somehow, my blood always rose at the sight or sound of danger; perhaps, because my life had been so peaceful. Poor Madame de Créquy! it was otherwise with her; she despaired while I hoped and Clément trusted.

"'Dear Madame de Créquy," said I, "he will return safely to us; every precaution shall be taken, that either he or you, or my lord, or Monkshaven can think of; but he cannot leave a girl – his nearest relation save you – his betrothed, is she not?"

"'His betrothed!" cried she, now at the utmost pitch of her excitement. "Virginie betrothed to Clément? – no! thank Heaven, not so bad as that! Yet it might have been. But mademoiselle scorned my son! She would have nothing to do with him. Now is the time for him to have nothing to do with her!"

'Clement had entered at the door behind his mother as she thus spoke. His face was set and pale, till it looked as grey and immovable as if it had been carved in stone. He came forward and stood before his mother. She stopped her walk, threw back her haughty head, and the two looked each other steadily in the face. After a minute or two in this attitude, her proud and resolute gaze never flinching or wavering, he went down upon one knee, and, taking her hand – her hard, stony hand, which never closed on his, but remained straight and stiff –

"'Mother," he pleaded, "withdraw you prohibition. Let me go!"

"'What were her words?" Madame de Créquy replied slowly, as if forcing her memory to the extreme of accuracy. "'My cousin," she said, "when I marry, I marry a man, not a petit-maître. I marry a man who, whatever his rank may be, will add dignity to the human race by his virtues, and not be content to live in an effeminate court on the traditions of past grandeur." She borrowed her words from the infamous

Jean-Jacques Rousseau, the friend of her scarce less infamous father, – nay! I will say it – if not her words, she borrowed her principles. And my son to request her to marry him!"

"'It was my father's written wish," said Clément.

"'But did you not love her? You plead your father's words – words written twelve years before – and as if that were your reason for being indifferent to my dislike to the alliance. But you requested her to marry you – and she refused you with insolent contempt; and now you are ready to leave me – leave me to desolate in a foreign land."

"'Desolate! my mother! and the Countess Ludlow stands there!"

"'Pardon madame! But all the earth, though it were full of kind hearts, is but a desolation and a desert place to a mother when her only child is absent. And you, Clément, would leave me for this Virginie – this degenerate De Créquy, tainted with the atheism of the Encyclopédistes! She is only reaping some of the fruit of the harvest whereof her friends have sown the seed. Let her alone! Doubtless she has friends – it may be lovers – among these demons, who, under the cry of liberty, comit every license. Let her alone, Clément! She refused you with scorn: be too proud to notice her now."

"'Mother, I cannot think of myself; only of her.'

"'Think of me, then! I, your mother, forbid you to go."

'Clement bowed low, and went out of the room instantly, as one blinded She saw his groping movement, and, for an instant, I think, her heart was touched. But she turned to me, and tried to exculpate her past violence by dilating upon her wrongs, and they certainly were many. The Count, her husband's younger brother, had invariably tried to make mischief between husband and wife. He had been the cleverer man of the two, and had possessed extraordinary influence over her husband. She suspected him of having instigated that clause in her husband's will, by which the Marquis expressed his wish for the marriage of the cousins. The Count had had some interest in the management of the De Créquy property during her son's minority. Indeed, I remembered then, that it was through the Count de Créquy that Lord Ludlow had first heard of the apartment which we afterwards took in the Hôtel de Créquy; and then the recollection of a past feeling came distinctly out of the mist, as it were; and I called to mind how, when we first took up our abode in the Hôtel de Créquy, both Lord Ludlow and I imagined that the arrangement was displeasing to our hostess; and how it had taken us a considerable time before we had been able to establish relations of friendship with her. Years after our visit, she began to suspect that Clément (whom she could not forbid to visit at his uncle's house, considering the terms on which his father had been with his brother; though she herself never set foot over the Count de Créquy's threshold) was attaching himself to mademoiselle, his cousin; and she made cautious inquiries as to the appearance, character and disposition of the young lady. Mademoiselle was not handsome, they said: but of a fine figure, and generally considered as having a very noble and attractive presence. In character she was daring and wilful (said one set); original and independent (said another). She was much indulged by her father, who had given her something of a man's education, and selected for her intimate friend a young lady below her in rank, one of the Bureaucratie, a Mademoiselle Necker, daughter of the Minister of Finance. Mademoiselle de Créquy was thus introduced into all the free-thinking salons of Paris; among people who were always full of plans for subverting society. "And did Clément affect such people?" Madame de Créquy had asked with some anxiety. No! Monsieur de Créquy had neither eyes nor ears, nor thought, for anything but his cousin, while she was by. And she? She hardly took notice of his devotion, so evident to every one else. The proud creature! But perhaps that was her haughty way of concealing what she felt. And so Madame de Créquy listened, and questioned, and learnt nothing decided, until one day she surprised Clément with the note in his hand, of which she remembered the stinging words so well, in which Virginie had said, in reply to a proposal Clément had sent her through her father, that "When she married, she married a man, not a petit-maître."

'Clément was justly indignant at the insulting nature of the answer Virginie had sent to a proposal, respectful in its tone, and which was, after all, but the cool, hardened lava over a burning heart. He acquiesced in his mother's desire, that he should not again present himself in his uncle's salons; but he did not forget Virginie, though he never mentioned her name.

'Madame de Créquy and her son were among the earliest *proscrits,* as they were of the strongest possible royalists, and aristocrats, as it was the custom of the horrid Sansculottes to term those who adhered to the habits of expression and action in which it was their pride to have been educated. They had left Paris some weeks before they had arrived in England, and Clément's belief at the time of quitting the Hôtel de Créquy had certainly been, that his uncle was not merely safe, but rather a popular man with the party in power. And, as all communication having relation to private individuals of a reliable kind was intercepted, Monsieur de Créquy had felt but little anxiety for his uncle and cousin, in comparison with what he did for many other friends of very different opinions in politics, until the day when he was stunned by the fatal information that even his progressive uncle was guillotined, and learnt that his cousin was imprisoned by the license of the mob, whose rights (as she called them) she was always advocating.

'When I heard all this story, I confess I lost in sympathy for Clément what I gained for his mother. Virginie's life did not seem to me worth the risk that Clément's would run. But when I saw him – sad, depressed, nay, hopeless – going about like one oppressed by a heavy dream which he cannot shake off; caring neither to eat, drink, nor sleep, yet bearing all with silent dignity, and even trying to force a poor, faint smile when he caught my anxious eyes; I turned round again and wondered how Madame de Créquy could resist this mute pleading of her son's altered appearance. As for my Lord Ludlow and Monkshaven, as soon as they understood the case, they were indignant that any mother should attempt to keep a son out of honourable danger; and it was honourable, and a clear duty (according to them), to try to save the life of a helpless orphan girl, his next-of-kin. None but a Frenchman, said my lord, would hold himself bound by an old woman's whimsies and fears, even though she were his mother. As it was, he was chafing himself to death under the restraint. If he went, to be sure, the — wretches might make an end of him, as they had done of many a fine fellow; but my lord would take heavy odds, that, instead of being guillotined, he would save the girl, and bring her safe to England, just desperately in love with her preserver, and then we would have a jolly wedding down at Monkshaven. My lord repeated his opinion so often that it became a certain prophecy in his mind of what was to take place; and, one day, seeing Clément look even paler and thinner than he had ever done before, he sent a message to Madame de Créquy, requesting permission to speak to her in private.

'"For, by George!" said he, "she shall hear my opinion and not let that lad of hers kill himself by fretting. He's too good for that. If he had been an English lad, he would have been off to his sweetheart long before this, without saying with your leave or by your leave; but, being a Frenchman, he is all for Æneas and filial piety — filial fiddlesticks!" (My lord had run away to sea, when a boy, against his father's consent, I am sorry to say; and, as all had ended well, and he had come back to find both parents alive, I do not think he was ever as much aware of his fault as he might have been under other circumst-ances.) "No, my lady," he went on, "don't come with me. A woman can manage a man best when he has a fit of obstinacy, and a man can persuade a woman out of her tantrums, when all her own sex, the whole army of them, would fail. Allow me to go alone to my *tête-à-tête* with madame."

'What he said, what passed, he never could repeat; but he came back graver than he went. However, the point was gained; Madame de Créquy withdrew her prohibition, and had given him leave to tell Clément as much.

'"But she is an old Cassandra," said he. "Don't let the lad be much with her; her talk would destroy the courage of the bravest man; she is so given over to superstition." Something that she had said had touched a chord in my lord's nature which he inherited from his Scotch ancestors. Long after-wards, I heard what this was. Medlicott told me.

'However, my lord shook off all fancies that told against the fulfilment of Clément's wishes. All that afternoon we three sat together, planning; and Monkshaven passed in and out, executing our commissions, and preparing everything. To-wards nightfall all was ready for Clément's start on his journey towards the coast.

'Madame had declined seeing any of us since my lord's

stormy interview with her. She sent word that she was fatigued, and desired repose. But, of course, before Clément set off, he was bound to wish her farewell, and to ask for her blessing. In order to avoid an agitating conversation between mother and son, my lord and I resolved to be present at the interview. Clément was already in his travelling-dress, that of a Norman fisherman, which Monkshaven had, with infinite trouble, discovered in the possession of one of the emigrés who thronged London, and who had made his escape from the shores of France in this disguise. Clément's plan was to go down to the coast of Sussex, and get one of the fishing or smuggling boats to take him across to the French coast near Dieppe. There again he would have to change his dress. Oh, it was so well planned! His mother was startled by his disguise (of which we had not thought to forewarn her) as he entered her apartment. And either that, or the being suddenly roused from the heavy slumber into which she was apt to fall when she was left alone, gave her manner an air of wildness that was almost like insanity.

"'Go, go!' she said to him, almost pushing him away as he knelt to kiss her hand. "Virginie is beckoning to you, but you don't see what kind of a bed it is."

"'Clément, make haste!' said my lord, in a hurried manner, as if to interrupt madame. "The time is later than I thought, and you must not miss the morning's tide. Bid your mother good-bye at once, and let us be off." For my lord and Monkshaven were to ride with him to an inn near the shore, from whence he was to walk to his destination. My lord almost took him by the arm to pull him away; and they were gone, and I was left alone with Madame de Créquy. When she heard the horses' feet, she seemed to find out the truth, as if for the first time. She set her teeth together. "He has left me for her!" she almost screamed. "Left me for her!" she kept muttering; and then, as the wild look came back into her eyes, she said, almost with exultation, "But I did not give him my blessing!"

CHAPTER VI

'All night Madame de Créquy raved in delirium. If I could, I would have sent for Clément back again. I did sent off one man, but I suppose my directions were confused, or they were wrong, for he came back after my lord's return, on the following afternoon. By this time Madame de Créquy was quieter; she was, indeed, asleep from exhaustion when Lord Ludlow and Monkshaven came in. They were in high spirits, and their hopefulness brought me round to a less dispirited state. All had gone well: they had accompanied Clément on foot along the shore, until they had met with a lugger, which my lord had hailed in good nautical language. The captain had responded to these freemason terms by sending a boat to pick up his passenger, and by an invitation to breakfast sent through a speaking-trumpet. Monkshaven did not approve of either the meal or the company, and had returned to the inn; but my lord had gone with Clément, and breakfasted on board, upon grog, biscuit, fresh-caught fish – "the best breakfast he ever ate," he said; but that was probably owing to the appetite his night's ride had given him. However, his good fellowship had evidently won the captain's heart, and Clément had set sail under the best auspices. It was agreed that I should tell all this to Madame de Créquy, if she inquired; otherwise, it would be wiser not to renew her agitation by alluding to her son's journey.

'I sat with her constantly for many days; but she never spoke of Clément. She forced herself to talk of the little occurences of Parisian society in former days; she tried to be conversational and agreeable, and to betray no anxiety or even interest in the object of Clément's journey; and, as far as unremitting efforts could go, she succeeded. But the tones of her voice were sharp and yet piteous, as if she were in constant pain; and the glance of her eye hurried and fearful, as if she dared not let it rest on any object.

'In a week we heard of Clément's safe arrival on the French coast. He sent a letter to this effect by the captain of the smuggler, when the latter returned. We hoped to hear again; but week after week elapsed, and there was no news of Clément. I had told Lord Ludlow in Madame de Créquy's presence, as he and I had arranged, of the note I had received from her son, informing us of his landing in France. She heard, but she took no notice, and evidently began to wonder that we did not mention any further intelligence of him in the same manner before her; and daily I began to fear that her pride would give way, and that she would supplicate for news before I had any to give her.

'One morning, on my awakening, my maid told me that Madame de Créquy had passed a wretched night, and had bidden Medlicott (whom, as understanding French, and speaking it pretty well, though with that horrid German accent, I had put about her) request that I would go to madame's room as soon as I was dressed.

'I knew what was coming, and I trembled all the time they were doing my hair, and otherwise arranging me. I was not encouraged by my lord's speeches. He had heard the message, and kept declaring that he would rather be shot than have to tell her that there was no news of her son; and yet he said, every now and then, when I was at the lowest pitch of uneasiness, that he never expected to hear again: that some day soon we should see him walking in and introducing Mademoiselle de Créquy to us.

'However, at last I was ready to go and go I must.

'Her eyes were fixed on the door by which I entered. I went up to the bedside. She was not rouged – she had left it off now for several days, – she no longer attempted to keep up the vain show of not feeling, and loving, and fearing.

'For a moment or two she did not speak, and I was glad of the respite.

'"Clément?" she said at length, covering her mouth with a handkerchief the minute she had spoken, that I might not see it quiver.

'"There has been no news since the first letter, saying how well the voyage was performed, and how safely he had landed – near Dieppe, you know." I replied as cheerfully as possible.

"My lord does not expect that we shall have another letter; he thinks that we shall see him soon."

'There was no answer. As I looked, uncertain whether to do or say more, she slowly turned hersself in bed, and lay with her face to the wall; and, as if that did not shut out the light of day and the busy, happy world enough, she put out her trembling hands, and covered her face with her handkerchief. There was no violence: hardly any sound.

'I told her what my lord had said about Clément's coming in some day, and taking us all by surprise. I did not believe it myself, but it was just possible – and I had nothing else to say. Pity, to one who was striving so hard to conceal her feelings, would have been impertinent. She let me talk; but she did not reply. She knew that my words were vain and idle, and had no root in my belief, as well as I did myself.

'I was very thankful when Medlicott came in with madame's breakfast, and gave me an excuse for leaving.

'But I think that conversation made me feel more anxious and impatient than ever. I felt almost pledged to Madame de Créquy for the fulfilment of the vision I had held out. She had taken entirely to her bed by this time; not from illness, but because she had no hope within her to stir her up to the effort of dressing. In the same way she hardly cared for food. She had no appetite – why eat to prolong a life of despair? But she let Medlicott feed her, sooner than take the trouble of resisting.

'And so it went on – for weeks, months – I could hardly count the time, it seemed so long. Medlicott told me she noticed a preternatural sensitiveness of ear in Madame de Créquy, induced by the habit of listening silently for the slightest unusual sound in the house. Medlicott was always a minute watcher of any one whom she cared about: and one day, she made me notice by a sign madame's acuteness of hearing, although the quick expectation was but evinced for a moment in the turn of the eye, the hushed breath – and then, when the unusual footstep turned into my lord's apartments, the soft quivering sigh and the closed eyelids.

'At length the intendant of the De Créquy's estates – the old man, you will remember, whose information respecting Virginie de Créquy first gave Clément the desire to return to

Paris – came to St. James's Square, and begged to speak to me. I made haste to go down to him in the housekeeper's room, sooner than that he should be ushered into mine, for fear of madame hearing any sound.

'The old man stood – I see him now – with his hat held before him in both his hands; he slowly bowed till his face touched it when I came in. Such long excess of courtesy augured ill. He waited for me to speak.

'"Have you any intelligence?" I inquired. He had been often to the house before, to ask if we had received any news; and once or twice I had seen him but this was the first time he had begged to see me.

'"Yes, madame," he replied, still standing with his head bent down, like a child in disgrace.

'"And is it bad!" I exclaimed.

'"It is bad." For a moment I was angry at the cold tone in which my words were echoed; but directly afterwards I saw the large, slow, heavy tears of age falling down the old man's cheeks, and on to the sleeves of his poor, threadbare coat.

'I asked him how he had heard it. it seemed as though I could not all at once bear to hear what it was. He told me that the night before, in crossing Long Acre, he had stumbled upon an old acquaintance of his; one who, like himself, had been a dependent upon the De Créquy family, but had managed their Paris affairs, while Fléchier had taken charge of their estates in the country. Both were now emigrants, and living on the proceeds of such small available talents as they possessed. Fléchier, as I knew, earned a very fair livelihood by going about to dress salads for dinner parties. His compatriot, Le Fébvre, had begun to give a few lessons as a dancing-master. One of them took the other home in his lodgings; and there, when their most immediate personal adventures had been hastily talked over, came the inquiry from Fléchier as to Monsieur de Créquy.

'"Clément was dead – guillotined. Virginie was dead – guillotined."

'When Fléchier had told me thus much, he could not speak for sobbing; and I, myself, could hardly tell how to restrain my tears sufficiently, until I could go to my own room, and be at liberty to give way. He asked my leave to bring in his friend

Le Fébvre, who was walking in the square, awaiting a possible summons to tell his story. I heard afterwards a good many details, which filled up the account, and made me feel – which brings me back to the point I started from – how unfit the lower orders are for being trusted indiscriminately with the dangerous powers of education. I have made a long preamble, but now I am coming to the moral of my story.'

My lady was trying to shake off the emotion which she evidently felt in recurring to this sad history of Monsieur de Créquy's death. She came behind me and arranged my pillows, and then, seeing I had been crying – for, indeed, I was weak-spirited at the time, and a little served to unloose my tears – she stooped down, and kissed my forehead, and said 'Poor child!' almost as if she thanked me for feeling that old grief of hers.

'Being once in France, it was no difficult thing for Clément to get into Paris. The difficulty in those days was to leave, not to enter. He came in dressed as a Norman peasant, in charge of a load of fruit and vegetables, with which one of the Seine barges was freighted. He worked hard with his companions in landing and arranging their produce on the quays; and then, when they dispersed to get their breakfasts at some of the estaminets near the old Marché aux Fleurs, he sauntered up a street which conducted him, by many an odd turn, through the Quartier Latin to a horrid back-alley, leading out of the Rue l'Ecole de Médecine: some atrocious place, as I have heard, not far from the shadow of that terrible Abbaye, where so many of the best blood of France awaited their deaths. But here some old man lived, on whose fidelity Clément thought that he might rely. I am not sure if he had not been gardener in those very gardens behind the Hôtel Créquy where Clément and Urian used to play together years before. But, whatever the old man's dwelling might be, Clément was only too glad to reach it, you may be sure. He had been kept in Normandy, in all sorts of disguises, for many days after landing in Dieppe, through the difficulty of entering Paris unsuspected by the many ruffians who were always on the look-out for aristocrats.

'The old gardener was, I believe, both faithful and tried, and sheltered Clément in his garret as well as might be. Before he could stir out, it was necessary to procure a fresh disguise, and one more in character with an inhabitant of Paris than that of a Norman carter was procured; and, after waiting indoors for one or two days, to see if any suspicion was excited, Clément set off to discover Virginie.

'He found her at the old concierge's dwelling. Madame Babette was the name of this woman, who must have been a less faithful – or rather, perhaps, I should say, a more interested – friend to her guest than the old gardener Jacques was to Clément.

'I have seen a miniature of Virginie, which a French lady of quality happened to have in her possession at the time of her flight from Paris, and which she brought with her to England unwittingly; for it belonged to the Count de Créquy, with whom she was slightly acquainted. I should fancy from it, that Virginie was taller and of a more powerful figure for a woman than her cousin Clément was for a man. Her dark-brown hair was arranged in short curls – the way of dressing the hair announced the politics of the individual in those days, just as patches did in my grandmother's time: and Virginie's hair was not to my taste, or according to my principles: it was too classical. Her large, black eyes looked out at you steadily. One cannot judge of the shape of a nose from a full-faced minia-ture, but the nostrils were clearly cut and largely opened. I do not fancy her nose could have been pretty; but her mouth had a character all its own, and which would, I think, have redeemed a plainer face. It was wide, and deep set into the cheeks at the corners; the upper lip was very much arched, and hardly closed over the teeth; so that the whole face looked (from the serious, intent look in the eyes, and the sweet intelligence of the mouth) as if she were listening eagerly to something to which her answer was quite ready, and would come out of those red, opening lips as soon as ever you had done speaking; and you longed to know what she would say.

'Well: this Virginie de Créquy was living with Madame Babette in the conciergerie of an old French inn, somewhere to the north of Paris, so, far enough from Clément's refuge. The inn had been frequented by farmers from Brittany and such kind of people, in the days when that sort of intercourse went on between Paris and the provinces, which had nearly stopped now. Few Bretons came near it now, and the inn had fallen into the hands of Madame Babette's brother, as payment for a bad wine debt of the last proprietor. He put his sister and her child in it, to keep it open, as it were, and sent all the people he could to occupy the half-furnished rooms of the house. They paid Babette for their lodging every morning as they went out to breakfast, and returned or not as they chose, at night. Every three days, the wine-merchant or his son came to Madame Babette, and she accounted to them for the money she had received. She and her child occupied the porter's office (in which the lad slept at nights) and a little miserable bedroom which opened out of it, and received all the light and air that was admitted through the door of communication, which was half glass. Madame Babette must have had a kind of attachment for the De Créquys – her De Créquys, you understand – Virginie's father, the Count; for, at some risk to herself, she had warned both him and his daughter of the danger impending over them. But he, infatuated, would not believe that his dear Human Race could ever do him harm; and, as long as he did not fear, Virginie was not afraid. It was by some ruse, the nature of which I never heard, that Madame Babette induced Virginie to come to her abode at the very hour in which the Count had been recognised in the streets, and hurried off to the Lanterne. It was after Babette had got her there, safe shut up in the little black den, that she told her what had befallen her father.

From that day, Virginie had never stirred out of the gates, or crossed the threshold of the porter's lodge. I do not say that Madame Babette was tired of her continual presence, or regretted the impulse which made her rush to the De Créquy's well-known house – after being compelled to form one of the mad crowds that saw the Count de Créquy seized and hung – and hurry his daughter out, through alleys and backways, until at length she had the orphan safe in her own dark sleeping-room, and could tell her her tale of horror: but Madame Babette was poorly paid for her porter's work by her avaricious brother; and it was hard enough to find food for herself and her growing boy; and, though the poor girl ate little enough, I dare say, yet there seemed no end to the burthen

that Madame Babette had imposed upon herself; the De
Créquys were plundered, ruined, had become an extinct race,
all but a lonely, friendless girl, in broken health and spirits:
and though she lent no positive encouragement to his suit, yet,
at the time when Clément re-appeared in Paris, Madame
Babette was beginning to think that Virginie might do worse
than encourage the attentions of Monsieur Morin Fils, her
nephew, and the wine-merchant's son. Of course, he and his
father had the entrée into the conciergerie of the hôtel that
belonged to them, in right of being both proprietors and
relations. The son, Morin, had seen Virginie in this manner.
He was fully aware that she was far above him in rank, and
guessed from her whole aspect that she had lost her natural
protectors by the terrible guillotine: but he did not know her
exact name or station, nor could he persuade his aunt to tell
him. However, he fell head over ears in love with her,
whether she were princess or peasant; and, though at first
there was something about her which made his passionate love
conceal itself with shy, awkward reserve, and then made it
only appear in the guise of deep, respectful devotion; yet,
by-and-by – by the same process of reasoning, I suppose, that
his aunt had gone through even before him – Jean Morin
began to let Hope oust Despair from his heart. Sometimes he
thought – perhaps years hence, that solitary, friendless lady,
pent up in squalor, might turn to him as to a friend and
comforter – and then – and then –. Meanwhile Jean Morin
was most attentive to his aunt, whom he had rather slighted
before. He would linger over the accounts; would bring her
little presents; and, above all, he made a pet and favourite of
Pierre, the little cousin, who could tell him about all the ways
of going on of Mam'selle Cannes, as Virginie was called.
Pierre was thoroughly aware of the drift and cause of his
cousin's inquiries; and was his ardent partisan, as I have heard,
even before Jean Morin had exactly acknowledged his wishes
to himself.

'It must have required some patience and diplomacy, before
Clément de Créquy found out the exact place where his cousin
was hidden. The old gardener took the cause very much to
heart; as, judging from my recollections, I imagine he would
have forwarded any fancy, however wild, of Monsieur Clé-

ment's. (I will tell you afterwards how I came to know all
these particulars so well.)

'After Clément's return, on two succeeding days, from his
dangerous search, without meeting with any good result,
Jacques entreated Monsieur de Créquy to let him take it in
hand. He represented that he, as gardener for the space of
twenty years and more at the Hôtel de Créquy, had a right to
be acquainted with all the successive conciérges at the Count's
house; that he should not go among them as a stranger, but as
an old friend, anxious to renew pleasant intercourse; and that
if the Intendant's story, which he had told Monsieur de
Créquy in England, was true, that mademoiselle was in hiding
at the house of a former concierge, why, something relating to
her would surely drop out in the course of conversation. So he
persuaded Clément to remain indoors, while he set off on his
round, with no apparent object but to gossip.

'At night he came home, – having seen mademoiselle. He
told Clément much of the story relating to Madame Babette
that I have told to you. Of course, he had heard nothing of the
ambitious hopes of Morin Fils – hardly of his existence, I
should think. Madame Babette had received him kindly;
although, for some time, she had kept him standing in the
carriage gateway outside her door. But, on his complaining of
the draught and his rheumatism, she had asked him in; first
looking round with some anxiety, to see who was in the room
behind her. No one was there when he entered and sat down.
But, in a minute or two, a tall thin young lady, with great, sad
eyes, and pale cheeks, came from the inner room, and seeing
him, retired. "It is Mademoiselle Cannes," said Madame
Babette, rather unnecessarily; for, if he had not been on the
watch for some sign of Mademoiselle de Créquy, he would
hardly have noticed the entrance and withdrawal.

'Clément and the good old gardener were always rather
perplexed by Madame Babette's evident avoidance of all
mention of the De Créquy family. If she were so much
interested in one member as to be willing to undergo the pains
and penalties of a domiciliary visit, it was strange that she
never inquired after the existence of her charge's friends and
relations from one who might very probably have heard
something of them. They settled that Madame Babette must

believe that the Marquise and Clément were dead; and admired her for her reticence in never speaking of Virginie. The truth was, I suspect, that she was so desirous of her nephew's success by this time, that she did not like letting anyone into the secret of Virginie's whereabouts who might interfere with their plan. However, it was arranged between Clément and his humble friend, that the former, dressed in the peasant's clothes in which he had entered Paris but smartened up in one or two particulars, as if, although a countryman, he had money to spare, should go and engage a sleeping-room in the old Breton Inn, where, as I told you, accommodation for the night was to be had. This was accordingly done, without exciting Madame Babette's suspicions, for she was unacquainted with the Normandy accent, and consequently did not perceive the exaggeration of it which Monsieur de Créquy adopted in order to disguise his pure Parisian. But after he had for two nights slept in a queer dark closet, at the end of one of the numerous short galleries in the Hôtel Duguesclin, and paid his money for such accommodation each morning at the little bureau under the window of the conciergerie, he found himself no nearer to his object. He stood outside in the gateway; Madame Babette opened a pane in her window, counted out the change, gave polite thanks, and shut to the pane with a clack, before he could ever find out what to say that might be the means of opening a conversation. Once in the streets, he was in danger from the bloodthirsty mob, who were ready in those days to hunt to death every one who looked like a gentleman, as an aristocrat: and Clément, depend upon it, looked a gentleman, whatever dress he wore. Yet it was unwise to traverse Paris to his old friend the gardener's grenier, so he had to loiter about, where I hardly know. Only he did leave the Hôtel Duguesclin, and he did not go to old Jacques, and there was not another house in Paris open to him. At the end of two days, he had made out Pierre's existence; and he began to try to make friends with the lad. Pierre was too sharp and shrewd not to suspect something from the confused attempts at friendliness. It was not for nothing that the Norman farmer lounged in the court and doorway, and brought home presents of galette. Pierre accepted the galette, reciprocated the civil speeches, but kept his eyes open. Once, returning home pretty late at night, he surprised the Norman studying the shadows on the blind, which was drawn down when Madame Babette's lamp was lighted. On going in, he found Mademoiselle Cannes with his mother, sitting by the table, and helping in the family mending.

'Pierre was afraid that the Norman had some view upon the money which his mother, as concierge, collected for her brother. But the money was all safe next evening, when his cousin, Monsieur Morin Fils, came to collect it. Madame Babette asked her nephew to sit down, and skilfully barred the passage to the inner door, so that Virginie, had she been ever so much disposed, could not have retreated. She sat silently sewing. All at once the little party were startled by a very sweet tenor voice, just close to the street window, singing one of the airs out of Beaumarchais' operas, which, a few years before, had been popular all over Paris. But after a few moments of silence, and one or two remarks, the talking went on again. Pierre, however, noticed an increased air of abstraction in Virginie, who, I suppose, was recurring to the last time that she had heard the song, and did not consider, as her cousin had hoped she would have done, what were the words set to the air, which he imagined she would remember, and which would have told her so much. For, only a few years before, Adam's opera of Richard le Roi had made the story of the minstrel Blondel and our English Cœur de Lion familiar to all the opera-going part of the Parisian public, and Clément had bethought him of establishing a communication with Virginie by some such means.

'The next night, about the same hour, the same voice was singing outside the window again. Pierre, who had been irritated by the proceeding the evening before, as it had diverted Virginie's attention from his cousin, who had been doing his utmost to make himself agreeable, rushed out to the door, just as the Norman was ringing the bell to be admitted for the night. Pierre looked up and down the street; no one else was to be seen. The next day, the Norman mollified him somewhat by knocking at the door of the conciergerie, and begging Monsieur Pierre's acceptance of some knee-buckles, which had taken the country farmer's fancy the day before, as he had been gazing into the shops, but, which, being too small for his purpose, he took the liberty of offering to Monsieur Pierre. Pierre, a French boy, inclined to foppery, was charmed, ravished by the beauty of the present and with monsieur's goodness, and he began to adjust them to his breeches immediately, as well as he could, at least, in his mother's absence. The Norman, whom Pierre kept carefully on the outside of the threshold, stood by, as if amused at the boy's eagerness.

'"Take care," said he, clearly and distinctly; "take care, my little friend, lest you become a fop; and, in that case, some day, years hence, when your heart is devoted to some young lady, she may be inclined to say to you" – here he raised his voice – "No thank you; when I marry, I marry a man, not a petit-maître; I will marry a man, who, whatever his position may be, will add dignity to the human race by his virtues." Farther than that in his quotation Clément dared not go. His sentiments (so much above the apparent occasion) met with applause from Pierre, who liked to contemplate himself in the light of a lover, even though it should be a rejected one, and who hailed the mention of the words "virtues" and "dignity of the human race" as belonging to the cant of a good citizen.

'But Clément was more anxious to know how the invisible lady took his speech. There was no sign at the time. But when he returned at night, he heard a voice, low singing, behind Madame Babette, as she handed him his candle, the very air he had sung without effect for two nights past. As if he had caught it up from her murmuring voice, he sang it loudly and clearly as he crossed the court.

'"Here is our opera-singer!" exclaimed Madame Babette. "Why, the Norman grazier sings like Boupré," naming a favourite singer at the neighbouring theatre.

'Pierre was struck by the remark, and quietly resolved to look after the Norman; but again, I believe, it was more because of his mother's deposit of money than with any thought of Virginie.

'However, the next morning, to the wonder of both mother and son, Mademoiselle Cannes proposed, with much hesitation, to go out and make some little purchase for herself. A month or two ago, this was what Madame Babette had been never weary of urging. But now she was as much surprised as if she had expected Virginie to remain a prisoner in her rooms all the rest of her life. I suppose she had hoped that her first time of quitting it would be when she left it for Monsieur Morin's house as his wife.

'A quick look from Madame Babette towards Pierre was all that was needed to encourage the boy to follow her. He went out cautiously. She was at the end of the street. She looked up and down, as if waiting for some one. No one was there. Back she came, so swiftly that she nearly caught Pierre before he could retreat through the porte-cochère. There he looked out again. The neighbourhood was low and wild, and strange; and some one spoke to Virginie – nay, laid his hand upon her arm – whose dress and aspect (he had emerged out of a side-street) Pierre did not know; but, after a start, and (Pierre could fancy) a little scream, Virginie recognised the stranger, and the two turned up the side street whence the man had come. Pierre stole swiftly to the corner of the street; no one was there: they had disappeared up some of the alleys. Pierre returned home to excite his mother's infinite surprise. But they had hardly done talking when Virginie returned, with a colour and a radiance in her face, which they had never seen there since her father's death.

CHAPTER VII

'I have told you that I heard much of this story from a friend of
the Intendant of the De Créquy's, whom he met with in
London. Some years afterwards – the summer before my
lord's death – I was travelling with him in Devonshire, and we
went to see the French prisoners of war on Dartmoor. We fell
into conversation with one of them, whom I found out to be
the very Pierre of whom I had heard before, as having been
involved in the fatal story of Clément and Virginie, and by
him I was told much of their last days, and thus I learnt how to
have some sympathy with all those who were concerned in
those terrible events; yes, even with the younger Morin
himself, on whose behalf Pierre spoke warmly, even after so
long a time had elapsed.

'For, when the younger Morin called at the porter's lodge,
on the evening of the day when Virginie had gone out for the
first time after so many months' confinement to the conciergerie, he was struck with the improvement in her appearance. It seems to have hardly been that he thought her beauty
greater; for, in addition, to the fact that she was not beautiful,
Morin had arrived at that point of being enamoured when it
does not signify whether the beloved one is plain or handsome
– she has enchanted one pair of eyes, which henceforward see
her through their own medium. But Morin noticed the faint
increase of colour and light in her countenance. It was as
though she had broken through her thick cloud of hopeless
sorrow, and was dawning forth into a happier life. And so
whereas during her grief he had revered and respected it even
to a point of silent sympathy, now that she was gladdened his
heart rose on the wings of strengthened hopes. Even in the
dreary monotony of this existence in his Aunt Babette's
conciergerie Time had not failed in his work, and now,
perhaps, soon he might humbly strive to help Time. The very

next day he returned – on some pretence of business – to the Hôtel Duguesclin, and made his aunt's room, rather than his aunt herself, a present of roses and geraniums tied up in a bouquet with a tricolour ribbon. Virginie was in the room, sitting at the coarse sewing she liked to do for Madame Babette. He saw her eyes brighten at the sight of the flowers: she asked his aunt to let her arrange them; he saw her untie the ribbon, and with a gesture of dislike, throw it on the ground, and give it a kick with her little foot, and even in this girlish manner of insulting his dearest prejudices he found something to admire.

'As he was coming out Pierre stopped him. The lad had been trying to arrest his cousin's attention by futile grimaces and signs played off behind Virginie's back; but Monsieur Morin saw nothing but Mademoiselle Cannes. However, Pierre was not to be baffled, and Monsieur Morin found him in waiting just outside the threshold. With his finger on his lips, Pierre walked on tiptoe by his companion's side till they would have been long past sight or hearing of the conciergerie, even had the inhabitants devoted themselves to the purposes of spying or listening.

'"Chut!" said Pierre at last. "She goes out walking."

'"Well?" said Monsieur Morin, half curious, half annoyed at being disturbed in the delicious reverie of the future into which he longed to fall.

'"Well! It is not well. It is bad."

'"Why? I do not ask who she is, but I have my ideas. She is an aristocrat. Do the people about here begin to suspect her?"

'"No, no!" said Pierre. "But she goes out walking. She has gone these two mornings. I have watched her. She meets a man – she is friends with him, for she talks to him as eagerly as he does to her – mamma cannot tell who he is."

'"Has my aunt seen him?"

'"No, not so much as a fly's wing of him. I myself have only seen his back. It strikes me like a familiar back, and yet I cannot think who it is. But they separate with sudden darts, like two birds who have been together to feed their young ones. One moment they are in close talk, their heads together chuchotting; the next he has turned up some by-street, and Mademoiselle Cannes is close upon me – has almost caught me."

"'But she did not see you?" inquired Monsieur Morin in so altered a voice that Pierre gave him one of his quick penetrating looks. He was struck by the way in which his cousin's features — always coarse and commonplace — had become contracted and pinched; struck, too, by the livid look on his sallow complexion. But, as if Morin was conscious of the manner in which his face belied his feelings, he made an effort, and smiled, and patted Pierre's head, and thanked him for his intelligence, and gave him a five-franc piece, and bade him go on with his observations of Mademoiselle Cannes' movements and report all to him.

'Pierre returned home with a light heart, tossing up his five-franc piece as he ran. Just as he was at the conciergerie door, a great tall man bustled past him, and snatched his money away from him, looking back with a laugh, which added insult to injury. Pierre had no redress; no one had witnessed the impudent theft, and, if they had, no one to be seen in the street was strong enough to give him redress. Besides, Pierre had seen enough of the state of the streets of Paris at that time to know that friends, not enemies, were required, and the man had a bad air about him. But all these considerations did not keep Pierre from bursting out into a fit of crying when he was once more under his mother's roof; and Virginie, who was alone there (Madame Babette having gone out to make her daily purchases), might have imagined him pommelled to death by the loudness of his sobs.

"'What is the matter?" asked she. "Speak, my child. What hast thou done?"

"'He has robbed me! he has robbed me!" was all Pierre could gulp out.

"'Robbed thee! and of what, my poor boy?" said Virginie, stroking his hair gently.

"'Of my five-franc piece – of a five-franc piece," said Pierre, correcting himself, and leaving out the word my, half fearful lest Virginie should inquire how he became possessed of such a sum, and for what services it had been given him. But, of course, no such idea came into her head, for it would have been impertinent, and she was gentle-born.

"'Wait a moment, my lad," and going to the one small drawer in the inner apartment, which held all her few possessions, she brought back a little ring – a ring just with one ruby in it – which she had worn in the days when she cared to wear jewels. "Take this," said she, "and run with it to a jeweller's. It is but a poor, valueless thing, but it will bring you in your five francs, at any rate. Go! I desire you."

'"But I cannot," said the boy, hesitating; some dim sense of honour flitting through his misty morals.

'"Yes, you must!" she continued, urging him with her hand to the door. "Run! if it brings you in more than five francs, you shall return the surplus to me."

'Thus tempted by her urgency, and, I suppose, reasoning with himself to the effect that he might as well have the money, and then see whether he thought it right to act as a spy upon her or not – the one action did not pledge him to the other, nor yet did she make any conditions with her gift – Pierre went off with her ring; and, after repaying himself his five francs, he was enabled to bring Virginie back two more so well had he managed his affairs. But, although the whole transaction did not leave him bound, in any way, to discover or forward Virginie's wishes, it did leave him pledged, according to his code, to act according to her advantage, and he considered himself the judge of the best course to be pursued to this end. And, moreover, this little kindness attached him to her personally. He began to think how pleasant it would be to have so kind and generous a person for a relation; how easily his troubles might be borne if he had always such a ready helper at hand; how much he should like to make her like him, and come to him for the protection of his masculine power! First of all his duties, as her self-appointed squire, came the necessity of finding out who her strange new acquaintance was. Thus, you see, he arrived at the same end, viâ supposed duty, that he was previously pledged to viâ interest. I fancy a good number of us, when any line of action will promote our own interest, can make ourselves believe that reasons exist which compel us to it as a duty.

'In the course of a very few days, Pierre had so circumvented Virginie as to have discovered that her new friend was no other than the Norman farmer in a different dress. This was a great piece of knowledge to impart to Morin. But Pierre was not prepared for the immediate physical effect it had on his cousin. Morin sat suddenly down on one of the seats in the Boulevards – it was there Pierre had met with him accidently – when he heard who it was that Virginie met. I do not suppose the man had the faintest idea of any relationship or even previous acquaintanceship between Clément and Virginie If he thought of anything beyond the mere fact presented to him, that his idol was in communication with another, younger, handsomer man than himself, it must have been that the Norman farmer had seen her at the conciergerie, and had been attracted by her, and, as was but natural, had tried to make her acquaintance, and had succeeded. But, from what Pierre told me, I should not think that even this much thought had passed through Morin's mind. He seems to have been a man of rare and concentrated attachments; violent, though restrained and undemonstrative passions; and, above all, a capability of jealousy, of which his dark oriental complexion must have been a type. I could fancy that, if he had married Virginie, he would have coined his life-blood for luxuries to make her happy; would have watched over and petted her, at every sacrifice to himself, as long as she would have been content to live with him alone. But, as Pierre expressed it to me: "When I saw what my cousin was, when I learned his nature too late, I perceived that he would have strangled a bird if she whom he loved was attracted by it from him."

'When Pierre had told Morin of his discovery, Morin sat down, as I said, quite suddenly, as if he had been shot. He found out that the first meeting between the Norman and Virginie was no accidental, isolated circumstance. Pierre was torturing him with his accounts of daily rendezvous: if, but for a moment, they were seeing each other every day, sometimes twice a day. And Virginie could speak to this man, though to himself she was so coy and reserved as hardly to utter a sentence. Pierre caught these broken words while his cousin's complexion grew more and more livid, and then purple, as if some great effect were produced on his circulation by the news he had just heard. Pierre was so startled by his cousin's wandering, senseless eyes, and otherwise disordered looks, that he rushed into a neighbouring cabaret for a glass of absinthe, which he paid for, as he recollected afterwards, with a portion of Virginie's five francs. By-and-by Morin recovered his natural appearance; but he was gloomy and silent; and all that Pierre could get out of him was, that the Norman farmer should not sleep another night at the Hôtel Duguesclin, giving him such opportunities of passing and repassing by the conciergerie door. He was too much absorbed in his own thoughts to repay Pierre the half-franc he had spent on the absinthe, which Pierre perceived, and seems to have noted down in the ledger of his mind as on Virginie's balance of favour.

'Altogether, he was much disappointed at his cousin's mode of receiving intelligence, which the lad thought worth another five-franc piece at least; or, if not paid for in money, to be paid for in open-mouthed confidence and expression of feeling; and thus he was, for a time, so far a partisan of Virginie's – unconscious Virginie's – against his cousin, as to feel regret when the Norman returned no more to his night's lodging, and when Virginie's eager watch at the crevice of the close-drawn blind ended only with a sigh of disappointment. If it had not been for his mother's presence at the time, Pierre thought he should have told her all. But how far was his mother in his cousin's confidence as regarded the dismissal of the Norman?

'In a few days, however, Pierre felt almost sure that they had established some new means of communication. Virginie went out for a short time every day; but, though Pierre followed her as closely as he could without exciting her observation, he was unable to discover what kind of intercourse she held with the Norman. She went, in general, the same short round among the little shops in the neighbourhood; not entering any, but stopping at two or three. Pierre afterwards remembered that she had invariably paused at the nosegays displayed in a certain window, and studied them long; but, then, she stopped and looked at caps, hats, fashions, confectionery (all of the humble kind common in that quarter) so how should he have known that any particular attraction existed among the flowers? Morin came more regularly than ever to his aunt's; but Virginie was apparently unconscious that she was the attraction. She looked healthier and more hopeful than she had done for months, and her manners to all were gentler and not so reserved. Almost as if she wished to

manifest her gratitude to Madame Babette for her long
continuance of kindness, the necessity for which was nearly
ended, Virginie showed an unusual alacrity in rendering the
old woman any little service in her power, and evidently tried
to respond to Monsieur Morin's civilities, he being Madame
Babette's nephew, with a soft graciousness which must have
made one of her principal charms; for all who knew her speak
of the fascination of her manners, so winning and attentive to
others, while yet her opinions, and often her actions, were of
so decided a character. For, as I have said, her beauty was by
no means great; yet every man who came near her seems to
have fallen into the sphere of her influence. Monsieur Morin
was deeper than ever in love with her during these last few
days: he was worked up into a state capable of any sacrifice,
either of himself or others, so that he might obtain her at last.
He sat "devouring her with his eyes" (to use Pierre's expression) wenever she could not see him; but, if she looked towards
him, he looked to the ground – anywhere – away from her,
and almost stammered in his replies if she addressed any
question to him.

'He had been, I should think, ashamed of his extreme
agitation on the Boulevards, for Pierre thought that he
absolutely shunned him for these few succeeding days. He
must have believed that he had driven the Norman (my poor
Clément!) off the field, by banishing him from his inn; and
have thought that the intercourse between him and Virginie,
which he had thus interrupted, was of so slight and transient a
character as to be quenched by a little difficulty.

'But he appears to have felt that he had made but little way,
and he awkwardly turned to Pierre for help – not yet
confessing his love, though; he only tried to make friends
again with the lad after their silent estrangement. And Pierre
for some time did not choose to perceive his cousin's adv-
ances. He would reply to all the roundabout questions Morin
put to him respecting household conversations when he was
not present, or household occupations and tone of thought,
without mentioning Virginie's name any more than his ques-
tioner did. The lad would seem to suppose that his cousin's
strong interest in their domestic ways of going on was all on
account of Madame Babette. At last he worked his cousin up

to the point of making him a confidant; and then the boy was half frightened at the torrent of vehement words he had unloosed. The lava came down with a greater rush for having been pent up so long. Morin cried out his words in a hoarse, passionate voice, clenched his teeth, his fingers, and seemed almost convulsed, as he spoke out his terrible love for Virginie, which would lead him to kill her sooner than see her another's; and if another stepped in between him and her! – and then he smiled a fierce triumphant smile, but did not say any more.

'Pierre was, as I said, half frightened; but also half admiring. This was really love – a "grande passion" – a really fine dramatic thing – like the plays they acted at the little theatre yonder. He had a dozen times the sympathy with his cousin now that he had had before, and readily swore by the infernal gods – for they were far too enlightened to believe in one God, or Christianity, or anything of the kind – that he would devote himself, body and soul, to forwarding his cousin's views. Then his cousin took him to a shop, and bought him a smart second-hand watch, on which they scratched the word Fidélité, and thus was the compact sealed. Pierre settled in his own mind that, if he were a woman, he should like to be beloved as Virginie was by his cousin, and that it would be an extremely good thing for her to be the wife of so rich a citizen as Morin Fils – and for Pierre himself, too, for doubtless their gratitude would lead them to give him rings and watches *ad infinitum*.

'A day or two afterwards, Virginie was taken ill. Madame Babette said it was because she had persevered in going out in all weathers, after confining herself to two warm rooms for so long; and very probably this was really the cause, for, from Pierre's account, she must have been suffering from a feverish cold, aggravated, no doubt, by her impatience at Madame Babette's familiar prohibitions of any more walks until she was better. Every day, in spite of her trembling, aching limbs, she would fain have arranged her dress for her walk at the usual time; but Madame Babette was fully prepared to put physical obstacles in her way, if she was not obedient in remaining tranquil on the little sofa by the side of the fire. The third day, she called Pierre to her, when his mother was not attending (having, in fact, locked up Mademoiselle Cannes' out-of-door things).

'"See, my child," said Virginie. "Thou must do me a great favour. Go to the gardener's shop in the Rue des Bons-Enfans, and look at the nosegays in the window. I long for pinks; they are my favourite flower. Here are two francs. If thou seest a nosegay of pinks displayed in the window, if it be ever so faded, – nay, if thou seest two or three nosegays of pinks, remember, buy them all, and bring them to me, I have so great a desire for the smell." She fell back weak and exhausted. Pierre hurried out. Now was the time; here was the clue to the long inspection of the nosegay in this very shop.

'Sure enough, there was a drooping nosegay of pinks in the window. Pierre went in, and, with all his impatience, he made as good a bargain as he could, urging that the flowers were faded, and good for nothing. At last he purchased them at a very moderate price. And now you will learn the bad consequences of teaching the lower orders anything beyond what is immediately necessary to enable them to earn their daily bread! The silly Count de Créquy, – he who had been sent to his bloody rest by the very canaille of whom he thought so much – he who had made Virginie (indirectly, it is true) reject such a man as her cousin Clément, by inflating her mind with his bubbles of theories – this Count de Créquy had long ago taken a fancy to Pierre, as he saw the bright sharp child playing about his courtyard. Monsieur de Créquy had even begun to educate the boy himself, to try to work out certain opinions of his into practice – but the drudgery of the affair wearied him, and, besides, Babette had left his employment. Still the Count took a kind of interest in his former pupil; and made some sort of arrangement by which Pierre was to be taught reading and writing, and accounts, and Heaven knows what besides – Latin, I dare say. So Pierre, instead of being an innocent messenger, as he ought to have been, – (as Mr. Horner's little lad Gregson ought to have been this morning) – could read writing as well as either you or I. So what does he do, on obtaining the nosegay, but examine it well. The stalks of the flowers were tied up with slips of matting in wet moss. Pierre undid the strings, unwrapped the moss, and out fell a piece of wet paper, with the writing all blurred with moisture.

It was but a torn piece of writing-paper, apparently, but Pierre's wicked mischievous eyes read what was written on it – written so as to look like a fragment – "Ready, every and any night at nine. All is prepared. Have no fright. Trust one who, whatever hopes he might once have had, is content now to serve you as a faithful cousin;" and a place was named, which I forget, but which Pierre did not, as it was evidently the rendezvous. After the lad had studied every word, till he could say it off by heart, he placed the paper where he had found it, enveloped it in moss, and tied the whole up again carefully. Virginie's face coloured scarlet as she received it. She kept smelling at it, and trembling: but she did not untie it, although Pierre suggested how much fresher it would be if the stalks were immediately put into water. But once, after his back had been turned for a minute, he saw it untied when he looked round again, and Virginie was blushing, and hiding something in her bosom.

'Pierre was now all impatience to set off and find his cousin. But his mother seemed to want him for small domestic purposes even more than usual: and he had chafed over a multitude of errands connected with the Hôtel before he could set off and search for his cousin at his usual haunts. At last the two met; and Pierre related all the events of the morning to Morin. He said the note off word by word. (That lad this morning had something of the magpie look of Pierre – it made me shudder to see him, and hear him repeat the note by heart.) Then Morin asked him to tell him all over again. Pierre was struck by Morin's heavy sighs as he repeated the story. When he came the second time to the note, Morin tried to write the words down; but either he was not a good, ready scholar, or his fingers trembled too much. Pierre hardly remembered, but, at any rate, the lad had to do it, with his wicked reading and writing. When this was done, Morin sat heavily silent. Pierre would have preferred the expected outburst, for this impenetrable gloom perplexed and baffled him. He had even to speak to his cousin to rouse him; and when he replied, what he said had so little apparent connection with the subject which Pierre had expected to find uppermost in his mind, that he was half afraid that his cousin had lost his wits.

'"My Aunt Babette is out of coffee."

"'I am sure I do not know,' said Pierre.

"'Yes, she is. I heard her say so. Tell her that a friend of mine has just opened a shop in the Rue Saint Antoine, and that, if she will join me there in an hour, I will supply her with a good stock of coffee, just to give my friend encouragement. His name is Antoine Meyer, Number One hundred and Fifty, at the sign of the Cap of Liberty.'

"'I could go with you now. I can carry a few pounds of coffee better than my mother,' said Pierre, all in good faith. He told me he should never forget the look on his cousin's face, as he turned round, and bade him begone, and give his mother the message without another word. It had evidently sent him home promptly to obey his cousin's command. Morin's message perplexed Madame Babette.

"'How could he know I was out of coffee?' said she. 'I am; but I only used the last up this morning. How could Victor know about it?'

"'I am sure I can't tell,' said Pierre, who by this time had recovered his usual self-possession. 'All I know is, that monsieur is in a pretty temper, and that if you are not sharp to your time at this Antoine Meyer's you are likely to come in for some of his black looks.'

"'Well, it is very kind of him to offer to give me some coffee, to be sure! But how could he know I was out?'

'Pierre hurried his mother off impatiently, for he was certain that the offer of the coffee was only a blind to some hidden purpose on his cousin's part; and he made no doubt that, when his mother had been informed of what his cousin's real intention was, he, Pierre, could extract it from her by coaxing or bullying. But he was mistaken. Madame Babette returned home, grave, depressed, silent, and loaded with the best coffee. Some time afterwards he learnt why his cousin had sought for this interview. It was to extract from her, by promises and threats, the real name of Mam'selle Cannes, which would give him a clue to the true appellation of the "faithful cousin". He concealed this second purpose from his aunt, who had been quite unaware of his jealousy of the Norman farmer, or of his identification of him with any relation of Virginie's. But Madame Babette instinctively shrank from giving him any information: she must have felt that, in the lowering mood in which she found him, his desire for greater knowledge of Virginie's antecedents boded her no good. And yet he made his aunt his confidante – told her what she only suspected before – that he was deeply enamoured of Mam'selle Cannes, and would gladly marry her. He spoke to Madame Babette of his father's hoarded riches; and of the share which he, as partner, had in them at the present time; and of the prospect of the succession to the whole, which he had, as only child. He told his aunt of the provision for her (Madame Babette's) life, which he would make on the day when he married Mam'selle Cannes. And yet – and yet – Babette saw that in his eye and look which made her more and more reluctant to confide in him. By-and-by he tried threats. She should leave the conciergerie, and find employment where she liked. Still silence. Then he grew angry, and swore that he would inform against her at the bureau of the Directory, for harbouring an aristocrat; an aristocrat he knew Mademoiselle was, whatever her real name might be. His aunt should have a domiciliary visit, and see how she liked that. The officers of the Government were the people for finding out secrets. In vain she reminded him that, by doing so, he would expose to imminent danger the lady whom he had professed to love. He told her, with a sudden relapse into silence after his vehement outpouring of passion, never to trouble herself about that. At last he wearied out the old woman, and frightened alike of herself, and of him, she told him all – that Mam'selle Cannes was Mademoiselle Virginie de Créquy, daughter of the Count of that name. Who was the Count? Younger brother of the Marquis. Where was the Marquis? Dead long ago, leaving a widow and child. A son? (eagerly). Yes, a son. Where was he? Parbleu! how should she know? – for her courage returned a little as he talk went away from the only person of the De Créquy family that she cared about. But, by dint of some small glasses out of a bottle of Antoine Meyer's, she told him more about the De Créquys than she liked afterwards to remember. For the exhilaration of the brandy lasted but a very short time, and she came home, as I have said, depressed, with a presentiment of coming evil. She would not answer Pierre, but cuffed him about in a manner to which the spoilt boy was quite unaccustomed. His

cousin's short, angry words, and sudden withdrawal of
confidence – his mother's unwonted crossness and fault-
finding; all made Virginie's kind, gentle treatment more than
ever charming to the lad. He half resolved to tell her how he
had been acting as a spy upon her actions, and at whose desire
he had done it. But he was afraid of Morin, and of the
vengeance which he was sure would fall upon him for any
breach of confidence. Towards half-past eight that evening,
Pierre, watching, saw Virginie arrange several little things –
she was in the inner room, but he sat where he could see her
through the glazed partition. His mother sat – apparently
sleeping – in the great easy-chair; Virginie moved about
softly, for fear of disturbing her. She made up one or two little
parcels of the few things she could call her own; one packet she
concealed about herself – the others she directed, and left on
the shelf. "She is going," thought Pierre, and (as he said in
giving me the account) his heart gave a spring, to think that he
should never see her again. If either his mother or his cousin
had been more kind to him, he might have endeavoured to
intercept her; but as it was, he held his breath, and when she
came out he pretended to read, scarcely knowing whether he
wished her to succeed in the purpose which he was almost sure
she entertained, or not. She stopped by him, and passed her
hand over his head. He told me that his eyes filled wth tears at
this caress. Then she stood for a moment, looking at the
sleeping Madame Babette, and stooped down and softly
kissed her on the forehead. Pierre dreaded lest his mother
should awake (for by this time the wayward, vacillating boy
must have been quite on Virginie's side), but the brandy she
had drunk made her slumber heavily. Virginie went. Pierre's
heart beat fast. He was sure his cousin would try to intercept
her; but how, he could not imagine. He longed to run out and
see the catastrophe – but he had let the moment slip; he was
also afraid of re-awakening his mother to her usual state of
anger and violence.

CHAPTER VIII

'Pierre went on pretending to read, but in reality listening with acute tension of ear to every little sound. His perceptions became so sensitive in this respect that he was incapable of measuring time, every moment had seemed so full of noises, from the beating of his heart up to the roll of the heavy carts in the distance. He wondered whether Virginie would have reached the place of rendezvous, and yet he was unable to compute the passage of minutes. His mother slept soundly: that was well. By this time Virginie must have met the "faithful cousin;" if, indeed, Morin had not made his appearance.

'At length, he felt as if he could no longer sit still, awaiting the issue, but must run out and see what course events had taken. In vain his mother, half rousing herself, called after him to ask whither he was going: he was already out of hearing before she had ended her sentence, and he ran on until stopped by the sight of Mademoiselle Cannes walking along at so swift a pace that it was almost a run; while at her side, resolutely keeping by her, Morin was striding abreast. Pierre had just turned the corner of the street when he came upon them. Virginie would have passed him without recognising him, she was in such passionate agitation, but for Morin's gesture, by which he would fain have kept Pierre from interrupting them. Then, when Virginie saw the lad, she caught at his arm, and thanked God, as if in that boy of twelve or fourteen she held a protector. Pierre felt her tremble from head to foot, and was afraid lest she would fall, there where she stood, in the hard rough street.

'"Begone, Pierre!" said Morin.

'"I cannot," replied Pierre, who indeed was held firmly by Virginie. "Besides, I won't," he added. "Who has been frightening mademoiselle in this way?" asked he, very much inclined to brave his cousin at all hazards.

"'Mademoiselle is not accustomed to walk in the streets alone," said Morin sulkily. "She came upon a crowd attracted by the arrest of an aristocrat, and their cries alarmed her. I offered to take charge of her home. Mademoiselle should not walk in these streets alone. We are not like the cold-blooded people of the Faubourg Saint-German."

'Virginie did not speak. Pierre doubted if she heard a word of what they were saying. She leant upon him more and more heavily.

"'Will mademoiselle condescend to take my arm?" said Morin, with sulky, and yet humble, uncouthness. I dare say he would have given worlds if he might have had that little hand within his arm; but, though she still kept silence, she shuddered up away from him, as you shrink from touching a toad. He had said something to her during that walk, you may be sure, which had made her loathe him. He marked and understood the gesture. He held himself aloof, while Pierre gave her all the assistance he could in their slow progress homewards. But Morin accompanied her all the same. He had played too desperate a game to be baulked now. He had given information against the çi-devant Marquis de Créquy, as a returned emigré, to be met with at such a time, in such a place. Morin had hoped that all sign of the arrest would have been cleared away before Virginie reached the spot – so swiftly were terrible deeds done in those days. But Clément defended himself desperately; Virginie was punctual to a second; and, though the wounded man was borne off to the Abbaye, amid a crowd of the unsympathising jeerers who mingled with the armed officials of the Directory, Morin feared lest Virginie had recognised him; and he would have preferred that she should have thought that the "faithful cousin" was faithless, than that she should have seen him in bloody danger on her account. I suppose he fancied that, if Virginie never saw or heard more of him, her imagination would not dwell on his simple disappearance, as it would do if she knew what he was suffering for her sake.

'At any rate, Pierre saw that his cousin was deeply mortified by the whole tenor of his behaviour during their walk home. When they arrived at Madame Babette's, Virginie fell fainting on the floor; her strength had but just sufficed for this exertion of reaching the shelter of the house. Her first sign of restoring consciousness consisted in avoidance of Morin. He had been most assiduous in his efforts to bring her round; quite tender in his way, Pierre said; and this marked, instinctive repugnance to him evidently gave him extreme pain. I suppose Frenchmen are more demonstrative than we are; for Pierre declared that he saw his cousin's eyes fill with tears, as she shrank away from his touch, if he tried to arrange the shawl they had laid under her head like a pillow, or as she shut her eyes when he passed before her. Madame Babette was urgent with her to go and lie down on the bed in the inner room; but it was some time before she was strong enough to rise and do this.

'When Madame Babette returned from arranging the girl comfortably, the three relations sat down in silence: a silence which Pierre thought would never be broken. He wanted his mother to ask his cousin what had happened. But Madame Babette was afraid of her nephew, and thought it more discreet to wait for such crumbs of intelligence as he might think fit to throw to her. But, after she had twice reported Virginie to be asleep, without a word being uttered in reply to her whispers by either of her companions, Morin's powers of self-containment gave way.

"It is very hard!" he said.

"What is hard?" asked Madame Babette, after she had paused for a time, to enable him to add to, or to finish, his sentence if he pleased.

"It is hard for a man to love a woman as I do," he went on. "I did not seek to love her, it came upon me before I was aware – before I had ever thought about it at all, I loved her better than all the world beside. All my life, before I knew her, seems a dull blank. I neither know nor care for what I did before then. And now there are just two lives before me. Either I have her, or I have not. That is all, but that is everything. And what can I do to make her have me? Tell me, aunt," and he caught at Madame Babette's arm, and gave it so sharp a shake, that she half screamed out, Pierre said, and evidently grew alarmed at her nephew's excitement.

"Hush Victor!" said she. "There are other women in the world, if this one will not have you."

"'None other for me," he said, sinking back as if hopeless. "I am plain and coarse, not one of the scented darlings of the aristocrats. Say that I am ugly, brutish; I did not make myself so, any more than I made myself love her. It is my fate. But am I to submit to the consequences of my fate without a struggle? Not I. As strong as my love is, so strong is my will. It can be no stronger," continued he gloomily. "Aunt Babette, you must help me – you must make her love me." He was so fierce here, that Pierre said he did not wonder that his mother was frightened.

"'I, Victor!" she exclaimed. "I make her love you? How can I? Ask me to speak for you to Mademoiselle Didot, or to Mademoiselle Cauchois even, or to such as they, and I'll do it, and welcome. But to Mademoiselle de Créquy, why, you don't know the difference! These people – the old nobility, I mean – why, they don't know a man from a dog, out of their own rank! And no wonder, for the young gentlemen of quality are treated differently to us from their very birth. If she had you tomorrow, you would be miserable. Let me alone for knowing the aristocracy. I have not been a concierge to a duke and three counts for nothing. I tell you, all your ways are different to her ways."

"'I would change my 'ways' as you call them."

"'Be reasonable, Victor."

"'No, I will not be reasonable, if by that you mean giving her up. I tell you two lives are before me; one with her, one without her. But the latter will be but a short career for both of us. You said, aunt, that the talk went in the conciergerie of her father's hôtel, that she would have nothing to do with this cousin whom I put out of the way today?"

"'So the servants said. How could I know? All I know is, that he left off coming to our hotel, and that at one time before then he had never been two days absent."

"'So much the better for him. He suffers now for having come between me and my object – in trying to snatch her away out of my sight. Take you warning, Pierre! I did not like your meddling tonight." And so he went off, leaving Madame Babette rocking herself backwards and forwards, in all the depression of spirits consequent upon the reaction after the brandy, and upon her knowledge of her nephew's threatened purpose, combined.

'In telling you most of this, I have simply repeated Pierre's account, which I wrote down at the time. But here what he had to say came to a sudden break; for, the next morning, when Madame Babette rose, Virginie was missing, and it was some time before either she, or Pierre, or Morin, could get the slightest clue to the missing girl.

'And now I must take up the story as it was told to the Intendant Fléchier by the old gardener Jacques, with whom Clément had been lodging on his first arrival in Paris. The old man could not, I dare say, remember half as much of what had happened as Pierre did; the former had the dulled memory of age, while Pierre had evidently thought over the whole series of events as a story – as a play, if one may call it so – during the solitary hours in his after-life, wherever they were passed, whether in lonely camp watches, or in the foreign prison, where he had to drag out many years. Clément had, as I said, returned to the gardener's garret after he had been dismissed from the Hôtel Duguesclin. There were several reasons for his thus doubling back. One was, that he put nearly the whole breadth of Paris between him and an enemy; though why Morin was an enemy, and to what extent he carried his dislike or hatred, Clément could not tell, of course. The next reason for returning to Jacques was, no doubt, the conviction that, in multiplying his residences, he multiplied the chances against his being suspected and recognised. And then, again, the old man was in his secret, and his ally, although perhaps but a feeble kind of one. It was through Jacques that the plan of communication, by means of a nosegay of pinks, had been devised; and it was Jacques who procured him the last disguise that Clément was to use in Paris – as he hoped and trusted. It was that of a respectable shopkeeper of no particular class: a dress that would have seemed perfectly suitable to the young man who would naturally have worn it; and yet, as Clément put it on, and adjusted it – giving it a sort of finish and elegance which I always noticed about his appearance, and which I believe was innate in the wearer – I have no doubt it seemed like the usual apparel of a gentleman. No coarseness of texture, nor clumsiness of cut could disguise the nobleman of thirty descents, it appeared; for immediately on arriving at the place of rendezvouz he was recognised by the men placed there on Morin's information to seize him. Jacques, following at a little distance, with a bundle under his arm containing articles of feminine disguise for Virginie, saw four men attempt Clément's arrest – saw him, quick as lightning, draw a sword hitherto concealed in a clumsy stick – saw his agile figure spring to his guard – and saw him defend himself with the rapidity and art of a man skilled in arms. "But what good did it do?" as Jacques piteously used to ask, Monsieur Fléchier told me. A great blow from a heavy club on the sword-arm of Monsieur de Créquy laid it helpless and immmovable by his side. Jacques always thought that that blow came from one of the spectators, who by this time had collected round the scene of the affray. The next instant, his master – his little marquis – was down among the feet of the crowd, and though he was up again before he had received much damage – so active and light was my poor Clément – it was not before the old gardener had hobbled forwards, and, with many an old-fashioned oath and curse, proclaimed himself a partisan of the losing side – a follower of a ci-devant aristocrat. It was quite enough. He received one or two good blows, which were, in fact, aimed at his master; and then, almost before he was aware, he found his arms pinioned behind him with a woman's garter, which one of the viragos in the crowd had made no scruple of pulling off in public as soon as she heard for what purpose it was wanted. Poor Jacques was stunned and unhappy – his master was out of sight, on before; and the old gardener scarce knew whither they were taking him. His head ached from the blows which had fallen upon it; it was growing dark – June day though it was – and, when first he seems to have become exactly aware of what had happened to him, it was when he was turned into one of the larger rooms of the Abbaye, in which all were put who had no other allotted place wherein to sleep. One or two iron lamps hung from the ceiling by chains, giving a dim light for a little circle. Jacques stumbled forwards over a sleeping body lying on the ground. The sleeper wakened up enough, to complain; and the apology of the old man in reply caught the ear of his master, who, until this time, could hardly have been aware of

the straits and difficulties of his faithful Jacques. And there
they sat – against a pillar, the livelong night, holding one
another's hands, and each restraining expressions of pain, for
fear of adding to the other's distress. That night made them
intimate friends, in spite of the difference of age and rank. The
disappointed hopes, the acute suffering of the present, the
apprehensions of the future, made them seek solace in talking
of the past. Monsieur de Créquy and the gardener found
themselves disputing with interest in which chimney of the
stack the starling used to build – the starling whose nest
Clément sent to Urian, you remember – and discussing the
merits of different espalier-pears which grew, and may grow
still, in the old garden of the Hôtel de Créquy. Towards
morning both fell asleep. The old man wakened first. His
frame was deadened to suffering, I suppose, for he felt relieved
of his pain; but Clément moaned and cried in feverish
slumber. His broken arm was beginning to inflame his blood.
He was, besides, much injured by some kicks from the crowd
as he fell. As the man looked sadly on the white, baked lips,
and the flushed cheeks, contorted with suffering even in his
sleep, Clément gave a sharp cry, which disturbed his miserable neighbours, all slumbering around in uneasy attitudes.
They bade him with curses be silent; and then, turning round,
tried again to forget their own misery in sleep. For you see,
the bloodthirsty canaille had not been sated with guillotining
and hanging all the nobility they could find, but were now
informing, right and left, even against each other; and when
Clément and Jacques were in the prison, there were few of
gentle blood in the place, and fewer still of gentle manners. At
the sound of the angry words and threats, Jacques thought it
best to awaken his master from his feverish, uncomfortable
sleep, lest he should provoke more enmity; and tenderly
lifting him up, he tried to adjust his own body, so that it
should serve as a rest and a pillow for the younger man. The
motion aroused Clément, and he began to talk in a strange,
feverish way, of Virginie, too – whose name he would not
have breathed in such a place had he been quite himself. But
Jacques had as much delicacy of feeling as any lady in the land,
although, mind you, he knew neither how to read nor write –
and bent his head low down, so that his master might tell him

in a whisper what messages he was to take to Mademoiselle de Créquy, in case – Poor Clément, he knew it must come to that! No escape for him now, in Norman disguise or otherwise! Either by gathering fever or guillotine, death was sure of his prey. Well! when that happened, Jacques was to go and find Mademoiselle de Créquy, and tell her that her cousin loved her at the last as he had loved her at the first; but that she should never have heard another word of his attachment from his living lips; that he knew he was not good enough for her, his queen; and that no thought of earning her love by his devotion had prompted his return to France, only that, if possible, he might have the great privilege of serving her whom he loved. And then he went off into rambling talk about petit-maîtres, and such kind of expressions, said Jacques to Fléchier, the Intendant, little knowing what a clue that one word gave to much of the poor lad's suffering.

'The summer morning came slowly on in that dark prison, and when Jacques could look round – his master was now sleeping on his shoulder, still the uneasy, starting sleep of fever – he saw that there were many women among the prisoners. (I have heard some of those who have escaped from the prisons say, that the look of despair and agony that came into the faces of the prisoners on first wakening, as the sense of their situation grew upon them, was what lasted the longest in the memory of the survivors. This look, they said, passed away from the women's faces sooner than it did from those of the men.)

'Poor old Jacques kept falling asleep, and plucking himself up again, for fear lest, if he did not attend to his master, some harm might come to the swollen, helpless arm. Yet his weariness grew upon him in spite of all his efforts, and at last he felt as if he must give way to the irresistible desire, if only for five minutes. But just then there was a bustle at the door. Jacques opened his eyes wide to look.

'"The gaoler is early with breakfast," said some one lazily.

'"It is the darkness of this cursed place that makes us think it early," said another.

'All this time a parley was going on at the door. Some one came in; not the gaoler – a woman. The door was shut to and locked behind her. She only advanced a step or two, for it was too sudden a change, out of the light into the dark shadow, for any one to see clearly for the first few minutes. Jacques had his eyes fairly open now, and was wide awake. It was Mademoiselle de Créquy, looking bright, clear, and resolute. The faithful heart of the old man read that look like an open page. Her cousin should not die there on her behalf, without at least the comfort of her sweet presence.

"'Here he is," he whispered, as her gown would have touched him in passing, without her perceiving him, in the heavy obscurity of the place.

"'The good God bless you, my friend!" she murmured, as she saw the attitude of the old man, propped against a pillar, and holding Clément in his arms, as if the young man had been a helpless baby, while one of the poor gardener's hands supported the broken limb in the easiest position. Virginie sat down by the old man, and held out her arms. Softly she moved Clément's head to her own shoulder; softly she transferred the task of holding the arm to herself. Clément lay on the floor, but she supported him, and Jacques was at liberty to arise and stretch and shake his stiff, weary old body. He then sat down at a little distance, and watched the pair until he fell asleep. Clément had muttered "Virginie," as they half-aroused him by their movements out of his stupor; but Jacques thought he was only dreaming; nor did he seem fully awake when once his eyes opened, and he looked full at Virginie's face bending over him, and growing crimson under his gaze, though she never stirred, for fear of hurting him if she moved. Clément looked in silence, until his heavy eyelids came slowly down, and he fell into his oppressive slumber again. Either he did not recognise her, or she came in too completely as a part of his sleeping visions for him to be disturbed by her appearance there.

'When Jacques awoke it was full daylight – at least as full as it would ever be in that place. His breakfast – the gaol-allowance of bread and vin ordinaire – was by his side. He must have slept soundly. He looked for his master. He and Virginie had recognised each other now – hearts, as well as appearance. They were smiling into each other's faces, as if that dull vaulted room in the grim Abbaye were the sunny gardens of Versailles, with music and festivity all abroad.

Apparently they had much to say to each other; for whispered questions and answers never ceased.

'Virginie had made a sling for the poor broken arm: nay, she had obtained two splinters of wood in some way, and one of their fellow-prisoners – having, it appeared, some knowledge of surgery – had set it. Jacques felt more desponding by far than they did, for he was suffering from the night he had passed, which told upon his aged frame; while they must have heard some good news, as it seemed to him so bright and happy did they look. Yet Clément was still in bodily pain and suffering, and Virginie, by her own act and deed, was a prisoner in that dreadful Abbaye, whence the only issue was the guillotine. But they were together; they loved; they understood each other at length.

'When Virginie saw that Jacques was awake, and languidly munching his breakfast, she rose from the wooden stool on which she was sitting, and went to him, holding out both hands, and refusing to allow him to rise, while she thanked him with pretty eagerness for all his kindness to Monsieur. Monsieur himself came towards him, following Virginie, but with tottering steps, as if his head was weak and dizzy, to thank the poor old man, who, now on his feet, stood between them, ready to cry while they gave him credit for faithful actions which he felt to have been almost involuntary on his part – for loyalty was like an instinct in the good old days, before your educational cant had come up. And so two days went on. The only event was the morning call for the victims, a certain number of whom were summoned to trial every day. And to be tried was to be condemned. Every one of the prisoners became grave, as the hour for their summons approached. Most of the victims went to their doom with uncomplaining resignation, and for a while after their departure there was comparative silence in the prison. But, by-and-by – so said Jacques – the conversation or amusement began again. Human nature cannot stand the perpetual pressure of such keen anxiety, without an effort to relieve itself by thinking of something else. Jacques said that Monsieur and Mademoiselle were for ever talking together of the past days – it was "Do you remember this?" or, "Do you remember that?" perpetually. He sometimes thought they forgot where they were, and what was before them. But Jacques did not, and every day he trembled more and more as the list was called over.

'The third morning of their incarceration, the gaoler brought in a man whom Jacques did not recognise, and therefore did not at once observe; for he was waiting, as in duty bound, upon his master and his sweet young lady (as he always called her in repeating the story). He thought that the new introduction was some friend of the gaoler, as the two seemed well acquainted, and the latter stayed a few minutes talking with his visitor before leaving him in prison. So Jacques was surprised when, after a short time had elapsed, he looked round, and saw the fierce stare with which the stranger was regarding Monsieur and Mademoiselle de Créquy, as the pair sat at breakfast – the said breakfast being laid as well as Jacques knew how, on a bench fastened into the prison wall – Virginie sitting on her low stool, and Clément half lying on the ground by her side, and submitting gladly to be fed by her pretty white fingers; for it was one of her fancies, Jacques said, to do all she could for him, in consideration of his broken arm. And, indeed, Clément was wasting away daily; for he had received other injuries, internal and more serious than that to his arm, during the *mêlée* which had ended in his capture. The stranger made Jacques conscious of his presence by a sign, which was almost a groan. All three prisoners looked round at the sound. Clément's face expressed little but scornful indifference; but Virginie's face froze into stony hate. Jacques said he never saw such a look, and hoped that he never should again. Yet after that first revelation of feeling, her look was steady and fixed in another direction to that in which the stranger stood – still motionless – still watching. He came a step nearer at last.

'"Mademoiselle," he said. Not the quivering of an eyelash showed that she heard him. "Mademoiselle!" he said again, with an intensity of beseeching that made Jacques – not knowing who he was – almost pity him, when he saw his young lady's obdurate face.

'There was perfect silence for a space of time which Jacques could not measure. Then again the voice, hesitatingly, saying, "Monsieur!" Clément could not hold the same icy countenance as Virginie; he turned his head with an impatient gesture of disgust; but even that emboldened the man.

'"Monsieur, do ask mademoiselle to listen to me – just two words."

'"Mademoiselle de Créquy only listens to whom she chooses." Very haughtily my Clément would say that, I am sure.

'"But, mademoiselle," lowering his voice; and coming a step or two nearer. Virginie must have felt his approach, though she did not see it; for she drew herself a little on one side, so as to put as much space as possible between him and her – "Mademoiselle, it is not too late. I can save you; but tomorrow your name is down on the list. I can save you, if you will listen."

'Still no word or sign. Jacques did not understand the affair. Why was she so obdurate to one who might be ready to include Clément in the proposal, as far as Jacques knew?

'The man withdrew a little, but did not offer to leave the prison. He never took his eyes off Virginie; he seemed to be suffering from some acute and terrible pain as he watched her.

'Jacques cleared away the breakfast-things as well as he could. Purposely, as I suspect, he passed near the man.

'"Hist!" said the stranger. "You are Jacques, the gardener, arrested for assisting an aristocrat. I know the gaoler. You shall escape, if you will. Only take this message from me to mademoiselle. You heard. She will not listen to me; I did not want her to come here. I never knew she was here, and she will die tomorrow. They will put her beautiful throat under the guillotine. Tell her, good old man, tell her how sweet life is; and how I can save her; and how I will not ask for more than just to see her from time to time. She is so young; and death is annihilation, you know. Why does she hate me so? I want to save her; I have done her no harm. Good old man, tell her how terrible death is; and that she will die tomorrow, unless she listens to me."

'Jacques saw no harm in repeating the message. Clément listened in silence, watching Virginie with an air of infinite tenderness.

'"Will you not try him, my cherished one?" he said. "Towards you he may mean well" (which makes me think that Virginie had never repeated to Clément the conversation which she had overheard that last night at Madame Babette's); "you would be in no worse a situation than you were before!"

'"No worse, Clément! and I should have known what you were, and have lost you. My Clément!" said she reproachfully.

'"Ask him," said she, turning to Jacques suddenly, "if he can save Monsieur de Créquy as well, – if he can? – O Clément, we might escape to England; we are but young." And she hid her face on his shoulder.

'Jacques returned to the stranger, and asked him Virginie's question. His eyes were fixed on the cousins; he was very pale, and the twitchings or contortions, which must have been involuntary whenever he was agitated, convulsed his whole body.

'He made a long pause. "I will save mademoiselle and monsieur, if she will go straight from prison to the mairie, and be my wife."

'"Your wife!" Jacques could not help exclaiming, "That she will never be – never."

'"Ask her!" said Morin hoarsely.

'But almost before Jacques thought he could have fairly uttered the words, Clément caught their meaning.

'"Begone!" said he; "not one word more." Virginie touched the old man as he was moving away. "Tell him he does not know how he makes me welcome death." And smiling, as if triumphant, she turned again to Clément.

'The stranger did not speak as Jacques gave him the meaning, not the words, of their replies. He was going away, but stopped. A minute or two afterwards, he beckoned to Jacques. The old gardener seems to have thought it undesirable to throw away even the chance of assistance from such a man as this, for he went forward to speak to him.

'"Listen! I have influence with the gaoler. He shall let thee pass out with the victims tomorrow. No one will notice it, or miss thee –. They will be led to trial – even at the last moment, I will save her, if she sends me word she relents. Speak to her, as the time draws on. Life is very sweet – tell her how sweet. Speak to him; he will do more with her than thou canst. Let him urge her to live. Even at the last, I will be at the

Palais de Justice — at the Grève. I have followers — I have interest. Come among the crowd that follow the victims — I shall see thee. It will be no worse for him, if she escapes — "

'"Save my master, and I will do all," said Jacques.

'"Only on my one condition," said Morin doggedly; and Jacques was hopeless of that condition ever being fulfilled. But he did not see why his own life might not be saved. By remaining in prison until the next day, he should have rendered every service in his power to the master and the young lady. He, poor fellow, shrank from death; and he agreed with Morin to escape, if he could, by the means that Morin had suggested, and to bring him word if Mademoiselle de Créquy relented. (Jacques had no expectation that she would; but I fancy he did not think it necessary to tell Morin of this conviction of his.) This bargaining with so base a man for so slight a thing as life, was the only flaw that I heard of in the old gardener's behaviour. Of course, the mere re-opening of the subject was enough to stir Virginie to displeasure. Clément urged her, it is true; but the light he had gained upon Morin's motions made him rather try to set the case before her in as fair a manner as possible than use any persuasive arguments. And, even as it was, what he said on the subject made Virginie shed tears — the first that had fallen from her since she entered the prison. So, they were summoned and went together, at the fatal call of the muster-roll of the victims the next morning. He, feeble from his wounds, and his injured health; she, calm and serene, only petitioning to be allowed to walk next to him, in order that she might hold him up when he turned faint and giddy from his extreme suffering.

'Together they stood at the bar; together they were condemned. As the words of judgment were pronounced, Virginie turned to Clément, and embraced him with passionate fondness. Then, making him lean on her, they marched out towards the Place de la Grève.

'Jacques was free now. He had told Morin how fruitless his efforts at persuasion had been; and scarcely caring to note the effect of his information upon the man, he had devoted himself to watching Monsieur and Mademoiselle de Créquy. And now he followed them to the Place de la Grève. He saw them mount the platform; saw them kneel down together till plucked up by the impatient officials; could see that she was urging some request to the executioner; the end of which seemed to be, that Clément advanced first to the guillotine, was executed (and just at this moment there was a stir among the crowd, as of a man pressing forward towards the scaffold). Then she, standing with her face to the guillotine, slowly made the sign of the cross, and knelt down.

'Jacques covered his eyes, blinded with tears. The report of a pistol made him look up. She was gone – another victim in her place – and where there had been a little stir in the crowd not five minutes before, some men were carrying off a dead body. A man had shot himself, they said. Pierre told me who that man was.'

CHAPTER IX

After a pause, I ventured to ask what became of Madame de Créquy, Clément's mother.

'She never made any inquiry about him,' said my lady. 'She must have known that he was dead; though how, we never could tell. Medlicott remembered afterwards that it was about, if not on – Medlicott to this day declares that it was on the very Monday, June the nineteenth, when her son was executed, that Madame de Créquy left off her rouge and took to her bed, as one bereaved and hopeless. It certainly was about that time; and Medlicott – who was deeply impressed by that dream of Madame de Créquy's (the relation of which I told you had had such an effect on my lord), in which she had seen the figure of Virginie, as the only light object amid much surrounding darkness as of night, smiling and beckoning Clément on – on – till at length the bright phantom stopped, motionless, and Madame de Créquy's bright eyes began to penetrate the murky darkness, and to see closing round her the gloomy dripping walls which she had once seen and never forgotten – the walls of the vault of the chapel of the De Créquy's in Saint German l'Auxerrois; and there the two last of the Créquys laid them down among their forefathers, and Madame de Créquy had awakened to the sound of the great door, which led to the open air, being locked upon her – I say Medlicott, who was predisposed by this dream to look out for the supernatural, always declared that Madame de Créquy was made conscious, in some mysterious way, of her son's death, on the very day and hour when it occurred, and that after that she had no more anxiety, but was only conscious of a kind of stupefying despair.

'And what became of her, my lady?' I again asked.

'What could become of her?' replied Lady Ludlow. 'She never could be induced to rise again, though she lived more than a year after her son's departure. She kept her bed; her room darkened, her face turned towards the wall, whenever any one besides Medlicott was in the room. She hardly ever spoke, and would have died of starvation but for Medlicott's tender care, in putting a morsel to her lips every now and then, feeding her in fact, just as an old bird feeds her young ones. In the height of summer my lord and I left London. We would fain have taken her with us into Scotland, but the doctor (we had the old doctor from Leicester Square) forbade her removal; and this time he gave such good reason against it that I acquiesced. Medlicott and a maid were left with her. Every care was taken of her. She survived till our return. Indeed, I thought she was in much the same state as I had left her in, when I came back to London. But Medlicott spoke of her as much weaker; and one morning, on awakening, they told me she was dead. I sent for Medlicott, who was in sad distress, she had become so fond of her charge. She said that, about two o'clock, she had been awakened by unusual res-lessness on Madame de Créquy's part; that she had gone to her bedside, and found the poor lady feebly but perpetually moving her wasted arm up and down – and saying to herself in a wailing voice – "I did not bless him when he left me – I did not bless him when he left me!" Medlicott gave her a spoonful or two of jelly, and sat by her, stroking her hand, and soothing her till she seemed to fall asleep. But in the morning she was dead.'

'It is a sad story, your ladyship,' said I, after a while.

'Yes, it is. People seldom arrive at my age without having watched the beginning, middle and end of many lives and many fortunes. We do not talk about them, perhaps; for they are often so sacred to us, from having touched into the very quick of our own hearts, as it were, or into those of others who are dead and gone, and veiled over from human sight, that we cannot tell the tale as if it was a mere story. But young people should remember that we have had this solemn experience of life, on which to base our opinions and form our judgments, so that they are not mere untried theories. I am not alluding to Mr. Horner just now, for he is nearly as old as I am – within ten years, I dare say – but I am thinking of Mr. Gray, with his endless plans for some new thing – schools, education, Sabbaths, and what not. Now he has not see what all this leads to.'

'It is a pity he has not heard your ladyship tell the story of poor Monsieur de Créquy'.

'Not at all a pity, my dear. A young man like him, who, both by position and age, must have had his experience confined to a very narrow circle, ought not to set up his opinion against mine; he ought not to require reasons from me, nor to need such explanation of my arguments (if I condescend to argue), as going into relation of the circumstances on which my arguments are based in my own mind would be.'

'But my lady, it might convince him,' I said, with perhaps injudicious perseverance.

'And why should he be convinced?' she asked, with gentle inquiry in her tone. 'He has only to acquiesce. Though he is appointed by Mr. Croxton, I am the lady of the manor, as he must know. But it is with Mr. Horner that I must have to do about this unfortunate lad Gregson. I am afraid there will be no method of making him forget his unlucky knowledge. His poor brains will be intoxicated with the sense of his powers, without any counterbalancing principles to guide him. Poor fellow! I am quite afraid it will end in his being hanged!'

The next day Mr. Horner came to apologise and explain. He was evidently – as I could tell from his voice, as he spoke to my lady in the next room – extremely annoyed at her ladyship's discovery of the education he had been giving to this boy. My lady spoke with great authority, and with reasonable grounds of complaint. Mr. Horner was well acquainted with her thoughts on the subject, and had acted in defiance of her wishes. He acknowledged as much, and should on no account have done it, in any other instance, without her leave.

'Which I could never have granted you,' said my lady.

But this boy had extraordinary capabilities; would, in fact, have taught himself much that was bad, if he had not been rescued, and another direction given to his powers. And in all Mr. Horner had done, he had had her ladyship's service in view. The business was getting almost beyond his power, so many letters and so much account-keeping was required by the complicated state in which things were.

Lady Ludlow felt what was coming – a reference to the mortgage for the benefit of my lord's Scottish estates, which, she was perfectly aware, Mr. Horner considered as having been a most unwise proceeding – and she hastened to observe –

'All this may be very true, Mr. Horner, and I am sure I should be the last person to wish you to overwork or distress yourself; but of that we will talk another time. What I am now anxious to remedy is, if possible, the state of this poor little Gregson's mind. Would not hard work in the fields be a wholesome and excellent way of enabling him to forget?'

'I was in hopes, my lady, that you would have permitted me to bring him up to act as a kind of clerk,' said Mr. Horner, jerking out his project abruptly.

'A what?' asked my lady, in infinite surprise.

'A kind of – of assistant, in the way of copying letters and doing up accounts. He is already an excellent penman and very quick at figures.'

' Mr. Horner,' said my lady, with dignity, 'the son of a poacher and vagabond ought never to have been able to copy letters relating to the Hanbury estates; and, at any rate, he shall not. I wonder how it is that, knowing the use he has made of his power of reading a letter, you should venture to propose such an employment for him as would require his being in your confidence, and you the trusted agent of this family. Why, every secret (and every ancient and honourable family has its secrets, as you know, Mr. Horner!) would be learnt off by heart, and repeated to the first comer!'

'I should have hoped to have trained him, my lady, to understand the rules of discretion.'

'Trained! Train a barn-door fowl to be a pheasant, Mr. Horner! That would be the easiest task. But you did right to speak of discretion rather than honour. Discretion looks to the consequences of actions – honour looks to the action itself, and is an instinct rather than a virtue. After all, it is possible you might have trained him to be discreet.'

Mr. Horner was silent. My lady was softened by his not replying, and began, as she always did in such cases, to fear lest she had been too harsh. I could tell that by her voice and by her next speech, as well as if I had seen her face.

'But I am sorry you are feeling the pressure of the affairs; I am quite aware that I have entailed much additional trouble upon you by some of my measures: I must try and provide you with some suitable assistance. Copying letters and doing up accounts, I think you said?'

Mr. Horner had certainly had a distant idea of turning the little boy, in process of time, into a clerk; but he had rather urged this possibility of future usefulness beyond what he had at first intended, in speaking of it to my lady as a palliation of his offence; and he certainly was very much inclined to retract his statement that the letter-writing, or any other business, had increased, or that he was in the slightest want of help of any kind, when my lady, after a pause of consideration, suddenly said –

'I have it. Miss Galindo will, I am sure, be glad to assist you. I will speak to her myself. The payment we should make to a clerk would be of real service to her!'

I could hardly help echoing Mr. Horner's tone of surprise as he said –

'Miss Galindo!'

For, you must be told who Miss Galindo was; at least, told as much as I know. Miss Galindo had lived in the village for many years, keeping house on the smallest possible means, yet always managing to maintain a servant. And this servant was invariably chosen because she had some infirmity that made her undesirable to every one else. I believe Miss Galindo had had lame and blind and hump-backed maids. She had even at one time taken in a girl hopelessly gone in consumption, because, if not, she would have had to go to the workhouse, and not have had enough to eat. Of course the poor creature could not perform a single duty usually required of a servant, and Miss Galindo herself was both servant and nurse.

Her present maid was scarcely four feet high, and bore a terrible character for ill-temper. Nobody but Miss Galindo would have kept her; but, as it was, mistress and servant squabbled perpetually, and were, at heart, the best of friends. For it was one of Miss Galindo's peculiarities to do all manner of kind and self-denying actions, and to say all manner of provoking things. Lame, blind, deformed, and dwarf, all came in for scoldings without number; it was only the consumptive girl that never had heard a sharp word. I don't think any of her servants liked her the worse for her peppery temper, and passionate odd ways, for they knew her real and beautiful kindness of heart; and, besides, she had so great a turn for humour, that very often her speeches amused as much or more than they irritated; and, on the other side, a piece of witty impudence from her servant would occasionally tickle her so much and so suddenly, that she would burst out laughing in the middle of her passion.

But the talk about Miss Galindo's choice and management of her servants was confined to village gossip, and had never reached my Lady Ludlow's ears, though doubtless Mr. Horner was well acquainted with it. What my lady knew of her amounted to this. It was the custom in those days for the wealthy ladies of the county to set on foot a repository, as it was called, in the assize-town. The ostensible manager of this repository was generally a decayed gentlewoman, a clergyman's widow, or so forth. She was, however, controlled by a committee of ladies: and paid by them in proportion to the amount of goods she sold; and these goods were the small manufactures of ladies of little or no fortune, whose names, if they chose it, were only signified by initials.

Poor water-colour drawings, indigo and Indian ink, screens, ornamented with moss and dried leaves, paintings on velvet and such faintly ornamental works, were displayed on one side of the shop. It was always reckoned a mark of characteristic gentility in the repository to have only common heavy-framed sash-windows, which admitted very little light; so I never was quite certain of the merit of these Works of Art, as they were entitled. But, on the other side, where the Useful Work placard was put up, there was a great variety of articles, of whose unusual excellence every one might judge. Such fine sewing, and stitching, and button-holing! Such bundles of soft delicate knitted stockings and socks; and above all, in Lady Ludlow's eyes, such hanks of the finest spun flaxen thread!

And the most delicate dainty work of all was done by Miss Galindo, as Lady Ludlow very well knew. Yet, for all their fine sewing, it sometimes happened that Miss Galindo's patterns were of an old-fashioned kind; and the dozen night-caps, may be, on the materials for which she had expended

bonâ-fida money, and on the making-up, no little time and
eyesight, would lie for months in a yellow neglected heap; and
at such times, it was said, Miss Galindo was more amusing
than usual, more full of dry drollery and humour; just as at the
times when an order came in to X (the initial she had chosen)
for a stock of well-paying things, she sat and stormed at her
servant as she stiched away. She herself explained her practice
in this way –

'When everything goes wrong, one would give up brea-
thing if one could not lighten one's heart by a joke. But when
I've to sit still from morning till night, I must have something
to stir my blood, or I should go off into an apoplexy; so I set
to, and quarrel with Sally.'

Such were Miss Galindo's means and manner of living in
her own house. Out of doors, and in the village, she was not
popular, although she would have been sorely missed had she
left the place. But she asked too many home questions (not to
say impertinent) respecting the domestic economies (for even
the very poor liked to spend their bit of money their own
way), and would open cupboards to find out hidden extrava-
gances, and question closely respecting the weekly amount of
butter; till one day she met with what would have been a
rebuff to any other person, but was by her rather enjoyed than
otherwise.

She was going into a cottage, and in the doorway met the
good woman chasing out a duck, and apparently unconscious
of her visitor.

'Get out, Miss Galindo!' she cried, addressing the duck. 'Get
out! Oh I ask your pardon,' she continued, as if seeing the lady
for the first time. 'It's only that weary duck will come in. Get
out Miss Gal –' (to the duck).

'And so you call it after me, do you?' inquired her visitor.

'Oh, yes, ma'am; my master would have it so; for, he said,
sure enough the unlucky bird was always poking herself
where she was not wanted.'

'Ha, ha! very good! And so your master is a wit, is he? Well!
tell him to come up and speak to me tonight about my parlour
chimney; for there is no one like him for chimney doctoring.'

And the master went up, and was so won over by Miss
Galindo's merry ways, and sharp insight into the mysteries of

his various kinds of business (he was a mason, chimney sweeper, and ratcatcher), that he came home and abused his wife the next time she called the duck the name by which he himself had christened her.

But, odd as Miss Galindo was in general, she could be as well-bred a lady as any one when she chose. And choose she always did when my Lady Ludlow was by. Indeed, I don't know the man, woman, or child, that did not instinctively turn out its best side to her ladyship. So she had no notion of the qualities which, I am sure, made Mr. Horner think that Miss Galindo would be most unmanageable as a clerk, and heartily wish that the idea had never come into my lady's head. But there it was, and he had annoyed her ladyship already more than he liked today; so he could not directly contradict her, but only urge difficulties which he hoped might prove insuperable. But every one of them Lady Ludlow knocked down. 'Letters to copy?' Doubtless. Miss Galindo could come up to the Hall; she should have a room to herself; she wrote a beautiful hand; and writing would save her eyesight. 'Capability with regard to accounts?' My lady would answer for that too; and for more than Mr. Horner seemed to think it necessary to inquire about. Miss Galindo was by birth and breeding a lady of the strictest honour, and would, if possible, forget the substance of any letters that passed through her hands: at any rate, no one would ever hear of them again from her. 'Remuneration?' Oh! as for that, Lady Ludlow would herself take care that it was managed in the most delicate manner possible. She would send to invite Miss Galindo to tea at the Hall that very afternoon, if Mr. Horner would only give her ladyship the slightest idea of the average length of time that my lady was to request Miss Galindo to sacrifice to her daily. 'Three hours? Very well.' Mr. Horner looked very grave as he passed the windows of the room where I lay. I don't think he liked the idea of Miss Galindo as a clerk.

Lady Ludlow's invitations were like royal commands. Indeed, the village was too quiet to allow the inhabitants to have many evening engagements of any kind. Now and then, Mr. and Mrs. Horner gave a tea and supper to the principal tenants and their wives, to which the clergyman was invited,

and Miss Galindo, Mrs. Medlicott, and one or two other
spinsters and widows. The glory of the supper-table on these
occasions were invariably furnished by her ladyship: it was a
cold roasted peacock, with its tail stuck out as if in life. Mrs.
Medlicott would take up the whole morning arranging the
feathers in the proper semicircle, and was always pleased with
the wonder and admiration it excited. It was considered a due
reward and fitting compliment to her exertions that Mr.
Horner always took her in to supper, and placed her opposite
to the magnificent dish, at which she sweetly smiled all the
time they were at table. But since Mrs. Horner had had the
paralytic stroke these parties had been given up; and Miss
Galindo wrote a note to Lady Ludlow in reply to her
invitation, saying that she was entirely disengaged, and would
have great pleasure in doing herself the honour of waiting
upon her ladyship.

Whoever visited my lady took their meals with her, sitting
on the dais, in the presence of all my former companions. So I
did not see Miss Galindo until some time after tea; as the
young gentlewomen had had to bring her their sewing and
spinning, to hear the remarks of so competent a judge. At
length her ladyship brought her visitor into the room where I
lay – it was one of my bad days, I remember – in order to have
her little bit of private conversation. Miss Galindo was dressed
in her best gown, I am sure, but I had never seen anything like
it except in a picture, it was so old-fashioned. She wore a
white muslin apron, delicately embroidered, and put on a little
crookedly, in order, as she told us, even Lady Ludlow, before
the evening was over, to conceal a spot whence the colour had
been discharged by a lemon-stain. This crookedness had an
odd effect, especially when I saw that it was intentional;
indeed, she was so anxious about her apron's right adjustment
in the wrong place, that she told us straight out why she wore
it so, and asked her ladyship if the spot was properly hidden,
at the same time lifting up her apron and showing her how
large it was.

'When my father was alive, I always took his right arm, so,
and used to remove any spotted or discoloured breadths to the
left side, if it was a walking-dress. That's the convenience of a
gentleman. But widows and spinsters must do what they can.

Ah, my dear!' (to me) 'when you are reckoning up the blessings in your lot – though you may think it a hard one in some respects – don't forget how little your stockings want darning, as you are obliged to lie down so much! I would rather knit two pairs of stockings than darn one, any day.'

'Have you been doing any of your beautiful knitting lately?' asked my lady, who had now arranged Miss Galindo in the pleasantest chair, and taken her own little wicker-work one, and, having her work in her hands, was ready to try and open the subject.

'No, and alas! your ladyship. It is partly the hot weather's fault, for people seem to forget that winter must come; and partly, I suppose, that every one is stocked who has the money to pay four-and-sixpence a pair for stockings.'

'Then may I ask if you have any time in your active days at liberty?' said my lady, drawing a little nearer to her proposal, which I fancy she found it a little awkward to make.

'Why the village keeps me busy, your ladyship, when I have neither knitting nor sewing to do. You know I took X, for my letter at the repository, because it stands for Xantippe, who was a great scold in old times, as I have learnt. But I'm sure I don't know how the world would get on without scolding, your ladyship. It would go to sleep, and the sun would stand still.'

'I don't think I could bear to scold, Miss Galindo,' said her ladyship, smiling.

'No! because your ladyship has people to do it for you. Begging your pardon, my lady, it seems to me the generality of people may be divided into saints, scolds, and sinners. Now, your ladyship is a saint, because you have a sweet and holy nature, in the first place; and you have people to do your anger and vexation for you, in the second place. And Jonathan Walker is a sinner, because he is sent to prison. But here am I, half way, having but a poor kind of disposition at best, and yet hating sin, and all that leads to it, such as wasting, and extravagance, and gossiping – and yet all this lies right under my nose in the village, and I am not saint enough to be vexed at it; and so I scold. And though I had rather be a saint, yet I think I do good in my way.'

'No doubt you do, dear Miss Galindo,' said Lady Ludlow.

'But I am sorry to hear that there is so much that is bad going on in the village – very sorry,'

'Oh, your ladyship! then I am sorry I brought it out. It was only by way of saying that when I have no particular work to do at home, I take a turn abroad, and set my neighbours to rights, just by way of steering clear of Satan.

> "For Satan finds some mischief still
> For idle hands to do."

you know, my lady.'

There was no leading into the subject by delicate degrees, for Mis Galindo was evidently so fond of talking that, if asked a question, she made her answer so long that before she came to an end of it, she had wandered far away from the original starting-point. So Lady Ludlow plunged at once into what she had to say.

'Miss Galindo, I have a great favour to ask of you.'

'My lady, I wish I could tell you what a pleasure it is to hear you say so,' replied Miss Galindo, almost with tears in her eyes; so glad were we all to do anything for her ladyship, which could be called a free service and not merely a duty.

'It is this Mr. Horner tells me that the business letters, relating to the estate, are multiplying so much that he finds it impossible to copy them all himself; and I therefore require the services of some confidential and discreet person to copy these letters, and occasionally to go through certain accounts. Now, there is a very pleasant little sitting-room very near to Mr. Horner's office (you know Mr. Horner's office – on the other side of the stone hall?) – and, if I could prevail upon you to come here to breakfast and afterwards to sit there for three hours every morning, Mr. Horner should bring or send you the papers –'

Lady Ludlow stopped. Miss Galindo's countenance had fallen. There was some great obstacle in her mind to her wish for obliging Lady Ludlow.

'What would Sally do?' she asked at length. Lady Ludlow had not a notion who Sally was. Nor, if she had had a notion, would she have had a conception of the perplexities that poured into Miss Galindo's mind, at the idea of leaving her

rough, forgetful dwarf, without the perpetual monitorship of
her mistress. Lady Ludlow, accustomed to a household where
everything went on noiselessly, perfectly, and by clockwork,
conducted by a number of highly-paid, well-chosen and
accomplished servants, had not a conception of the nature of
the rough material from which her servants came. Besides, in
her establishment, so that the result was good, no one inquired
if the small economies had been observed in the production.
Whereas every penny – every halfpenny – was of consequence
to Miss Galindo; and visions of squandered drops of milk and
wasted crusts of bread filled her mind with dismay. But she
swallowed all her apprehensions down, out of her regard for
Lady Ludlow, and desire to be of service to her. No one
knows how great a trial it was to her when she thought of
Sally, unchecked and unscolded for three hours every morning. But all she said was –

"'Sally, go to the Deuce.' I beg your pardon, my lady, if I
was talking to myself; it's a habit I have got into of keeping
my tongue in practice, and I am not quite aware when I do it.
Three hours every morning! I shall be only too proud to do
what I can for your ladyship; and I hope Mr. Horner will not
be too impatient with me at first. You know, perhaps, that I
was nearly being an authoress once, and that seems as if I was
destined to "employ my time in writing."'

'No, indeed; we must return to the subject of the clerkship
afterwards, if you please. An authoress, Miss Galindo! You
surprise me!'

'But, indeed I was. All was quite ready. Doctor Burney
used to teach me music: not that I ever could learn, but it was a
fancy of my poor father's. And his daughter wrote a book,
and they said she was but a very young lady, and nothing but a
music-master's daughter; so why should not I try?'

'Well?'

'Well! I got paper and half-a-hundred good pens, a bottle of
ink, all ready.'

'And then –'

'Oh, it ended in my having nothing to say, when I sat down
to write. But sometimes, when I get hold of a book, I wonder
why I let such a poor reason stop me. It does not others.'

'But I think it was very well it did, Miss Galindo,' said her ladyship. 'I am extremely against women usurping men's employments, as they are very apt to do. But perhaps, after all, the notion of writing a book improved your hand. It is one of the most legible I ever saw.'

'I despise z's without tails,' said Miss Galindo, with a good deal of gratified pride at my lady's praise. Presently, my lady took her to look at a curious old cabinet, which Lord Ludlow had picked up at the Hague; and, while they were out of the room on this errand, I suppose the question of remuneration was settled, for I heard no more of it.

When they came back, they were talking of Mr. Gray. Miss Galindo was unsparing in her expressions of opinion about him: going much farther than my lady – in her language, at least.

'A little blushing man like him, who can't say bo to a goose without hesitating and colouring, to come to this village – which is as good a village as ever lived – and cry us down for a set of sinners, as if we had all committed murder and that other thing! – I have no patience with him, my lady. And then, how is he to help us to heaven, by teaching us our a b, ab – b a, ba? And yet, by all accounts, that's to save poor children's souls. Oh, I knew your ladyship would agree with me. I am sure my mother was as good a creature as ever breathed the blessed air; and she could not spell a letter decently. And does Mr. Gray think God took note of that?'

'I was sure you would agree with me, Miss Galindo,' said my lady. 'You and I can remember how this talk about education – Rousseau, and his writings – stirred up the French people to their Reign of Terror, and all those bloody scenes '

'I'm afraid that Rousseau and Mr. Gray are birds of a feather,' replied Miss Galindo, shaking her head. 'And yet there is some good in the young man too. He sat up all night with Billy Davis, when his wife was fairly worn out with nursing him.'

'Did he, indeed?' said my lady, her face lighting up, as it always did when she heard of any kind or generous action, no matter who performed it. 'What a pity he is bitten with these new revolutionary ideas, and is so much for disturbing the established order of society!'

When Miss Galindo went, she left so favourable an impress-

ion of her visit on my lady, that she said to me with a pleased
smile –

'I think I have provided Mr. Horner with a far better clerk
than he would have made of that lad Gregson in twenty years.
And I will send the lad to my lord's grieve, in Scotland, that he
may be kept out of harm's way.'

But something happened to the lad before this purpose
could be accomplished.

CHAPTER X

The next morning, Miss Galindo made her appearance, and, by some mistake, unusual to my lady's well-trained servants, was shown into the room where I was trying to walk; for a certain amount of exercise was prescribed for me, painful although the exertion had become.

She brought a little basket along with her; and while the footman was gone to inquire my lady's wishes (for I don't think that Lady Ludlow expected Miss Galindo so soon to assume her clerkship; nor, indeed, had Mr. Horner any work of any kind ready for his new assistant to do), she launched out into conversation with me.

'It was a sudden summons, my dear! However, as I have often said to myself, ever since an occasion long ago; if Lady Ludlow ever honours me by asking for my right hand, I'll cut it off, and wrap the stump up so tidily she shall never find it bleeds. But, if I had had a little more time, I could have mended my pens better. You see, I have had to sit up pretty late to get these sleeves made' and she took out of her basket a pair of brown-holland over-sleeves, very much such as a grocer's assistant wears – 'and I had only time to make seven or eight pens, out of some quills Father Thomson gave me last autumn. As for ink, I'm thankful to say, that's always ready: an ounce of steel filings, an ounce of nut-gall, and a pint of water (tea, if you're extravagant, which, thank Heaven! I'm not); put all in a bottle, and hang it up behind the house door, so that the whole gets a good shaking every time you slam it to – and even if you are in a passion and bang it, as Sally and I often do, it is all the better for it – and there's my ink ready for use; ready to write my lady's will with, if need be.'

'Oh, Miss Galindo!' said I, 'don't talk so; my lady's will! and she not dead yet.'

'And if she were, what would be the use of talking of

making her will? Now, if you were Sally, I should say,
"Answer me that, you goose!" But, as you're a relation of my
lady's, I must be civil, and only say, "I can't think how you
can talk so like a fool!" To be sure, poor thing, you're lame!'

I do not know how long she would have gone on; but my
lady came in, and I, released from my duty of entertaining
Miss Galindo, made my limping way into the next room. To
tell the truth, I was rather afraid of Miss Galindo's tongue, for
I never knew what she would say next.

After a while my lady came in, and began to look in the
bureau for something: and as she looked she said –

'I think Mr. Horner must have made some mistake when he
said he had so much work that he almost required a clerk, for
this morning he cannot find anything for Miss Galindo to do;
and there she is, sitting with her pen behind her ear, waiting
for something to write. I am come to find her my mother's
letters, for I should like to have a fair copy made of them. Oh,
here they are: don't trouble yourself, my dear child.'

When my lady returned again, she sat down and began to
talk of Mr. Gray.

'Miss Galindo says she saw him going to hold a prayer-
meeting in a cottage. Now that really makes me unhappy, it is
so like what Mr. Wesley used to do in my younger days; and
since then we have had rebellion in the American colonies and
the French Revolution. You may depend upon it, my dear,
making religion and education common – vulgarising them,
as it were – is a bad thing for a nation. A man who hears
prayers read in the cottage where he has just supped on bread
and bacon, forgets the respect due to a church: he begins to
think that one place is as good as another, and, by-and-by,
that one person is as good as another, and after that, I always
find that people begin to talk of their rights, instead of
thinking of their duties. I wish Mr. Gray had been more
tractable, and had left well alone. What do you think I heard
this morning? Why, that the Home Hill estate, which niches
into the Hanbury property, was bought by a Baptist baker
from Birmingham!'

'A Baptist baker!' I exclaimed. I had never seen a Dissenter,
to my knowledge; but, having always heard them spoken of
with horror, I looked upon them almost as if they were

rhinoceroses. I wanted to see a live Dissenter, I believe, and yet I wished it were over. I was almost surprised when I heard that any of them were engaged in such peaceful occupations as baking.

'Yes! so Mr. Horner tells me. A Mr. Lambe, I believe, But, at any rate, he is a Baptist, and has been in trade. What with his schismatism and Mr. Gray's methodism, I am afraid all the primitive character of this place will vanish.'

From what I could hear, Mr. Gray seemed to be taking his own way; at any rate, more than he had done when he first came to the village, when his natural timidity had made him defer to my lady and seek her consent and sanction before embarking in any new plan. But newness was a quality Lady Ludlow especially disliked. Even in the fashions of dress and furniture, she clung to the old, to the modes which had prevailed when she was young; and, though she had a deep personal regard for Queen Charlotte (to whom, as I have already said, she had been maid-of-honour), yet there was a tinge of Jacobitism about her, such as made her extremely dislike to hear Prince Charles Edward, called the young Pretender, as many loyal people did in those days, and made her fond of telling of the thorn tree in my lord's park in Scotland, which had been planted by bonny Queen Mary herself, and before which every guest in the Castle of Monks-haven was expected to stand bare-headed, out of respect to the memory and misfortunes of the royal planter.

We might play at cards, if we chose, on a Sunday; at least, I suppose we might, for my lady and Mr. Mountford used to do so often when I first went. But we must neither play cards, nor read, nor sew, on the fifth of November and on the thirtieth of January, but must go to church, and meditate all the rest of the day – and very hard work meditating was. I would far rather have scoured a room. That was the reason, I suppose, why a passive life was seen to be better discipline for me than an active one.

But I am wandering away from my lady, and her dislike to all innovation. Now, it seemed to me, as far as I heard, that Mr. Gray was full of nothing but new things, and that what he first did was to attack all our established institutions, both in the village and the parish, and also in the nation. To be sure, I heard of his ways of going on principally from Miss Galindo, who was apt to speak more strongly than accurately.

'There he goes,' she said, 'clucking up the children just like an old hen, and trying to teach them about their salvation and their souls, and I don't know what – things that it is just blasphemy to speak about out of church. And he potters old people about reading their Bibles. I am sure I don't want to speak disrespectfully about the Holy Scriptures, but I found old Job Horton busy reading his Bible yesterday. Says I, "What are you reading, and where did you get it, and who gave it you?" So he made answer, "That he was reading Susannah and the Elders, for that he had read Bel and the Dragon til he could pretty near say it off by heart; and they were two as pretty stories as ever he had read, and that it was a caution to him what bad old chaps there were in the world." Now, as Job is bedridden, I don't think he is likely to meet with the Elders; and I say that I think repeating his Creed, the Commandments, and the Lord's Prayer, and, may be, throwing in a verse of the Psalms, if he wanted a bit of a change, would have done him far more good than his pretty stories, as he called them. And what's the next thing our young parson does? Why, he tries to make us all feel pitiful for the black slaves, and leaves little pictures of negroes about, with the question printed below, "Am I not a man and a brother?" just as if I was to be hail-fellow-well-met with every negro footman. They do say he takes no sugar in his tea, because he thinks he sees spots of blood in it. Now I call that superstition.'

The next day it was a still worse story.

'Well, my dear! and how are you? My lady sent me in to sit a bit with you, while Mr. Horner looks out some papers for me to copy. Between ourselves, Mr. Steward Horner does not like having me for a clerk. It is all very well he does not; for, if he were decently civil to me, I might want a chaperon, you know, now poor Mrs. Horner is dead.' This was one of Miss Galindo's grim jokes. 'As it is, I try to make him forget I'm a woman; I do everything as ship-shape as a masculine man-clerk. I see he can't find a fault – writing good, spelling correct, sums all right. And then he squints up at me with the tail of his eye, and looks glummer than ever, just because I'm a

woman – as if I could help that. I have gone good lengths to
set his mind at ease. I have stuck my pen behind my ear; I have
made him a bow instead of a curtsey; I have whistled – not a
tune, I can't pipe up that – nay, if you won't tell my lady, I
don't mind telling you that I have said "Confound it!" and
"Zounds!" I can't get any farther. For all that, Mr. Horner
won't forget I am a lady; and so I am not half the use I might
be, and, if it were not to please my Lady Ludlow, Mr. Horner
and his books might go hang (see how natural that came out!).
And there is an order for a dozen nightcaps for a bride, and I
am so afraid I shan't have time to do them. Worst of all,
there's Mr. Gray taking advantage of my absence to seduce
Sally!'

'To seduce Sally! Mr. Gray!'

'Pooh, pooh, child! There's many a kind of seduction. Mr.
Gray is seducing Sally to want to go to church. There has he
been twice at my house, while I have been away in the
mornings, talking to Sally about the state of her soul and that
sort of thing. But when I found the meat all roasted to a
cinder, I said, "Come, Sally, let's have no more praying when
beef is down at the fire. Pray at six o'clock in the morning and
nine at night, and I won't hinder you." So she sauced me, and
said something about Martha and Mary, implying that, because
she had let the beef get so overdone that I declare I could
hardly find a bit for Nancy Pole's sick grandchild, she had
chosen the better part. I was very much put about, I own, and
perhaps you'll be shocked at what I said – indeed, I don't
know if it was right myself – but I told her I had a soul as well
as she, and, if it was to be saved by my sitting still and
thinking about salvation and never doing my duty, I thought I
had as good a right as she had to be Mary, and save my soul.
So, that afternoon, I sat quite still and it was really a comfort,
for I am often too busy, I know, to pray as I ought. There is
first one person wanting me, and then another, and the house
and the food and the neighbours to see after. So, when
tea-time comes, there enters my maid with her hump on her
back, and her soul to be saved. "Please ma'am, did you order
the pound of butter?" "No Sally," I said, shaking my head,
"this morning I did not go round by Hale's farm, and this
afternoon I have been employed in spiritual things."

'Now, our Sally likes tea and bread-and-butter above
everything, and dry bread was not to her taste.

"'I'm thankful," said the impudent hussy, "that you have
taken a turn towards godliness. It will be my prayers, I trust,
that's given it you."

'I was determined not to give her an opening towards the
carnal subject of butter; so she lingered still, longing to ask
leave to run for it. But I gave her none, and munched my dry
bread myself, thinking what a famous cake I could make for
little Ben Pole with the bit of butter we were saving; and,
when Sally had had her butterless tea, and was in none of the
best of tempers because Martha had not bethought herself of
the butter, I just quietly said –

"'Now, Sally, tomorrow we'll try to hash that beef well,
and to remember the butter, and to work out our salvation all
at the same time, for I don't see why it can't all be done, as
God has set us to do it all." But I heard her at it again about
Mary and Martha, and I have no doubt that Mr. Gray will
teach her to consider me a lost sheep.'

I had heard so many little speeches about Mr. Gray from
one person or another, all speaking against him, as a mischief-
maker, a setter-up of new doctrines and of a fanciful standard
of life (and you may be sure that, where Lady Ludlow led,
Mrs. Medlicott and Adams were certain to follow, each in
their different way showing the influence my lady had over
them), that I believe I had grown to consider him as a very
instrument of evil, and to expect to perceive in his face marks
of his presumption, and arrogance, and impertinent interfer-
ence. It was now many weeks since I had seen him, and, when
he was one morning shown into the blue drawing-room, (into
which I had been removed for a change), I was quite surprised
to see how innocent and awkward a young man he appeared,
confused even more than I was at our unexpected *tête-à-tête*.
He looked thinner, his eyes more eager, his expression more
anxious, and his colour came and went more than it had done
when I had seen him last. I tried to make a little conversation,
as I was, to my own surprise, more at my ease than he was;
but his thoughts were evidently too much preoccupied for
him to do more than answer me with monosyllables.

Presently, my lady came in. Mr. Gray twitched and coloured more than ever; but plunged into the middle of his subject at once.

'My lady, I cannot answer it to my conscience, if I allow the children of this village to go on any longer the little heathens that they are. I must do something to alter their condition. I am quite aware that your ladyship disapproves of many of the plans which have suggested themselves to me; but nevertheless I must do something, and I am come now to your ladyship to ask respectfully, but firmly, what you would advise me to do.'

His eyes were dilated, and I could almost have said they were full of tears with his eagerness. But I am sure it is a bad plan to remind people of decided opinions which they have once expressed, if you wish them to modify those opinions. Now, Mr. Gray had done this with my lady; and, though I do not mean to say she was obstinate, yet she was not one to retract.

She was silent for a moment or two before she replied.

'You ask me to suggest a remedy for an evil of the existence of which I am not conscious,' was her answer – very coldly, very gently given. 'In Mr. Mountford's time, I heard no such complaints; whenever I see the village children (and they are not infrequent visitors at this house, on one pretext or another), they are well and decently behaved.'

'Oh, madam, you cannot judge,' he broke in. 'They are trained to respect you in word and deed; you are the highest they ever look up to; they have no notion of a higher.'

'Nay, Mr. Gray,' said my lady, smiling, 'They are as loyally disposed as any children can be. They come up here every fourth of June, and drink his Majesty's health, and have buns, and (as Margaret Dawson can testify) they take a great and respectful interest in all the pictures I can show them of the royal family.'

'But, madam, I think of something higher than any earthly dignities.'

My lady coloured at the mistake she had made; for she herself was truly pious. Yet, when she resumed the subject, it seemed to me as if her tone was a little sharper than before.

'Such want of reverence is, I should say, the clergyman's fault. You must excuse me, Mr. Gray, if I speak plainly.'

'My lady, I want plain speaking. I myself am not accustomed to those ceremonies and forms which are, I suppose, the etiquette in your lady's rank of life, and which seem to hedge you in from any power of mine to touch you. Among those with whom I have passed my life hitherto, it has been the custom to speak plainly out what we have felt earnestly. So, instead of needing any apology from your ladyship for straightforward speaking, I will meet what you say at once, and admit that it is the clergyman's fault, in a great measure, when the children of his parish swear, and curse, and are brutal, and ignorant of all saving grace; nay, some of them of the very name of God. And, because this guilt of mine, as the clergyman of this parish, lies heavy on my soul, and every day leads but from bad to worse, till I am utterly bewildered how to do good to children who escape from me as if I were a monster, and who are growing up to be men fit for and capable of any crime, but one requiring wit or sense, I come to you, who seem to me all-powerful as far as material power goes – for your ladyship only knows the surface of things, and barely that, that pass in your village – to help me with advice, and such outward help as you can give.'

Mr. Gray had stood up and sat down once or twice while he had been speaking, in an agitated, nervous kind of way; and now he was interrupted by a violent fit of coughing, after which he trembled all over.

My lady rang for a glass of water, and looked much distressed.

'Mr. Gray,' said she, 'I am sure you are not well; and that makes you exaggerate childish faults into positive evils. It is always the case with us when we are not strong in health. I hear of your exerting yourself in every direction: you overwork yourself, and the consequence is, that you imagine us all worse people than we are.'

And my lady smiled very kindly and pleasantly at him, as he sat, a little panting, a little flushed, trying to recover his breath. I am sure that, now they were brought face to face, she had quite forgotten all the offence she had taken at his doings when she heard of them from others; and, indeed, it was enough to soften anyone's heart to see that young, almost boyish face, looking in such anxiety and distress.

'Oh, my lady, what shall I do?' he asked, as soon as he could recover breath, and with such an air of humility that I am sure no one who had seen it could have ever thought him conceited again. 'The evil of this world is too strong for me. I can do so little. It is all in vain. It was only today' – and again the cough and agitation returned.

'My dear Mr. Gray,' said my lady (the day before I could never have believed she could have called him "my dear"), 'You must take the advice of an old woman about yourself. You are not fit to do anything just now but attend to your own health: rest, and see a doctor (but, indeed, I will take care of that); and when you are pretty strong again, you will find you have been magnifying evils to yourself.'

'But, my lady, I cannot rest. The evils do exist, and the burden of their continuance lies on my shoulders. I have no place to gather the children together in, that I may teach them the things necessary to salvation. The rooms in my own house are too small; but I have tried them. I have money of my own; and, as your ladyship knows, I tried to get a piece of leasehold property on which to build a school house at my own expense. Your ladyship's lawyer comes forward, at your instructions, to enforce some old feudal right, by which no building is allowed on leasehold property without the sanction of the lady of the manor. It may be all very true; but it was a cruel thing to do – that is, if your ladyship had known (which I am sure you do not) the real moral and spiritual state of my poor parishioners. And now I come to you to know what I am to do. Rest! I cannot rest, while children whom I could possibly save are being left in their ignorance, their blasphemy, their uncleanness, their cruelty. It is known through the village that your ladyship disapproves of my efforts, and opposes all my plans. If you think them wrong, foolish, ill-digested (I have been a student, living in a college, and eschewing all society but that of pious men, until now: I may not judge for the best, in my ignorance of this sinful human nature), tell me of better plans and wiser projects for accomplishing my end; but do not bid me rest, with Satan compassing me round, and stealing souls away.'

'Mr. Gray,' said my lady, 'there may be some truth in what you have said. I do not deny it, though I think, in your present state of indisposition and excitement, you exaggerate it much. I believe – nay, the experience of a pretty long life has convinced me – that education is a bad thing, if given indiscriminately. It unfits the lower orders for their duties, the duties to which they are called by God; of submission to those placed in authority over them; of contentment with that state of life to which it has pleased God to call them, and of ordering themselves lowly and reverently to all their betters. I have made this conviction of mine tolerably evident to you, and have expressed distinctly my disapprobation of some of your ideas. You may imagine, then, that I was not well pleased when I found that you had taken a rood or more of Farmer Hale's land, and were laying the foundations of a school house. You had done this without asking for my permission, which, as Farmer Hale's liege lady, ought to have been obtained legally, as well as asked for out of courtesy. I put a stop to what I believed to be calculated to do harm to a village, to a population, in which, to say the least of it, I may be disposed to take as much interest as you can do. How can reading, and writing, and the multiplication-table (if you choose to go so far), prevent blasphemy, and uncleanness, and cruelty? Really, Mr. Gray, I hardly like to express myself so strongly on the subject in your present state of health, as I should do at any other time. It seems to me that books do little; character much; and character is not formed from books.'

'I do not think of character: I think of souls. I must get some hold upon these children, or what will become of them in the next world? I must be found to have some power beyond what they have, and which they are rendered capable of appreciating, before they will listen to me. At present physical force is all they look up to; and I have none.'

'Nay, Mr. Gray, by your own admission, they look up to me.'

'They would not do anything your ladyship disliked if it was likely to come to your knowledge; but, if they could conceal it from you, the knowledge of your dislike to a particular line of conduct would never make them cease from pursuing it.'

'Mr. Gray' – surprise in her air, and some little indignation –

'they and their fathers have lived on the Hanbury land for generations!'

'I cannot help it, madam. I am telling you the truth, whether you believe me or not.' There was a pause; my lady looked perplexed, and somewhat ruffled; Mr. Gray as though hopeless and wearied out. 'Then, my lady,' said he at last, rising as he spoke, 'you can suggest nothing to ameliorate the state of things which, I do assure you, does exist on your lands, and among your tenants. Surely, you will not object to my using Farmer Hale's great barn every Sabbath? He will allow me the use of it, if your ladyship will grant your permission.'

'You are not fit for any extra work at present,' (and indeed he had been coughing very much all through the conversation). 'Give me time to consider it. Tell me what you wish to teach. You will be able to take care of your health, and grow stronger while I consider. It shall not be the worse for you, if you leave it in my hands for a time.'

My lady spoke very kindly; but he was in too excited a state to recognise the kindness, while the idea of delay was evidently a sorry irritation. I heard him say: 'And I have so little time in which to do my work. Lord! lay not this sin to my charge!'

But my lady was speaking to the old butler, for whom, at her sign, I had rung the bell some little time before. Now she turned round.

'Mr. Gray, I find I have some bottles of Malmsey, of the vintage of seventeen hundred and seventy-eight, yet left. Malmsey, as perhaps you know, used to be considered a specific for coughs arising from weakness. You must permit me to send you half-a-dozen bottles, and, depend upon it, you will take a more cheerful view of life and its duties before you have finished them, especially if you will be so kind as to see Dr. Trevor, who is coming to see me in the course of the week. By the time you are strong enough to work, I will try and find some means of preventing the children from using such bad language, and otherwise annoying you.'

'My lady, it is the sin, and not the annoyance. I wish I could make you understand!' He spoke with some impatience. Poor fellow! he was too weak, exhausted, and nervous. 'I am perfectly well; I can set to work tomorrow; I will do anything

not to be oppressed with the thought of how little I am doing.
I do not want your wine. Liberty to act in the manner I think
right, will do me far more good. But it is of no use. It is
pre-ordained that I am to be nothing but a cumberer of the
ground. I beg your ladyship's pardon for this call.'

He stood up, and then turned dizzy. My lady looked on,
deeply hurt, and not a litle offended. He held out his hand to
her, and I could see that she had a little hesitation before she
took it. He then saw me, I almost think, for the first time; and
put out his hand once more, drew it back, as if undecided, put
it out again, and finally took hold of mine for an instant in his
damp, listless hand, and was gone.

Lady Ludlow was dissatisfied with both him and herself, I
was sure. Indeed, I was dissatisfied with the result of the
interview myself. But my lady was not one to speak out her
feelings on the subject; nor was I one to forget myself, and
begin on a topic which she did not begin. She came to me, and
was very tender with me; so tender, that that, and the
thoughts of Mr. Gray's sick, hopeless, disappointed look,
nearly made me cry.

'You are tired, little one,' said my lady. 'Go and lie down in
my room, and hear what Medlicott and I can decide upon in
the way of strengthening dainties for that poor young man,
who is killing himself with his over-sensitive conscientiousness.'

'Oh, my lady!' said I, and then stopped.

'Well. What?' asked she.

'If you could but let him have Farmer Hale's barn at once, it
would do him more good than all.'

'Pooh, pooh, child!' though I don't think she was displeased, 'he is not fit for more work just now. I shall go and
write for Dr. Trevor.'

And for the next half-hour, we did nothing but arrange
physical comforts and cures for poor Mr. Gray. At the end of
the time, Mrs. Medlicott said –

'Has your ladyship heard that Harry Gregson has fallen
from a tree, and broken his thigh-bone, and is like to be a
cripple for life?'

'Harry Gregson! That black-eyed lad who read my letter? It
all comes from over-education.'

CHAPTER XI

But I don't see how my lady could think it was over-education that made Harry Gregson break his thigh, for the manner in which he met with the accident was this –

Mr. Horner, who had fallen sadly out of health since his wife's death, had attached himself greatly to Harry Gregson. Now, Mr. Horner had a cold manner to everyone, and never spoke more than was necessary, at the best of times And, latterly, it had not been the best of times with him. I dare say, he had had some causes for anxiety (of which I knew nothing) about my lady's affairs; and he was evidently annoyed by my lady's whim (as he once inadvertently called it) of placing Miss Galindo under him in the position of a clerk. Yet he had always been friends, in his quiet way, with Miss Galindo, and she devoted herself to her new occupation with diligence and punctuality, although more than once she had moaned to me over the orders for needlework which had been sent to her, and which, owing to her occupation in the service of Lady Ludlow, she had been unable to fulfil.

The only living creature to whom the staid Mr. Horner could be said to be attached, was Harry Gregson. To my lady he was a faithful and devoted servant, looking keenly after her interests, and anxious to forward them at any cost of trouble to himself. But the more shrewd Mr. Horner was, the more probability was there of his being annoyed at certain peculiarities of opinion which my lady held with a quiet, gentle pertinacity; against which no arguments, based on mere worldly and business calculations, made any way. This frequent opposition to views which Mr. Horner entertained, although it did not interfere with the sincere respect which the lady and the steward felt for each other, yet prevented any warmer feeling of affection from coming in. It seems strange to say it, but I must repeat it – the only person for whom,

141

since his wife's death, Mr. Horner seemed to feel any love, was the little imp Harry Gregson, with his bright, watchful eyes, his tangled hair hanging right down to his eyebrows, for all the world like a Skye terrier. This lad, half gypsy and whole poacher, as many people esteemed him, hung about the silent, respectable, staid Mr. Horner, and followed his steps with something of the affectionate fidelity of the dog which he resembled. I suspect, this demonstration of attachment to his person on Harry Gregson's part was what won Mr. Horner's regard. In the first instance, the steward had only chosen the lad out as the cleverest instrument he could find for his purpose; and I don't mean to say that, if Harry had not been almost as shrewd as Mr. Horner himself was, both by original disposition and subsequent experience, the steward would have taken to him as he did, let the lad have shown ever so much affection for him.

But even to Harry Mr. Horner was silent. Still, it was pleasant to find himself in many ways so readily understood; to perceive that the crumbs of knowledge he let fall were picked up by his little follower, and hoarded like gold; that here was one to hate the persons and things whom Mr. Horner coldly disliked, and to reverence and admire all those for whom he had any regard. Mr. Horner had never had a child, and unconsciously, I suppose, something of the paternal feeling had begun to develop itself in him towards Harry Gregson. I heard one or two things from different people, which have always made me fancy that Mr. Horner secretly and almost unconsciously hoped that Harry Gregson might be trained so as to be first his clerk, and next his assistant, and finally his successor in his stewardship to the Hanbury estates.

Harry's disgrace with my lady, in consequence of his reading the letter, was a deeper blow to Mr. Horner than his quiet manner would ever have led anyone to suppose, or than Lady Ludlow ever dreamed of inflicting, I am sure.

Probably Harry had a short, stern rebuke from Mr. Horner at the time, for his manner was always hard even to those he cared for the most. But Harry's love was not to be daunted or quelled by a few sharp words. I dare say, from what I heard of them afterwards that Harry accompanied Mr. Horner in his walk over the farm the very day of the rebuke; his presence

apparently unnoticed by the agent, by whom his absence
would have been painfully felt nevertheless. That was the way
of it, as I have been told. Mr. Horner never bade Harry go
with him; never thanked him for going, or being at his heels
ready to run on any errands, straight as the crow flies to his
point, and back to heel in as short a time as possible. Yet, if
Harry were away, Mr. Horner never inquired the reason from
any of the men who might be supposed to know whether he
was detained by his father, or otherwise engaged; he never
asked Harry himself where he had been. But Miss Galindo
said that those labourers who knew Mr. Horner well told her
that he was always more quick-eyed to shortcomings, more
savage-like in fault-finding, on those days when the lad was
absent.

Miss Galindo, indeed, was my great authority for most of
the village news which I heard. She it was who gave me the
particulars of poor Harry's accident.

'You see, my dear,' she said, 'the little poacher has taken
some unaccountable fancy to my master.' (This was the name
by which Miss Galindo always spoke of Mr. Horner to me,
ever since she had been, as she called it, appointed his clerk.)

'Now, if I had twenty hearts to lose, I never could spare a
bit of one of them for that good, grey, square, severe man.
But different people have different tastes, and here is that little
imp of a gipsy-tinker ready to turn slave for my master; and,
odd enough, my master – who, I should have said beforehand,
would have made short work of imp, and imp's family, and
have sent Hall, the Bang-beggar, after them in no time – my
master, as they tell me, is in his way quite fond of the lad, and,
if he could, without vexing my lady too much, he would have
made him what the folks here call a Latiner. However, last
night, it seems that there was a letter of some importance,
forgotten (I can't tell you what it was about, my dear, though
I know perfectly well, but *service oblige* as well as *noblesse*, and
you must take my word for it that it was important, and one
that I am surprised my master could forget), till too late for the
post. (The poor, good, orderly man is not what he was before
his wife's death.) Well, it seems that he was sore annoyed by
his forgetfulness, and well he might be. And it was all the
more vexatious, as he had no one to blame but himself. As for

that matter, I always scold somebody else when I'm in fault; but I suppose my master would never think of doing that, else it's a mighty relief. However, he could eat no tea, and was altogether put out and gloomy. And the little faithful imp-lad, perceiving all this, I suppose, got up like a page in an old ballad, and said he would run for his life across country to Comberford, and see if he could not get there before the bags were made up. So my master gave him the letter, and nothing more was heard of the poor fellow till this morning, for the father thought his son was sleeping in Mr. Horner's barn, as he does occasionally, it seems, and my master, as was very natural that he had gone to his father's.'

'And he had fallen down the old stone quarry, had he not?'

'Yes, sure enough. Mr. Gray had been up here fretting my lady with some of his new-fangled schemes; and, because the young man could not have it all his own way, from what I understand, he was put out, and thought he would go home by the back lane, instead of through the village, where the folks would notice if the parson looked glum. But, however, it was a mercy, and I don't mind saying so, ay, and meaning it too, though it may be like Methodism; for, as Mr. Gray walked by the quarry, he heard a groan; and at first he thought it was a lamb fallen down, and he stood still, and he heard it again; and then, I suppose he looked down and saw Harry. So he let himself down by the boughs of the trees to the ledge where Harry lay half-dead, and with his poor thigh broken. There he had laid ever since the night before: he had been returning to tell the master that he had safely posted the letter, and the first words he said, when they recovered him from the exhausted state he was in, were' (Miss Galindo tried hard not to whimper, as she said it), '"It was in time, sir, I see'd it put in the bag with my own eyes."'

'But where is he?' asked I. 'How did Mr. Gray get him out.'

'Ay! there it is, you see. Why, the old gentleman (I daren't say Devil in Lady Ludlow's house) is not so black as he is painted; and Mr. Gray must have a deal of good in him, as I say at times; and then at others, when he has gone against me, I can't bear him, and think hanging too good for him. But he lifted the poor lad, as if he had been a baby, I suppose, and carried him up the great ledges that were formerly used for

steps; and laid him soft and easy on the wayside grass, and ran
home and got help and a door, and had him carried to his
house, and laid on his bed; and then somehow, for the first
time either he or anyone else perceived it, he himself was all
over blood – his own blood – he had broken a blood-vessel;
and there he lies in the little dressing room, as white and as
still as if he were dead; and the little imp in Mr. Gray's own
bed, sound asleep, now his leg is set, just as if linen sheets and
a feather bed were his native element, as one may say. Really,
now he is doing so well, I've no patience with him, lying there
where Mr. Gray ought to be. It is just what my lady always
prophesied would come to pass, if there was any confusion of
ranks.'

'Poor Mr. Gray!' said I, thinking of his flushed face, and his
feverish, restless ways, when he had been calling on my lady
not an hour before his exertions on Harry's behalf. And I told
Miss Galindo how ill I had thought him.

'Yes,' said she. 'And that was the reason my lady had sent
for Doctor Trevor. Well, it has fallen out admirably, for he
looked well after that old donkey of a Prince, and saw that he
made no blunders.'

Now 'that old donkey of a Prince' meant the village
surgeon, Mr. Prince, between whom and Miss Galindo there
was war to the knife, as they often met in the cottages, when
there was illness, and she had laid her queer, odd recipes,
which he, with his grand pharmacopœia, held in infinite
contempt; and the consequence of their squabbling had been,
not long before this very time, that he had established a kind
of rule, that into whatever sick-room Miss Galindo was
admitted, there he refused to visit. But Miss Galindo's pre-
scriptions and visits cost nothing, and were often backed by
kitchen-physic; so, though it was true that she never came but
she scolded about something or other, she was generally
preferred as medical attendant to Mr. Prince.

'Yes, the old donkey is obliged to tolerate me, and be civil
to me; for, you see, I got there first, and had possession, as it
were, and yet my lord the donkey likes the credit of attending
the parson, and being in consultation with so grand a county-
town doctor as Doctor Trevor. And Doctor Trevor is an old
friend of mine' (she sighed a little, some time I may tell you

why), 'and treats me with infinite bowing and respect; so the donkey, not to be out of medical fashion, bows too, though it is sadly against the grain; and he pulled a face as if he had heard a slate-pencil gritting against a slate, when I told Doctor Trevor I meant to sit up with the two lads; for I call Mr. Gray little more than a lad, and a pretty conceited one, too, at times.'

'But why should you sit up, Miss Galindo? It will tire you sadly.'

'Not it. You see, there is Gregson's mother to keep quiet; for she sits by her lad, fretting and sobbing, so that I'm afraid of her disturbing Mr. Gray; and Mr. Gray to keep quiet, for Doctor Trevor says his life depends on it; and there is medicine to be given to the one, and bandages to be attended to for the other; and the wild horde of gipsy brothers and sisters to be turned out, and the father to be held in from showing too much gratitude to Mr. Gray, who can't bear it – and who is to do it all but me? The only servant is old lame Betty, who once lived with me, and *would* leave me because she said I was always bothering – (there was a good deal of truth in what she said, I grant, but she need not have said it; a good deal of truth is best let alone at the bottom of the well) and what can she do – deaf as ever she can be, too?'

So Miss Galindo went her ways; but not the less was she at her post in the morning; a little crosser and more silent than usual; but the first was not to be wondered at, and the last was rather a blessing.

Lady Ludlow had been extremely anxious both about Mr. Gray and Harry Gregson. Kind and thoughtful in any case of illness and accident she always was; but somehow, in this, the feeling that she was not quite – what shall I call it? – 'friends' seems hardly the right word to use, as to the possible feeling between the Countess Ludlow and the little vagabond messenger, who had only once been in her presence – that she had hardly parted from either as she could have wished to do, had death been near, made her more than usually anxious. Doctor Trevor was not to spare obtaining the best medical advice the county could afford; whatever he ordered in the way of diet, was to be prepared under Mrs. Medlicott's own eye, and sent down from the Hall to the Parsonage. As Mr. Horner had

given somewhat similar directions, in the case of Harry
Gregson at least, there was rather a multiplicity of counsellors
and dainties than any lack of them. And, the second night,
Mr. Horner insisted on taking the superintendence of the
nursing himself, and sat and snored by Harry's bedside, while
the poor, exhausted mother lay by her child – thinking that
she watched him, but in reality fast asleep, as Miss Galindo
told us; for, distrusting anyone's power of watching and
nursing but her own, she had stolen across the quiet village
street in cloak and dressing-gown, and found Mr. Gray in vain
trying to reach the cup of barley-water which Mr. Horner had
placed just beyond his reach.

In consequence of Mr. Gray's illness, we had to have a
strange curate to do duty: a man who dropped his *h*'s, and
hurried through the service, and yet had time enough to stand
in my lady's way, bowing to her as she came out of church,
and so subservient in manner that I believe that, sooner than
remain unnoticed by a countess, he would have preferred
being scolded, or even cuffed. Now I found out that, great as
was my lady's liking and approval of respect, nay, even
reverence, being paid to her as a person of quality – a sort of
tribute to her Order, which she had no individual right to
remit, or, indeed, not to exact – yet she, being personally
simple, sincere, and holding herself in low esteem, could not
endure anything like the servility of Mr. Crosse, the temporary curate. She grew absolutely to loathe his perpetual smiling
and bowing; his instant agreement with the slightest opinion
she uttered; his veering round as she blew the wind. I have
often said that my lady did not talk much, as she might have
done had she lived among her equals. But we all loved her so
much that we had learnt to interpret all her little ways pretty
truly; and I knew what particular turns of her head, and
contractions of her delicate fingers meant, as well as if she had
expressed herself in words. I began to suspect that my lady
would be very thankful to have Mr. Gray about again, and
doing his duty even with a conscientiousness that might
amount to worrying himself and fidgeting others; and,
although Mr. Gray might hold her opinions in as little esteem
as those of any simple gentlewoman, she was too sensible not
to feel how much flavour there was in his conversation,

compared to that of Mr, Crosse, who was only her tasteless echo.

As for Miss Galindo, she was utterly and entirely a partisan of Mr. Gray's, almost ever since she had begun to nurse him during his illness.

'You know, I never set up for reasonableness, my lady. So I don't pretend to say, as I might do if I were a sensible woman and all that – that I am convinced by Mr. Gray's arguments of this thing or t'other. For one thing, you see, poor fellow! he has never been able to argue, or hardly indeed to speak, for Doctor Trevor has been very peremptory. So there's been no scope for arguing! But what I mean is this: – When I see a sick man thinking always of others, and never of himself; patient, humble – a trifle too much at times, for I've caught him praying to be forgiven for having neglected his work as a parish priest' (Miss Galindo was making horrible faces, to keep back tears, squeezing up her eyes in a way which would have amused me at any other time but when she was speaking of Mr. Gray); 'when I see a downright good, religious man, I'm apt to think he's got hold of the right clue, and that I can do no better than hold on by the tails of his coat and shut my eyes, if we've got to go over doubtful places on our road to heaven. So, my lady, you must excuse me, if, when he gets about again, he is all agog about a Sunday-school; for, if he is, I shall be agog too, and perhaps twice as bad as him; for, you see, I've a strong constitution compared to his, and strong ways of speaking and acting. And I tell your ladyship this now, because I think from your rank – and still more, if I may say so, for all your kindness to me long ago, down to this very day – you've a right to be first told of anything about me. Change of opinion I can't exactly call it, for I don't see the good of schools and teaching A B C, any more than I did before, only Mr. Gray does, so I'm to shut my eyes, and leap over the ditch to the side of education. I've told Sally already, that if she does not mind her work, but stands gossiping with Nelly Mather, I'll teach her her lessons; and I've never caught her with old Nelly since.'

I think Miss Galindo's desertion to Mr. Gray's opinions in this matter hurt my lady just a little bit; but she only said –

'Of course, if the parishioners wish for it, Mr. Gray must

have his Sunday-school. I shall, in that case, withdraw my
opposition. I am sorry I cannot alter my opinions as easily as
you.'

My lady made herself smile as she said this. Miss Galindo
saw it was an effort to do so. She thought a minute before she
spoke again.

'Your ladyship has not seen Mr. Gray as intimately as I have
done. That's one thing. But, as for the parishioners, they will
follow your ladyship's lead in everything; so there is no chance
of their wishing for a Sunday-school.'

'I have never done anything to make them follow my lead,
as you call it, Miss Galindo,' said my lady gravely.

'Yes, you have,' replied Miss Galindo bluntly. And then
correcting herself, she said, 'Begging your ladyship's pardon,
you have. Your ancestors have lived here time out of mind,
and have owned the land on which their forefathers have lived
ever since there were forefathers. You yourself were born
amongst them, and have been like a little queen to them ever
since, I might say, and they've never known your ladyship do
anything but what was kind and gentle; but I'll leave fine
speeches about your ladyship to Mr. Crosse. Only you, my
lady, lead the thoughts of the parish, and save some of them a
world of trouble; for they could never tell what was right if
they had to think for themselves. It's all quite right that they
should be guided by you, my lady – if only you would agree
with Mr. Gray.'

'Well,' said my lady, 'I told him only the last day that he
was here, that I would think about it. I do believe I could make
up my mind on certain subjects better if I were left alone, than
while being constantly talked to about them.'

My lady said this in her usual soft tones, but the words had a
tinge of impatience about them; indeed, she was more ruffled
than I had often seen her; but, checking herself in an instant,
she said –

'You don't know how Mr. Horner drags in this subject of
education à-propos of everything. Not that he says much
about it at any time; it is not his way. But he cannot let the
thing alone.'

'I know why, my lady,' said Miss Galindo. 'That poor lad,
Harry Gregson, will never be able to earn his livelihood in any

active way, but will be lame for life. Now, Mr. Horner thinks
more of Harry than of any one else in the world – except,
perhaps, your ladyship.' Was it not a pretty companionship
for my lady? 'And he has schemes of his own for teaching
Harry; and, if Mr. Gray could but have his school, Mr.
Horner and he think Harry might be schoolmaster, as your
ladyship would not like to have him coming to you as
steward's clerk. I wish your ladyship would fall into this plan;
Mr. Gray has it so at heart.'

Miss Galindo looked wistfully at my lady, as she said this.
But my lady only said drily, and rising at the same time, as if
to end the conversation –

'So! Mr. Horner and Mr. Gray seem to have gone a long
way in advance of my consent to their plans.'

'There!' exclaimed Miss Galindo, as my lady left the room,
with an apology for going away; 'I have gone and done
mischief with my long, stupid tongue. To be sure, people plan
a long way ahead of today; more especially when one is a sick
man, lying all through the weary day on a sofa.'

'My lady will soon get over her annoyance,' said I, as it
were apologetically. I only stopped Miss Galindo's self-
reproaches to draw down her wrath upon myself.

'And has not she a right to be annoyed with me if she likes,
and to keep annoyed as long as she likes? Am I complaining of
her, that you need tell me that? Let me tell you, I have known
my lady these thirty years; and if she were to take me by the
shoulders, and turn me out of the house, I should only love
her the more. So don't you think to come between us with any
little mincing, peace-making speeches. I have been a mischief-
making parrot, and I like her the better for being vexed with
me. So goodbye to you, Miss; and wait till you know Lady
Ludlow as well as I do, before you next think of telling me she
will soon get over her annoyance!' And off Miss Galindo
went.

I could not exactly tell what I had done wrong; but I took
care never again to come in between my lady and her by any
remark about the one to the other; for I saw that some most
powerful bond of grateful affection made Miss Galindo almost
worship my lady.

Meanwhile Harry Gregson was limping a little about in the

village, still finding his home in Mr. Gray's house; for there he could most conveniently be kept under the doctor's eye, and receive the requisite care, and enjoy the requisite nourishment. As soon as he was a little better, he was to go to Mr. Horner's house; but, as the steward lived some distance out of the way, and was much from home, he had agreed to leave Harry at the house to which he had first been taken, until he was quite strong again; and the more willingly, I suspect, from what I heard afterwards, because Mr. Gray gave up all the little strength of speaking which he had, to teaching Harry in the very manner which Mr. Horner most desired.

As for Gregson the father, he – wild man of the woods, poacher, tinker, jack-of-all-trades – was getting tamed by this kindness to his child. Hitherto his hand had been against every man, as every man's had been against him. That affair before the justice, which I told you about, when Mr. Gray and even my lady had interested themselves to get him released from unjust imprisonment, was the first bit of justice he had ever met with: it attracted him to the people, and attached him to the spot on which he had but squatted for a time. I am not sure if any of the villagers were grateful to him for remaining in their neighbourhood, instead of decamping as he had often done before, for good reasons, doubtless, of personal safety. Harry was only one out of a brood of ten or twelve children, some of whom had earned for themselves no good character in service: one, indeed, had been actually transported, for a robbery committed in a distant part of the county; and the tale was yet told in the village of how Gregson the father came back from the trial in a state of wild rage, striding through the place, and uttering oaths of vengeance to himself, his great black eyes gleaming out of his matted hair, and his arms working by his side, and now and then tossed up in his impotent despair. As I heard the account, his wife followed him, child-laden and weeping. After this, they had vanished from the country for a time, leaving their mud hovel locked up, and the door-key, as the neighbours said, buried in a hedge-bank. The Gregsons had re-appeared much about the same time that Mr. Gray came to Hanbury. He had either never heard of their evil character, or considered that it gave them all the more claims upon his Christian care; and the end

of it was, that this rough, untamed, strong giant of a heathen
was loyal slave to the weak, hectic, nervous, self-distrustful
parson. Gregson had also a kind of grumbling respect for Mr.
Horner: he did not quite like the steward's monopoly of his
Harry; the mother submitted to that with a better grace,
swallowing down her maternal jealousy in the prospect of her
child's advancement to a better and more respectable position
than that in which his parents had struggled through life. But
Mr. Horner, the steward, and Gregson, the poacher and
squatter, had come into disagreeble contact too often in
former days for them to be perfectly cordial at any future
time. Even now, when there was no immediate cause for
anything but gratitude for his child's sake on Gregson's part,
he would skulk out of Mr. Horner's way, if he saw him
coming; and it took all Mr. Horner's natural reserve and
acquired self-restraint to keep him from occasionally holding
up his father's life as a warning to Harry. Now, Gregson had
nothing of this desire for avoidance with regard to Mr. Gray.
The poacher had a feeling of physical protection towards the
parson; while the latter had shown the moral courage, without
which Gregson would never have respected him, in coming
right down upon him more than once in the exercise of
unlawful pursuits, and simply and boldly telling him he was
doing wrong, with such a quiet reliance upon Gregson's better
feeling, at the same time, that the strong poacher could not
have lifted a finger against Mr. Gray, though it had been to
save himself from being apprehended and taken to the lock-
ups the very next hour. He had rather listened to the parson's
bold words with an approving smile, much as Mr. Gulliver
might have hearkened to a lecture from a Lilliputian. But
when brave words passed into kind deeds, Gregson's heart
mutely acknowledged its master and keeper. And the beauty
of it all was, that Mr. Gray knew nothing of the good work he
had done, or recognised himself as the instrument which God
had employed. He thanked God, it is true, fervently and often,
that the work was done, and loved the wild man for his rough
gratitude; but it never occurred to the poor young clergyman,
lying on his sick-bed, and praying, as Miss Galindo had told
us he did, to be forgiven for his unprofitable life, to think of
Gregson's reclaimed soul as anything with which he had had

to do. It was now more than three months since Mr. Gray had been at Hanbury Court. During all that time he had been confined to his house, if not to his sick-bed, and he and my lady had never met since their last discussion and difference about Farmer Hale's barn.

This was not my dear lady's fault, no one could have been more attentive in every way to the slightest possible want of either of the invalids, especially of Mr. Gray. And she would have gone to see him at his own house, as she sent him word, but that her foot had slipped upon the polished oak staircase, and her ankle had been sprained.

So we had never seen Mr. Gray since his illness, when one November day he was announced as wishing to speak to my lady. She was sitting in her room – the room in which I lay now pretty constantly – and I remember she looked startled, when word was brought to her of Mr. Gray's being at the Hall.

She could not go to him, she was too lame for that, so she bade him be shown into where she sat.

'Such a day for him to go out!' she exclaimed, looking at the fog which had crept up to the windows, and was sapping the little remaining life in the brilliant Virginian creeper leaves that draperied the house on the terrace side.

He came in white, trembling, his large eyes wild and dilated. He hastened up to Lady Ludlow's chair, and, to my surprise, took one of her hands and kissed it, without speaking, yet shaking all over.

'Mr. Gray!' said she quickly, with sharp, tremulous apprehension of some unknown evil. 'What is it? There is something unusual about you.'

'Something unusual has occurred,' replied he, forcing his words to be calm, as with a great effort. 'A gentleman came to my house, not half-an-hour ago – a Mr. Howard. He came straight from Vienna.'

'My son!' said my dear lady, stretching out her arms in dumb questioning attitude.

'The Lord gave and the Lord taketh away. Blessed be the name of the Lord.'

But my poor lady could not echo the words. He was the last remaining child. And once she had been the joyful mother of nine.

CHAPTER XII

I am ashamed to say what feeling became strongest in my mind about this time; next to the sympathy we all of us felt for my dear lady in her deep sorrow, I mean; for that was greater and stronger than anything else, however contradictory you may think it, when you hear all.

It might arise from my being so far from well at the time, which produced a diseased mind in a diseased body; but I was absolutely jealous for my father's memory, when I saw how many signs of grief there were for my lord's death, he having done next to nothing for the village and parish, which now changed, as it were, its daily course of life, because his lordship died in a far-off city. My father had spent the best years of his manhood in labouring hard, body and soul, for the people amongst whom he lived. His family, of course, claimed the first place in his heart; he would have been good for little, even in the way of benevolence, if they had not. But close after them he cared for his parishioners, and neighbours. And yet, when he died, though the church bells tolled, and smote upon our hearts with hard, fresh pain at every beat, the sounds of every day life still went on, close pressing around us – carts and carriages, street-cries, distant barrel-organs, (the kindly neighbours kept them out of our street): life, active, noisy life, pressed on our acute consciousness of Death, and jarred upon it as on a quick nerve.

And when we went to church – my father's own church – though the pulpit cushions were black, and many of the congregation had put on some humble sign of mourning, yet it did not alter the whole material aspect of the place. And yet what was Lord Ludlow's relation to Hanbury, compared to my father's work and place in –?

Oh! it was very wicked in me! I think if I had seen my lady – if I had dared to ask to go to her, I should not have felt so miserable, so discontented. But she sat in her own room, hung with black, all, even over the shutters. She saw no light but that which was artificial – candles, lamps and the like – for more than a month. Only Adams went near her. Mr. Gray was not admitted, though he called daily. Even Mrs. Medlicott did not see her for near a fortnight. The sight of my lady's griefs, or rather the recollection of it, made Mrs. Medlicott talk far more than was her wont. She told us, with many tears, and much gesticulation, even speaking German at times, when her English would not flow, that my lady sat there, a white figure in the middle of a darkened room; a shaded lamp near her, the light of which fell on an open Bible – the great family Bible. It was not open at any chapter or consoling verse, but at the page whereon were registered the births of her nine children. Five had died in infancy – sacrificed to the cruel system which forbade the mother to suckle her babies. Four had lived longer; Urian had been the first to die, Ughtred Mortimer, Earl Ludlow, the last.

My lady did not cry, Mrs. Medlicott said. She was quite composed; very still, very silent. She put aside everything that savoured of mere business: sent people to Mr. Horner for that. But she was proudly alive to every possible form which might do honour to the last of her race.

In those days, expresses were slow things, and forms still slower. Before my lady's directions could reach Vienna, my lord was buried. There was some talk (so Mrs. Medlicott said) about taking the body up, and bringing him to Hanbury. But his executors – connections on the Ludlow side – demurred to this. If he were removed to England, he must be carried on to Scotland, and interred with his Monkshaven forefathers. My lady, deeply hurt, withdrew from the discussion, before it degenerated to an unseemly contest. But all the more, for this understood mortification of my lady's, did the whole village, and estate of Hanbury assume every outward sign of mourning. The church bells tolled morning and evening. The church itself was draped in black inside. Hatchments were placed everywhere, where hatchments could be put. All the tenantry spoke in hushed voices for more than a week, scarcely daring to observe that all flesh, even that of an Earl Ludlow, and the last of the Hanburys, was but grass after all. The very Fighting

Lion closed its front door – front shutters it had none – and
those who needed drink stole in at the back, and were silent
and maudlin over their cups, instead of riotous and noisy.
Miss Galindo's eyes were swollen up with crying, and she told
me, with a fresh burst of tears, that even hump-backed Sally
had been found sobbing over her Bible, and using a pocket-
handkerchief for the first time in her life; her aprons having
hitherto stood her in the necessary stead, but not being
sufficiently in accordance with etiquette to be used when
mourning over an earl's premature decease.

If it was this way out of the Hall, 'you might work it by the
rule of three,' as Miss Galindo used to say, and judge what it
was in the Hall. We none of us spoke but in a whisper: we
tried not to eat; and indeed the shock had been so really great,
and we did really care so much for my lady, that for some days
we had but little appetite. But after that, I fear our sympathy
grew weaker, while our flesh grew stronger. But we still
spoke low, and our hearts ached whenever we thought of my
lady sitting there alone in the darkened room, with the light
ever falling on that one solemn page.

We wished, oh, how I wished that she would see Mr. Gray!
But Adams said, she thought my lady ought to have a bishop
come to see her. Still no one had authority enough to send for
one.

Mr. Horner all this time was suffering as much as any one.
He was too faithful a servant of the great Hanbury family,
though now the family had dwindled down to a fragile old
lady, not to mourn acutely over its probable extinction. He
had, besides, a deeper sympathy and reverence with, and for,
my lady, in all things than probably he ever cared to show, for
his manners were always measured and cold. He suffered from
sorrow. He also suffered from wrong. My lord's executors
kept writing to him continually. My lady refused to listen to
mere business, saying she intrusted all to him. But the 'all' was
more complicated than I ever thoroughly understood. As far
as I comprehended the case, it was something of this kind: –
There had been a mortgage raised on my lady's property of
Hanbury, to enable my lord, her husband, to spend money in
cultivating his Scottish estates, after some new fashion that
required capital. As long as my lord, her son, lived who was

to succeed to both the estates after her death, this did not signify; so she had said and felt; and she had refused to take any steps to secure the repayment of capital, or even the payment of the interest of the mortgage, from the possible representatives and possessors of the Scotch estates, to the possible owner of the Hanbury property; saying it ill became her to calculate on the contingency of her son's death.

But he had died childless, unmarried. The heir of the Monkshaven property was an Edinburgh advocate, a far-away kinsman of my lord's: the Hanbury property, at my lady's death, would go to the descendants of a third son of the Squire Hanbury in the days of Queen Anne.

This complication of affairs was most grievous to Mr. Horner. He had always been opposed to the mortgage; had hated the payment of the interest, as obliging my lady to practise certain economies which, though she took care to make them as personal as possible, he disliked as derogatory to the family. Poor Mr. Horner! He was so cold and hard in his manner, so curt and decisive in his speech, that I don't think we any of us did him justice. Miss Galindo was almost the first, at this time, to speak a kind word of him, or to take thought of him at all, any farther than to get out of his way when we saw him approaching.

'I don't think Mr. Horner is well,' she said one day, about three weeks after we had heard of my lord's death. 'He sits resting his head on his hand, and hardly hears me when I speak to him.'

But I thought no more of it, as Miss Galindo did not name it again. My lady came amongst us once more. From elderly she had become old: a little, frail, old lady, in heavy black drapery, never speaking about nor alluding to her great sorrow; quieter, gentler, paler than ever before; and her eyes dim with much weeping, never witnessed by mortal.

She had seen Mr. Gray at the expiration of the month of deep retirement. But I do not think that, even to him, she had said one word of her own particular individual sorrow. All mention of it seemed buried deep for evermore. One day, Mr. Horner sent word that he was too much indisposed to attend to his usual business at the Hall; but he wrote down some directions and requests to Miss Galindo, saying that he would be at his office early the next morning. The next morning he was dead.

Miss Galindo told my lady. Miss Galindo herself cried plentifully, but my lady, although very much distressed, could not cry. It seemed a physical impossibility, as if she had shed all the tears in her power. Moreover, I almost think her wonder was far greater that she herself lived than that Mr. Horner died. It was almost natural that so faithful a servant should break his heart, when the family he belonged to lost their stay, their heir, and their last hope.

Yes! Mr. Horner was a faithful servant. I do not think there are many so faithful now; but perhaps that is an old woman's fancy of mine. When his will came to be examined, it was discovered that, soon after Harry Gregson's accident, Mr. Horner had left the few thousands (three, I think) of which he was possessed, in trust for Harry's benefit, desiring his executors to see that the lad was well educated in certain things, for which Mr. Horner had thought that he had shown especial aptitude; and there was a kind of implied apology to my lady in one sentence, where he stated that Harry's lameness would prevent his being ever able to gain his living by the exercise of any mere bodily faculties, 'as had been wished by a lady whose wishes' he, the testator, 'was bound to regard.'

But there was a codicil in the will, dated since Lord Ludlow's death – feebly written by Mr. Horner himself, as if in preparation only for some more formal manner of bequest: or, perhaps, only as a mere temporary arrangement till he could see a lawyer, and have a fresh will made. In this he revoked his previous bequest to Harry Gregson. He only left two hundred pounds to Mr. Gray to be used, as that gentleman thought best, for Henry Gregson's benefit. With this one exception, he bequeathed all the rest of his savings to my lady, with a hope that they might form a nest-egg, as it were, towards the paying off of the mortgage which had been such a grief to him during his life. I may not repeat all this in lawyer's phrase; I heard it through Miss Galindo, and she might make mistakes. Though, indeed, she was very clear-headed, and soon earned the respect of Mr. Smithson, my lady's lawyer from Warwick. Mr. Smithson knew Miss Galindo a little before, both personally and by reputation; but I don't think he was prepared to find her installed as steward's clerk, and, at first, he was inclined to treat her, in this capacity, with polite contempt. But Miss Galindo was both a lady and a spirited, sensible woman, and she could put aside her self-indulgence in eccentricity of speech and manner whenever she chose. Nay, more; she was usually so talkative that, if she had not been amusing and warm-hearted, one might have thought her wearisome occasionally. But to meet Mr. Smithson she came out daily in her Sunday gown; she said no more than was required in answer to his questions; her books and papers were in thorough order, and methodically kept; her statements of matters of fact accurate, and to be relied on. She was amusingly conscious of her victory over his contempt of a woman-clerk and his preconceived opinion of her unpractical eccentricity.

'Let me alone,' said she, one day when she came in to sit awhile with me. 'That man is a good man – a sensible man – and I have no doubt he is a good lawyer; but he can't fathom women yet. I make no doubt he'll go back to Warwick, and never give credit again to those people who made him think me half-cracked to begin with. Oh, my dear, he did! He showed it twenty times worse than my poor dear master ever did. It was a form to be gone through to please my lady, and, for her sake, he would hear my statements and see my books. It was keeping a woman out of harm's way, at any rate, to let her fancy herself useful. I read the man. And, I am thankful to say, he cannot read me. At least, only one side of me. When I see an end to be gained, I can behave accordingly. Here was a man who thought that a woman in a black silk gown was a respectable, orderly kind of person; and I was a woman in a black silk gown. He believed that a woman could not write straight lines, and required a man to tell her that two and two made four. I was not above ruling my books, and had Cocker a little more at my fingers' ends than he had. But my greatest triumph has been holding my tongue. He would have thought nothing of my books, or my sums, or my black silk gown, if I had spoken unasked. So I have buried more sense in my bosom these ten days than ever I have uttered in the whole course of my life before. I have been so curt, so abrupt, so

abominably dull, that I'll answer for it he thinks me worthy to
be a man. But I must go back to him, my dear; so goodbye to
conversation and you.'

But though Mr. Smithson might be satisfied with Miss
Galindo, I am afraid she was the only part of the affair with
which he was content. Everything else went wrong. I could
not say who told me – but the conviction of this seemed to
pervade the house. I never knew how much we had all looked
up to the silent, gruff Mr. Horner for decisions, until he was
gone. My lady herself was a pretty good woman of business,
as women of business go. Her father, seeing that she would be
the heiress of the Hanbury property, had given her a training
which was thought unusual in those days; and she liked to feel
herself queen regnant, and to have to decide in all cases
between herself and her tenantry. But, perhaps, Mr. Horner
would have done it more wisely; not but what she always
attended to him at last. She would begin by saying, pretty
clearly and promptly, what she would have done, and what
she would not have done. If Mr. Horner approved of it, he
bowed, and set about obeying her directly; if he disapproved
of it, he bowed, and lingered so long before he obeyed her,
that she forced his opinion out of him with her 'Well, Mr.
Horner! and what have you to say against it?' For she always
understood his silence as well as if he had spoken. But the
estate was pressed for ready money, and Mr. Horner had
grown gloomy and languid since the death of his wife, and
even his own personal affairs were not in the order in which
they had been a year or two before, for his old clerk had
gradually become superannuated, or, at any rate, unable by
the superfluity of his own energy and wit to supply the spirit
that was wanting in Mr. Horner.

Day after day Mr. Smithson seemed to grow more fidgety,
more annoyed at the state of affairs. Like every one else
employed by Lady Ludlow, as far as I could learn, he had an
hereditary tie to the Hanbury family. As long as the Smithsons
had been lawyers, they had been lawyers to the Hanburys;
always coming in on all great family occasions, and better able
to understand the characters, and connect the links of what
had once been a large and scattered family, than any individual
thereof had ever been.

As long as a man was at the head of the Hanburys, the lawyers had simply acted as servants, and had only given their advice when it was required. But they had assumed a different position on the memorable occasion of the mortgage; they had remonstrated against it. My lady had resented this remonstrance, and a slight, unspoken coolness had existed between her and the father of this Mr. Smithson ever since.

I was very sorry for my lady. Mr. Smithson was inclined to blame Mr. Horner for the disorderly state in which he found some of the outlying farms, and for the deficiencies in the annual payment of the rents. Mr. Smithson had too much good feeling to put his blame into words; but my lady's quick instinct led her to reply to a thought, the existence of which she perceived; and she quietly told the truth, and explained how she had interfered repeatedly to prevent Mr. Horner from taking certain desirable steps, which were discordant to her hereditary sense of right and wrong between landlord and tenant. She also spoke of the want of ready money as a misfortune that could be remedied, by more economical personal expenditure on her own part; by which individual saving it was possible that a reduction of fifty pounds a year might have been accomplished. But as soon as Mr. Smithson touched on larger economies, such as either affected the welfare of others, or the honour and standing of the great House of Hanbury, she was inflexible. Her establishment consisted of somewhere about forty servants, of which nearly as many as twenty were unable to perform their work properly, and yet would have been hurt if they had been dismissed; so they had the credit of fullfilling duties, while my lady paid and kept their substitutes. Mr. Smithson made a calculation, and would have saved some hundreds a year by pensioning off these old servants. But my lady would not hear of it. Then, again I know privately that he urged her to allow some of us to return to our homes. Bitterly we should have regretted the separation from Lady Ludlow; but we would have gone back gladly, had we known at the time that her circumstances required it: but she would not listen to the proposal for a moment.

'If I cannot act justly towards every one, I will give up a plan which has been a source of much satisfaction; at least, I will

not carry it out to such an extent in future. But to these young
ladies who do me the favour to live with me at present, I stand
pledged. I cannot go back from my word, Mr. Smithson. We
had better talk no more of this.'

As she spoke, she entered the room where I lay. She and
Mr. Smithson were coming for some papers contained in the
bureau. They did not know I was there, and Mr. Smithson
started a little when he saw me, as he must have been aware
that I had overheard something. But my lady did not change a
muscle in her face. All the world might overhear her kind,
just, pure sayings, and she had no fear of their misconstruc-
tion. She came up to me, and kissed me on the forehead, and
then went to search for the required papers.

'I rode over the Conington farms yesterday, my lady. I
must say I was quite grieved to see the condition they are in;
all the land that is not waste is utterly exhausted with working
successive white crops. Not a pinch of manure laid on the
ground for years. I must say that a greater contrast could never
have been presented than that between Harding's farm and the
next fields – fences in perfect order, rotation crops, sheep
eating down the turnips on the waste lands – everything that
could be desired.'

'Whose farm is that?' asked my lady.

'Why, I am sorry to say, it was on none of your ladyship's
that I saw such good methods adopted. I hoped it was: I
stopped my horse to inquire. A queer-looking man, sitting on
his horse like a tailor, watching his men with a couple of the
sharpest eyes I ever saw, and dropping his *h*'s at every word,
answered my question, and told me it was his. I could not go
on asking him who he was; but I fell into conversation with
him, and I gathered that he had earned some money in trade in
Birmingham, and had bought the estate (five hundred acres, I
think he said) on which he was born, and now was setting
himself to cultivate it in downright earnest, going to Holkham
and Woburn, and half the country over, to get himself up on
the subject.'

'It would be Brooke, that dissenting baker from Birmingham,' said my lady in her most icy tone. 'Mr. Smithson I am
sorry I have been detaining you so long but I think these are
the letters you wished to see.'

If her ladyship thought by this speech to quench Mr. Smithson she was mistaken. Mr. Smithson just looked at the letters, and went on with the old subject.

'Now, my lady, it struck me that if you had such a man to take poor Horner's place, he would work the rents and the land round most satisfactorily. I should not despair of inducing this very man to undertake the work. I should not mind speaking to him myself on the subject, for we got capital friends over a snack of luncheon that he asked me to share with him.'

Lady Ludlow fixed her eyes on Mr. Smithson as he spoke, and never took them off his face until he had ended. She was silent a minute before she answered.

'You are very good, Mr. Smithson, but I need not trouble you with any such arrangements. I am going to write this afternoon to Captain James, a friend of one of my sons, who has, I hear, been severely wounded at Trafalgar, to request him to honour me by accepting Mr. Horner's situation.'

'A Captain James! a captain in the navy! going to manage your ladyship's estate!'

'If he will be so kind. I shall esteem it a condescension on his part; but I hear that he will have to resign his profession, his state of health is so bad, and a country life is especially prescribed for him. I am in some hopes of tempting him here, as I learn he has but little to depend on if he gives up his profession.'

'A Captain James! an invalid captain!'

'You think I am asking too great a favour,' continued my lady. (I never could tell how far it was simplicity, or how far a kind of innocent malice, that made her misinterpret Mr. Smithson's words and looks as she did.) 'But he is not a post-captain, only a commander, and his pension will be but small. I may be able, by offering him country air and a healthy occupation, to restore him to health.'

'Occupation! My lady, may I ask how a sailor is to manage land? Why, your tenants will laugh him to scorn.'

'My tenants, I trust, will not behave so ill as to laugh at any one I choose to set over them. Captain James has had experience in managing men. He has remarkable practical talents, and a great common sense, as I hear from every one.

But, whatever he may be, the affair rests between him and myself. I can only say I shall esteem myself fortunate if he comes.'

There was no more to be said, after my lady spoke in this manner. I had heard her mention Captain James before, as a middy who had been very kind to her son Urian. I thought I remembered then, that she had mentioned that his family circumstances were not very prosperous. But, I confess that, little as I knew of the management of land, I quite sided with Mr. Smithson. He, silently prohibited from again speaking to my lady on the subject, opened his mind to Miss Galindo, from whom I was pretty sure to hear all the opinions and news of the household and village. She had taken a great fancy to me, because she said I talked so agreeably. I believe it was because I listened so well.

'Well, have you heard the news,' she began, 'about this Captain James? A sailor – with a wooden leg, I have no doubt. What would the poor, dear, deceased master have said to it, if he had known who was to be his successor! My dear I have often thought of the postman's bringing me a letter as one of the pleasures I shall miss in heaven. But, really, I think Mr. Horner may be thankful he has got out of the reach of news; or else he would hear of Mr. Smithson's having made up to the Birmingham baker, and of this one-legged captain coming to dot-and-go-one over the estate. I suppose he will look after the labourers through a spy glass. I only hope he won't stick in the mud with his wooden leg; for I, for one, won't help him out. Yes, I would,' said she, correcting herself; 'I would, for my lady's sake.'

'But are you sure he has a wooden leg?' asked I. 'I heard Lady Ludlow tell Mr. Smithson about him, and she only spoke of him as wounded.'

'Well, sailors are almost always wounded in the leg. Look at Greenwich Hospital! I should say there were twenty one-legged pensioners to one without an arm there. But, say he has got half-a-dozen legs: what has he to do with managing land? I shall think him very impudent if he comes, taking advantage of my lady's kind heart.'

However, come he did. In a month from that time, the carriage was sent to meet Captain James; just as three years before it had been sent to meet me. His coming had been so much talked about that we were all as curious as possible to see him, and to know how so unusual an experiment, as it seemed to us, would answer. But, before I tell you anything about our new agent, I must speak of something quite as interesting, and I really think quite as important. And this was my lady's making friends with Harry Gregson. I do believe she did it for Mr. Horner's sake; but, of course, I can only conjecture why my lady did anything. But I heard one day, from Mary Legard, that my lady had sent for Harry to come and see her, if he was well enough to walk so far; and the next day he was shown into the room he had been in once before under such unlucky circumstances.

The lad looked pale enough, as he stood propping himself up on his crutch, and, the instant my lady saw him, she bade John Footman place a stool for him to sit down upon while she spoke to him. It might be his paleness that gave his whole face a more refined and gentle look; but I suspect it was that the boy was apt to take impressions, and that Mr. Horner's grave, dignified ways, and Mr. Gray's tender and quiet manners, had altered him; and then the thoughts of illness and death seem to turn many of us into·gentlemen and gentlewomen, as long as such thoughts are in our minds. We cannot speak loudly or angrily at such times; we are not apt to be eager about mere wordly things, for our very awe at our quickened sense of the nearness of the invisible world makes us calm and serene about the petty trifles of today. At least, I know that was the explanation Mr. Gray once gave me of what we all thought the great improvement in Harry Gregson's way of behaving.

My lady hesitated so long about what she had best say, that Harry grew a little frightened at her silence. A few months ago it would have surprised me more than it did now; but since my lord her son's death she had seemed altered in many ways – more uncertain and distrustful of herself, as it were.

At last she said, and I think the tears were in her eyes: 'My poor little fellow, you have had a narrow escape with your life since I saw you last.'

To this there was nothing to be said but 'Yes'; and again there was silence.

'And you have lost a good, kind friend in Mr. Horner.'

The boy's lips worked, and I think he said 'Please don't.'
But I can't be sure; at any rate, my lady went on –

'And so have I – a good, kind friend he was to both of us;
and to you he wished to show his kindness in even a more
generous way than he has done. Mr. Gray has told you about
his legacy to you, has he not?'

There was no sign of eager joy on the lad's face, as if he
realised the power and pleasure of having what to him must
have seemed like a fortune.

'Mr. Gray said as how he had left me a matter of money.'

'Yes, he has left you two hundred pounds.'

'But I would rather have had him alive, my lady,' he burst
out, sobbing as if his heart would break.

'My lad, I believe you. We would rather have had our dead
alive, would we not? and there is nothing in money that can
comfort us for their loss. But you know – Mr. Gray has told
you – who has appointed all our times to die. Mr. Horner was
a good, just man; and has done well and kindly, both by me
and you. You perhaps do not know,' (and now I understand
what my lady had been making up her mind to say to Harry,
all the time she was hesitating how to begin) 'that Mr. Horner,
at one time, meant to leave you a great deal more: probably all
he had, with the exception of a legacy to his old clerk,
Morrison. But he knew that this estate – on which my
forefathers had lived for six hundred years – was in debt, and
that I had no immediate chance of paying off this debt; and yet
he felt that it was a very sad thing for an old property like this
to belong in part to those other men, who had lent the money.
You understand me, I think, my little man?' said she, questioning Harry's face.

He had left off crying, and was trying to understand, with
all his might and main; and I think he had got a pretty good
general idea of the state of affairs; though probably he was
puzzled by the term 'the estate being in debt'. But he was
sufficiently interested to want my lady to go on; and he
nodded his head at her, to signify this to her.

'So Mr. Horner took the money which he once meant to be
yours, and has left the greater part of it to me, with the
intention of helping me to pay off this debt I have told you
about. It will go a long way, and I shall try hard to save the

rest, and then I shall die happy in leaving the land free from debt.' She paused. 'But I shall not die happy in thinking of you. I do not know if having money, or even having a great estate and much honour, is a good thing for any of us. But God sees fit that some of us should be called to this condition, and it is our duty then to stand to our posts, like brave soldiers. Now, Mr. Horner intended you to have this money first. I shall only call it borrowing from you, Harry Gregson, if I take it and use it to pay off the debt. I shall pay Mr. Gray interest on this money, because he is to stand as your guardian, as it were, till you come of age; and he must fix what ought to be done with it, so as to fit you for spending the principal rightly when the estate can repay it you. I suppose, now, it will be right for you to be educated. That will be another snare that will come with your money. But have courage, Harry. Both education and money may be used rightly, if we only pray against the temptations they bring with them.'

Harry could make no answer, though I am sure he understood it all. My lady wanted to get him to talk to her a little, by way of becoming acquainted with what was passing in his mind; and she asked him what he would like to have done with his money, if he could have part of it now? To such a simple question, involving no talk about feelings, his answer came readily enough.

'Build a cottage for father, with stairs in it, and give Mr. Gray a school-house. Oh, father does so want Mr. Gray for to have his wish! Father saw all the stones lying quarried and hewn on Farmer Hale's land; Mr. Gray had paid for them all himself. And father said he would work night and day, and little Tommy should carry mortar, if the parson would let him, sooner than that he should be fretted and frabbed as he was, with no one giving him a helping hand, or a kind word.'

Harry knew nothing of my lady's part in the affair; that was very clear. My lady kept silence.

'If I might have a piece of my money, I would buy land from Mr. Brooke; he has got a bit to sell just at the corner of Hendon Lane, and I would give it to Mr. Gray; and, perhaps, if your ladyship thinks I may be learn'd again, I might grow up into the schoolmaster.'

'You are a good boy,' said my lady. 'But there are more things to be thought of, in carrying out such a plan, than you are aware of. However, it shall be tried.'

'The school, my lady?' I exclaimed, almost thinking she did not know what she was saying.

'Yes, the school. For Mr. Horner's sake, for Mr. Gray's sake, and last, not least, for this lad's sake, I will give the new plan a trial. Ask Mr. Gray to come up to me this afternoon about the land he wants. He need not go to a Dissenter for it. And tell your father he shall have a good share in the building of it, and Tommy shall carry the mortar.'

'And I may be schoolmaster?' asked Harry eagerly.

'We'll see about that,' said my lady, amused. 'It will be some time before that plan comes to pass, my little fellow.'

And now to return to Captain James. My first account of him was from Miss Galindo.

'He's not above thirty; and I must just pack up my pens and my paper, and be off; for it would be the height of impropriety for me to be staying here as his clerk. It was all very well in the old master's days. But here am I, not fifty till next May, and this young, unmarried man, who is not even a widower! Oh, there would be no end of gossip. Besides, he looks as askance at me as I do at him. My black silk gown had no effect. He's afraid I shall marry him. But I won't; he may feel himself quite safe from that. And Mr. Smithson has been recommending a clerk to my lady. She would far rather keep me on; but I can't stop. I really could not think it proper.'

'What sort of a looking man is he?'

'Oh, nothing particular. Short, and brown, and sunburnt. I did not think it became me to look at him. Well, now for the nightcaps. I should have grudged any one else doing them, for I have got such a pretty pattern!'

But when it came to Miss Galindo's leaving, there was a great misunderstanding between her and my lady. Miss Galindo had imagined that my lady had asked her as a favour to copy the letters, and enter the accounts, and had agreed to do the work without the notion of being paid for so doing. She had, now and then, grieved over a very profitable order for needlework passing out of her hands on account of her not having time to do it, because of her occupation at the Hall; but

she had never hinted this to my lady, but gone on cheerfully at
her writing as long as her clerkship was required. My lady was
annoyed that she had not made her intention of paying Miss
Galindo more clear, in the first conversation she had had with
her; but I suppose that she had been too delicate to be very
explicit with regard to money matters; and now Miss Galindo
was quite hurt at my lady's wanting to pay her for what she
had done in such right-down good-will.

'No,' Miss Galindo said; 'my own dear lady, you may be as
angry with me as you like, but don't offer me money. Think
of six-and-twenty years ago, and poor Arthur, and as you
were to me then! Besides, I wanted money – I don't disguise it
– for a particular purpose; and when I found that (God bless
you for asking me!) I could do you a service, I turned it over in
my mind, and I gave up one plan, and took up another, and
it's all settled now. Bessy is to leave school and come and live
with me. Don't, please, offer me money again. You don't
know how glad I have been to do anything for you. Have not
I, Margaret Dawson? Did you not hear me say, one day, I
would cut off my hand for my lady; for am I a stock or a
stone, that I should forget kindness? Oh, I have been so glad to
work for you! And now Bessy is coming here; and no one
knows anything about her – as if she had done anything
wrong, poor child!'

'Dear Miss Galindo,' replied my lady, 'I will never ask you
to take money again. Only I thought it was quite understood
between us. And you know you have taken money for a set of
morning wrappers, before now.'

'Yes, my lady; but that was not confidential. Now I was so
proud to have something to do for you confidentially.'

'But who is Bessy?' asked my lady. 'I do not understand
who she is, or why she is to come and live with you. Dear
Miss Galindo, you must honour me by being confidential
with me in your turn!'

CHAPTER XIII

I had always understood that Miss Galindo had once been in much better circumstances, but I had never liked to ask any questions respecting her. But about this time many things came out respecting her former life, which I will try and arrange: not, however, in the order in which I heard them, but rather as they occurred.

Miss Galindo was the daughter of a clergyman in Westmoreland. Her father was the younger brother of a baronet, his ancestor having been one of those of James the First's creation. This baronet-uncle of Miss Galindo was one of the queer, out-of-the-way people who were bred at that time, and in that northern district of England. I never heard much of him from any one, besides this one great fact; that he had early disappeared from his family, which indeed only consisted of a brother and sister who died unmarried, and lived no one knew where – somewhere on the Continent, it was supposed, for he had never returned from the grand tour which he had been. sent to make, according to the general fashion of the day, as soon as he had left Oxford. He corresponded occasionally with his brother the clergyman; but the letters passed through a banker's hands; the banker being pledged to secrecy, and, as he told Mr. Galindo, having the penalty, if he broke his pledge, of losing the whole profitable business, and of having the management of the baronet's affairs taken out of his hands, without any advantage accruing to the inquirer; for Sir Lawrence had told Messrs. Graham that, in case his place of residence was revealed by them, not only would he cease to bank with them, but instantly take measures to baffle any future inquiries as to his whereabouts, by removing to some distant country.

Sir Lawrence paid a certain sum of money to his brother's account every year; but the time of this payment varied, and it

was sometimes eighteen or nineteen months between the
deposits; then, again, it would not be above a quarter of the
time, showing that he intended it to be annual; but, as this
intention was never expressed in words, it was impossible to
rely upon it, and a great deal of this money was swallowed up
by the necessity Mr. Galindo felt himself under of living in the
large, old, rambling family mansion, which had been one of
Sir Lawrence's rarely expressed desires. Mr. and Mrs. Galindo
often planned to live upon their own small fortune and the
income derived from the living (a vicarage, of which the great
tithes went to Sir Lawrence as lay impropriator), so as to put
by the payments made by the baronet, for the benefit of
Laurentia – our Miss Galindo. But I suppose they found it
difficult to live economically in a large house, even though
they had it rent free. They had to keep up with hereditary
neighbours and friends, and could hardly help doing it in the
hereditary manner.

One of these neighbours, a Mr. Gibson, had a son a few
years older than Laurentia. The families were sufficiently
intimate for the young people to see a good deal of each other;
and I was told that this young Mr. Mark Gibson was an
unusually prepossessing man (he seemed to have impressed
every one who spoke of him to me as being a handsome,
manly, kind-hearted fellow), just what a girl would be sure to
find most agreeable. The parents either forgot that their
children were growing up to man's and woman's estate, or
thought that the intimacy and probable attachment would be
no bad thing, even if it did lead to a marriage. Still, nothing
was ever said by young Gibson till later on, when it was too
late, as it turned out. He went to and from Oxford; he shot
and fished with Mr. Galindo, or came to the Mere to skate in
winter-time; was asked to accompany Mr. Galindo to the
Hall, as the latter returned to the quiet dinner with his wife
and daughter; and so, and so, it went on, nobody much knew
how, until one day, when Mr. Galindo received a formal letter
from his brother's bankers, announcing Sir Lawrence's death,
of malaria fever, at Albano, and congratulating Sir Hubert on
his accession to the estates and the baronetcy. 'The king is
dead – Long live the king!' as I have since heard that the French
express it.

Sir Hubert and his wife were greatly surprised. Sir Lawrence was but two years older than his brother; and they had never heard of any illness till they heard of his death. They were sorry; very much shocked; but still a little elated at the succession to the baronetcy and estates. The London bankers had managed everything well. There was a large sum of ready money in their hands, at Sir Hubert's service, until he should touch his rents, the rent-roll being eight thousand a year. And only Laurentia to inherit it all! Her mother, a poor clergyman's daughter, began to plan all sorts of fine marriages for her; nor was her father much behind his wife in his ambition. They took her up to London, when they went to buy new carriages, and dresses, and furniture. And it was then and there she made my lady's acquaintance. How it was that they came to take a fancy to each other I cannot say. My lady was of the old nobility – grand, composed, gentle, and stately in her ways. Miss Galindo must always have been hurried in her manner, and her energy must have shown itself in inquisitiveness and oddness even in her youth. But I don't pretend to account for things: I only narrate them. And the fact was this: – that the elegant, fastidious countess was attracted to the country girl, who on her part almost worshipped my lady. My lady's notice of their daughter made her parents think, I suppose, that there was no match that she might not command: she, the heiress of eight thousand a year, and visiting about among earls and dukes. So when they came back to their old Westmoreland Hall, and Mark Gibson rode over to offer his hand and his heart, and prospective estate of nine hundred a year, to his old companion and playfellow, Laurentia, Sir Hubert and Lady Galindo made very short work of it. They refused him plumply themselves; and, when he begged to be allowed to speak to Laurentia, they found some excuse for refusing him the opportunity of so doing, until they had talked to her themselves, and brought up every argument and fact in their power to convince her – a plain girl, and conscious of her plainness – that Mr. Mark Gibson had never thought of her in the way of marriage till after her father's accession to his fortune, and that it was the estate – not the young lady – that he was in love with. I suppose it will never be known in this world how far this supposition of theirs was true. My Lady

Ludlow had always spoken as if it was; but, perhaps events, which came to her knowledge about this time, altered her opinion. At any rate, the end of it was, Laurentia refused Mark, and almost broke her heart in doing so. He discovered the suspicions of Sir Hubert and Lady Galindo, and that they had persuaded their daughter to share in them. So he flung off with high words, saying that they did not know a true heart when they met with one; and that, although he had never offered till after Sir Lawrence's death, yet his father knew all along that he had been attached to Laurentia, only that he, being the eldest of five children, and having as yet no profession, had had to conceal, rather than to express, an attachment which, in those days, he had believed was recipro- cated. He had always meant to study for the bar, and the end of all he had hoped for had been to earn a moderate income, which he might ask Laurentia to share. This, or something like it, was what he said. But his reference to his father cut two ways. Old Mr. Gibson was known to be very keen about money. It was just as likely that he would urge Mark to make love to the heiress, now she was an heiress, as that he would have restrained him previously, as Mark said he had done. When this was repeated to Mark, he became proudly reserved, or sullen, and said that Laurentia, at any rate, might have known him better. He left the country, and went up to London to study law soon afterwards; and Sir Hubert and Lady Galindo thought they were well rid of him. But Laurentia never ceased reproaching herself, and never did to her dying day, as I believe. The words, 'She might have known me better,' told to her by some kind friend or other, rankled in her mind, and were never forgotten. Her father and mother took her up to London the next year; but she did not care to visit – dreaded going out even for a drive, lest she should see Mark Gibson's reproachful eyes – pined and lost her health. Lady Ludlow saw this change with regret, and was told the cause by Lady Galindo, who, of course, gave her own version of Mark's conduct and motives. My lady never spoke to Miss Galindo about it, but tried constantly to interest and please her. It was at this time that my lady told Miss Galindo so much about her own early life, and about Hanbury, that Miss Galindo re- solved, if ever she could, she would go and see the old place which her friend loved so well. The end of it all was, that she came to live there, as we know.

But a great change was to come first. Before Sir Hubert and Lady Galindo had left London on this, their second visit, they had a letter from the lawyer, whom they employed, saying that Sir Lawrence had left an heir, his legitimate child by an Italian woman of low rank; at least legal claims to the title and property had been sent in to him on the boy's behalf. Sir Lawrence had always been a man of adventurous and artistic, rather than of luxurious tastes; and it was supposed, when all came to be proved at the trial, that he was captivated by the free, beautiful life they lead in Italy, and had married this Neapolitan fisherman's daughter, who had people about her shrewd enough to see that the ceremony was legally performed. She and her husband had wandered about the shores of the Mediterranean for years, leading a happy, careless, irresponsible life, unencumbered by any duties except those connected with a rather numerous family. It was enough for her that they never wanted money, and that her husband's love was always continued to her. She hated the name of England – wicked, cold, heretic England – and avoided the mention of any subjects connected with her husband's early life. So that, when he died at Albano, she was almost roused out of her vehement grief to anger with the Italian doctor, who declared that he must write to a certain address to announce the death of Lawrence Galindo. For some time, she feared lest English barbarians might come down upon her, making a claim to the children. She hid herself and them in the Abruzzi, living upon the sale of what furniture and jewels Sir Lawrence had died possessed of. When these failed, she returned to Naples, which she had not visited since her marriage. Her father was dead; but her brother inherited some of his keenness. He interested the priests, who made inquiries and found that the Galindo succession was worth securing to an heir of the true faith. They stirred about it, obtained advice at the English Embassy; and hence that letter to the lawyers, calling upon Sir Hubert to relinquish title and property, and to refund what money he had expended. He was vehement in his opposition to this claim. He could not bear to think of his brother having married a foreigner – a Papist, a fisherman's daughter; nay, of his having become a Papist himself. He was in despair at the thought of his ancestral property going to the issue of such a marriage. He fought tooth and nail, making enemies of his relations, and losing almost all his own private property; for he would go on against the lawyer's advice, long after every one was convinced except himself and his wife. At last he was conquered. He gave up his living in gloomy despair. He would have changed his name if he could, so desirous was he to obliterate all ties between himself and the mongrel Papist baronet and his Italian mother who came to take possession of the Hall soon after Mr. Hubert Galindo's departure, stayed there one winter, and then flitted back to Naples with gladness and delight. Mr. and Mrs. Hubert Galindo lived in London. He had obtained a curacy somewhere in the city. They would have been thankful now if Mr. Mark Gibson had renewed his offer. No one could accuse him of mercenary motives if he had done so. Because he did not come forward, as they wished, they brought his silence up as a justification of what they had previously attributed to him. I don't know what Miss Galindo thought herself; but Lady Ludlow has told me how she shrank from hearing her parents abuse him. Lady Ludlow supposed that he was aware that they were living in London. His father must have known the fact, and it was curious if he had never named it to his son. Besides, the name was very uncommon; and it was unlikely that it should never come across him, in the advertisements of charity sermons which the new and rather eloquent curate of Saint Mark's East was asked to preach. All this time Lady Ludlow never lost sight of them, for Miss Galindo's sake. And when the father and mother died, it was my lady who upheld Miss Galindo in her determination not to apply for any provision to her cousin, the Italian baronet, but rather to live upon the hundred a year which had been settled on her mother and the children of his son Hubert's marriage by the old grandfather, Sir Lawrence.

Mr. Mark Gibson had risen to some eminence as a barrister on the Northern Circuit, but had died unmarried in the lifetime of his father, a victim (so people said) to intemperance. Doctor Trevor, the physician who had been called in to Mr. Gray and Harry Gregson, had married a sister of his. And

that was all my lady knew about the Gibson family. But who
was Bessy?

That mystery and secret came out, too, in process of time.
Miss Galindo had been to Warwick, some years before I
arrived at Hanbury, on some kind of business or shopping,
which can only be transacted in a county town. There was an
old Westmoreland connection between her and Mrs. Trevor,
though I believe the latter was too young to have been made
aware of her brother's offer to Miss Galindo at the time when
it took place; and such affairs, if they are unsuccessful, are
seldom spoken about in the gentleman's family afterwards.
But the Gibsons and Galindos had been county neighbours for
too long for the connection not to be kept up between two
members settled far away from their early homes. Miss
Galindo always desired her parcels to be sent to Doctor
Trevor's, when she went to Warwick for shopping purposes.
If she were going any journey, and the coach did not come
through Warwick as soon as she arrived (in my lady's coach or
otherwise) from Hanbury, she went to Doctor Trevor's to wait.
She was as much expected to sit down to the household meals
as if she had been one of the family; and in after years it was
Mrs. Trevor who managed her repository business for her.

So, on the day I spoke of, she had gone to Doctor Trevor's
to rest, and possibly to dine. The post, in those times, came in
at all hours of the morning; and Doctor Trevor's letters had
not arrived until after his departure on his morning round.
Miss Galindo was sitting down to dinner with Mrs. Trevor
and her seven children, when the Doctor came in. He was
flurried and uncomfortable, and hurried the children away as
soon as he decently could. Then (rather feeling Miss Galindo's
presence an advantage, both, as a present restraint on the
violence of his wife's grief, and as a consoler when he was
absent on his afternoon round) he told Mrs. Trevor of her
brother's death. He had been taken ill on circuit, and had
hurried back to his chambers in London only to die. She cried
terribly; but Doctor Trevor said afterwards, he never noticed
that Miss Galindo cared much about it one way or another.
She helped him to soothe his wife, promised to stay with her
all the afternoon instead of returning to Hanbury, and afterwards offered to remain with her while the Doctor went to

attend the funeral. When they heard of the old love-story between the dead man and Miss Galindo – brought up by mutual friends in Westmoreland, in the review which we are all inclined to take of the events of a man's life when he comes to die – they tried to remember Miss Galindo's speeches and ways of going on during this visit. She was a little pale, a little silent; her eyes were sometimes swollen, and her nose red; but she was at an age when such appearances are generally attributed to a bad cold in the head, rather than to any more sentimental reason. They felt towards her as towards an old friend, a kindly, useful, eccentric old maid. She did not expect more, or wish them to remember that she might once have had other hopes, and more youthful feelings. Doctor Trevor thanked her very warmly for staying with his wife, when he returned home from London (where the funeral had taken place). He begged Miss Galindo to stay with them, when the children were gone to bed, and she was preparing to leave the husband and wife by themselves. He told her and his wife many particulars – then paused – then went on –

'And Mark has left a child – a little girl –'

'But he never was married!' exclaimed Mrs. Trevor.

'A little girl,' continued her husband, 'whose mother, I conclude, is dead. At any rate, the child was in possession of his chambers; she and an old nurse, who seemed to have the charge of everything, and has cheated poor Mark, I should fancy, not a little.'

'But the child!' asked Mrs. Trevor, still almost breathless with astonishment. 'How do you know it is his.'

'The nurse told me it was, with great appearance of indignation at my doubting it. I asked the little thing her name, and all I could get was "Bessy!" and a cry of "Me wants papa!" The nurse said the mother was dead, and she knew no more about it than that Mr. Gibson had engaged her to take care of the little girl, calling it his child. One or two of his lawyer friends, whom I met with at the funeral, told me they were aware of the existence of the child.'

'What is to be done with her?' asked Mrs. Trevor.

'Nay, I don't know,' replied he. 'Mark has hardly left assets enough to pay his debts, and your father is not inclined to come forward.'

That night, as Doctor Trevor sat in his study, after his wife had gone to bed, Miss Galindo knocked on his door. She and he had a long conversation. The result was that he accompanied Miss Galindo up to town the next day; that they took possession of the little Bessy, and she was brought down, and placed at nurse at a farm in the country near Warwick; Miss Galindo undertaking to pay one-half of the expense, and to furnish her with clothes, and Dr Trevor undertaking that the remaining half should be furnished by the Gibson family, or by himself in their default.

Miss Galindo was not fond of children; and I dare say she dreaded taking this child to live with her for more reasons than one. My Lady Ludlow could not endure any mention of illegitimate children. It was a principle of hers that society ought to ignore them. And I believe Miss Galindo had always agreed with her until now, when the thing came home to her womanly heart. Still she shrank from having this child of some strange woman under her roof. She went over to see it from time to time; she worked at its clothes long after every one thought she was in bed; and, when the time came for Bessy to be sent to school, Miss Galindo laboured away more diligently than ever, in order to pay the increased expense. For the Gibson family had, at first, paid their part of the compact, but with unwillingness and grudging hearts; then they had left it off altogether, and it fell hard on Dr. Trevor with his twelve children; and, latterly, Miss Galindo had taken upon herself almost all the burden. One can hardly live and labour, and plan and make sacrifices, for any human creature, without learning to love it. And Bessy loved Miss Galindo, too, for all the poor girl's scanty pleasures came from her, and Miss Galindo had always a kind word, and latterly, many a kind caress, for Mark Gibson's child; whereas, if she went to Dr. Trevor's for her holiday, she was overlooked and neglected in that bustling family, who seemed to think that if she had comfortable board and lodging under their roof, it was enough.

I am sure, now, that Miss Galindo had often longed to have Bessy to live with her; but, as long as she could pay for her being at school, she did not like to take so bold a step as bringing her home, knowing what the effect of the consequent explanation would be on my lady. And as the girl was now more than seventeen, and past the age when young ladies are usually kept at school; and, as there was no great demand for governesses in those days, and as Bessy had never been taught any trade by which to earn her own living, why, I don't exactly see what could have been done but for Miss Galindo to bring her to her own home in Hanbury. For, although the child had grown up lately, in a kind of unexpected manner, into a young woman, Miss Galindo mght have kept her at school for a year longer, if she could have afforded it; but this was impossible when she became Mr. Horner's clerk, and relinquished all the payment of her repository work; and perhaps, after all, she was not sorry to be compelled to take the steps she was longing for. At any rate, Bessy came to live with Miss Galindo in a very few weeks from the time when Captain James set Miss Galindo free to superintend her own domestic economy again.

For a long time, I knew nothing about this new inhabitant of Hanbury. My lady never mentioned her in any way. This was in accordance with Lady Ludlow's well-known principles. She neither saw nor heard, nor was in any way cognisant of the existence of those who had no legal right to exist at all. If Miss Galindo had hoped to have an exception made in Bessy's favour, she was mistaken. My lady sent a note inviting Miss Galindo herself to tea one evening, about a month after Bessy came; but Miss Galindo 'had a cold and could not come.' The next time she was invited, she 'had an engagement at home' – a step nearer to the absolute truth. And the third time, she 'had a young friend staying with her whom she was unable to leave.' My lady accepted every excuse as bonâ fide, and took no further notice. I missed Miss Galindo very much; we all did; for, in the days when she was clerk, she was sure to come in and find the opportunity of saying something amusing to some of us before she went away. And I, as an invalid, or perhaps from natural tendency, was particularly fond of little bits of village gossip. There was no Mr. Horner – he even had come in, now and then, with formal, stately pieces of intelligence – and there was no Miss Galindo in these days. I missed her much. And so did my lady, I am sure. Behind all her quiet, sedate manner, I am certain her heart ached

sometimes for a few words from Miss Galindo, who seemed
to have absented herself altogether from the Hall now Bessy
was come.

Captain James might be very sensible, and all that; but not
even my lady could call him a substitute for the old familiar
friends. He was a thorough sailor, as sailors were in those days
– swore a good deal, drank a good deal (without its ever
affecting him in the least), and was very prompt and kind-
hearted in all his actions; but he was not accustomed to
women, as my lady once said, and would judge in all things
for himself. My lady had expected, I think, to find someone
who would take his notions on the management of her estate
from her ladyship's own self; but he spoke as if he were
responsible for the good management of the whole and must,
consequently, be allowed full liberty of action. He had been
too long in command over men at sea to like to be directed by
a woman in anything he undertook, even though that woman
was my lady. I suppose this was the commonsense my lady
spoke of; but, when common sense goes against us, I don't
think we value it quite so much as we ought to do.

Lady Ludlow was proud of her personal superintendence of
her own estate. She liked to tell us how her father used to
take her with him on his rides, and bid her observe this and
that, and on no account to allow such and such things to
be done. But I have heard that, the first time she told all this
to Captain James, he told her point-blank that he had heard
from Mr. Smithson that the farms were much neglected and
the rents sadly behindhand, and that he meant to set to in
good earnest and study agriculture, and see how he could
remedy the state of things. My lady would, I am sure, be
greatly surprised; but what could she do? Here was the very
man she had chosen herself, setting to with all his energy
to conquer the defect of ignorance, which was all that those
who had presumed to offer her ladyship advice had ever had
to say against him. Captain James read Arthur Young's
'Tours' in all his spare time, as long as he was an invalid; and
shook his head at my lady's accounts as to how the land had
been cropped or left fallow from time immemorial. Then he
set to, and tried too many experiments at once. My lady
looked on in dignified silence; but all the farmers and tenants

were in an uproar, and prophesied a hundred failures. Perhaps
fifty did occur; they were only half as many as Lady Ludlow
had feared; but they were twice as many – four, eight times
as many – as the captain had anticipated. His openly-expressed
disappointment made him popular again. The rough country-
people could not have understood silent and dignified regret
at the failure of his plans; but they sympathised with a man
who swore at his ill success – sympathised, even while they
chuckled over his discomfiture. Mr. Brooke, the retired
tradesman, did not cease blaming him for not succeeding,
and for swearing. 'But what could you expect from a sailor?'
Mr. Brooke asked, even in my lady's hearing; though he
might have known Captain James was my lady's own
personal choice, from the old friendship Mr. Urian had always
shown for him. I think it was this speech of the Birmingham
baker's that made my lady determine to stand by Captain
James, and encourage him to try again. For she would not
allow that her choice had been an unwise one, at the bidding
(as it were) of a dissenting tradesman; the only person in the
neighbourhood, too, who had flaunted about in coloured
clothes, when all the world was in mourning for my lady's
only son.

Captain James would have thrown the agency up at once, if
my lady had not felt herself bound to justify the wisdom of her
choice, by urging him to stay. He was much touched by her
confidence in him, and swore a great oath, that the next year
he would make the land such as it had never been before for
produce. It was not my lady's way to repeat anything she had
heard, especially to another person's disadvantage. So I don't
think she ever told Captain James of Mr. Brooke's speech
about a sailor's being likely to mismanage the property; and
the captain was too anxious to succeed in this, the second, year
of his trial, to be above going to the flourishing, shrewd Mr.
Brooke, and asking for his advice as to the best method of
working the estate. I dare say, if Miss Galindo had been as
intimate as formerly at the Hall, we should all of us have heard
of this new acquaintance of the agent's long before we did. As
it was, I am sure my lady never dreamed that the captain, who
held opinions that were even more Church and King than her
own, could ever have made friends with a Baptist baker from

Birmingham, even to serve her ladyship's own interests in the most loyal manner.

We heard of it first from Mr. Gray, who came now often to see my lady; for neither he nor she could forget the solemn tie which the fact of his being the person to acquaint her with my lord's death had created between them. For true and holy words spoken at that time, though having no reference to aught below the solemn subjects of life and death, had made her withdraw her opposition to Mr. Gray's wish about establishing a village school. She had sighed a little, it is true, and was even yet more apprehensive than hopeful as to the result; but, almost as if as a memorial to my lord, she had allowed a kind of rough school house to be built on the green, just by the church; and had gently used the power she undoubtedly had, in expressing her strong wish that the boys might only be taught to read and write, and the first four rules of arithmetic, while the girls were only to learn to read, and to add up in their heads, and the rest of the time to work at mending their own clothes, knitting stockings, and spinning. My lady presented the school with more spinning-wheels than there were girls, and requested that there might be a rule that they should have spun so many hanks of flax, and knitted so many pairs of stockings, before they ever were taught to read at all. After all, it was but making the best of a bad job with my poor lady – but life was not what it had been to her. I remember well the day that Mr. Gray pulled some delicately fine yarn (and I was a good judge of those things) out of his pocket, and laid it and a capital pair of knitted stockings before my lady, as the first-fruits, so to say, of his school. I recollect seeing her put on her spectacles, and carefully examine both productions. Then she passed them to me.

'This is well, Mr. Gray. I am much pleased. You are fortunate in your schoolmistress. She has had both proper knowledge of womanly things and much patience. Who is she? One out of our village?'

'My lady,' said Mr. Gray, stammering and colouring in his old fashion, 'Miss Bessy is so very kind as to teach all those sorts of things – Miss Bessy, and Miss Galindo, sometimes.'

My lady looked at him over her spectacles: but she only repeated the words 'Miss Bessy,' and paused, as if trying to remember who such a person could be: and he, if he had then intended to say more, was quelled by her manner, and dropped the subject. He went on to say that he had thought it his duty to decline the subscription to his school offered by Mr. Brooke, because he was a Dissenter; that he (Mr. Gray) feared that Captain James, through whom Mr. Brooke's offer of money had been made, was offended at his refusing to accept it from a man who held heterodox opinions; nay, whom Mr. Gray suspected of being infected by Dodwell's heresy.

'I think there must be some mistake,' said my lady, 'or I have misunderstood you. Captain James would never know enough of a schismatic to be employed by that man Brooke in distributing his charities. I should have doubted, until now, if Captain James knew him.'

'Indeed, my lady, he not only knows him, but is intimate with him, I regret to say. I have repeatedly seen the captain and Mr. Brooke walking together; going through the fields together; and people do say –'

My lady looked up in interrogation at Mr. Gray's pause.

'I disapprove of gossip, and it may be untrue; but people do say that Captain James is very attentive to Miss Brooke.'

'Impossible!' said my lady indignantly. 'Captain James is a loyal and religious man. I beg your pardon, Mr. Gray; but it is impossible.'

CHAPTER XIV

Like many other things which have been declared to be impossible, this report of Captain James being attentive to Miss Brooke turned out to be very true.

The mere idea of her agent being on the slightest possible terms of acquaintance with the Dissenter, the tradesman, the Birmingham democrat, who had come to settle in our good, orthodox, aristocratic, and agricultural Hanbury, made my lady very uneasy. Miss Galindo's misdemeanour in having taken Miss Bessy to live with her, faded into a mistake, a mere error of judgment, in comparison with Captain James's intimacy at Yeast House, as the Brookes called their ugly square-built farm. My lady talked herself quite into complacency with Miss Galindo, and even Miss Bessy was named by her, the first time I had ever been aware that my lady recognised her existence; but – I recollect it was a long rainy afternoon, and I sat with her ladyship, and we had time and opportunity for a long uninterrupted talk – whenever we had been silent for a little while she began again, with something like a wonder how it was that Captain James could ever have commenced an acquaintance with 'that man Brooke.' My lady recapitulated all the times she could remember, that anything had occurred, or been said by Captain James which she could now understand as throwing light upon the subject.

'He said once that he was anxious to bring in the Norfolk system of cropping, and spoke a good deal about Mr. Coke of Holkham (who, by the way, was no more a Coke than I am – collateral in the female line – which counts for little or nothing among the great old commoners' families of pure blood), and his new ways of cultivation; of course new men bring in new ways, but it does not follow that either are better than the old ways. However, Captain James has been very anxious to try turnips and bone-manure, and he really is a man of such good sense and energy, and was so sorry last year about the failure, that I consented; and now I begin to see my error. I have always heard that town bakers adulterate their flour with bone-dust; and, of course, Captain James would be aware of this, and go to Brooke to inquire where the article was to be purchased.'

My lady always ignored the fact which had sometimes, I suspect, been brought under her very eyes during her drives, that Mr. Brooke's few fields were in a state of far higher cultivation than her own; so she could not, of course, perceive that there was any wisdom to be gained from asking the advice of the tradesman turned farmer.

But, by-and-by, this fact of her agent's intimacy with the person whom in the whole world she most disliked (with that sort of dislike in which a large amount of uncomfortableness is combined – the dislike which conscientious people sometimes feel to another without knowing why, and yet which they cannot indulge in with comfort to themselves without having a moral reason why), came before my lady in many shapes. For, indeed, I am sure that Captain James was not a man to conceal or be ashamed of one of his actions. I cannot fancy his ever lowering his strong loud clear voice, or having a confidential conversation with any one. When his crops had failed, all the village had known it. He complained, he regretted, he was angry, or owned himself a   fool, all down the village street; and the consequence was that, although he was a far more passionate man than Mr. Horner, all the tenants liked him far better. People, in general, take a kindlier interest in any one the workings of whose mind and heart they can watch and understand, than in a man who only lets you know what he has been thinking about and feeling by what he does. But Harry Gregson was faithful to the memory of Mr. Horner. Miss Galindo has told me that she used to watch him hobble out of the way of Captain James, as if to accept his notice, however good naturedly given, would have been a kind of treachery to his former benefactor. But Gregson (the father) and the new agent rather took to each other; and one day, much to my surprise, I heard that the 'poaching, tinkering vagabond,' as the people used to call Gregson when I first had come to live at Hanbury, had been appointed game-keeper;

Mr. Gray standing godfather, as it were, to his trustworthi-
ness, if he were trusted with anything; which I thought at the
time was rather an experiment – only it answered, as many of
Mr. Gray's deeds of daring did. It was curious how he was
growing to be a kind of autocrat in the village; and how
unconscious he was of it. He was as shy and awkward and
nervous as ever in any affair that was not of some more moral
consequence to him. But, as soon as he was convinced that a
thing was right, he 'shut his eyes and ran and butted at it like a
ram,' as Captain James once expressed it, in talking over
something Mr. Gray had done. People in the village said,
'they never knew what the parson would be at next;' or, they
might have said, 'where his reverence would next turn up.'
For I have heard of his marching right into the middle of a set
of poachers, gathered together for some desperate midnight
enterprise, or walking into a public-house that lay just beyond
the bounds of my lady's estate, and in that extra-parochial
piece of ground I named long ago, and which was considered
the rendezvous of all the ne'er-do-well characters for miles
round, and where a parson and a constable were held in much
the same kind of esteem as unwelcome visitors. And yet Mr.
Gray had his long fits of depression, in which he felt as if he
were doing nothing, making no way in his work, useless and
unprofitable, and better out of the world than in it. In
comparison with the work he had set himself to do, what he
did seemed to be nothing. I suppose it was constitutional,
these attacks of lowness of spirits which he had about this
time; perhaps a part of the nervousness which made him
always so awkward when he came to the Hall. Even Mrs.
Medlicott, who almost worshipped the ground he trod on, as
the saying is, owned that Mr. Gray never entered one of my
lady's rooms without knocking down something, and too
often breaking it. He would much sooner have faced a
desperate poacher than a young lady any day. At least so we
thought.

I do not know how it was that it came to pass that my lady
become reconciled to Miss Galindo about this time. Whether
it was that her ladyship was weary of the unspoken coolness
with her old friend; or that the specimens of delicate sewing
and fine spinning at the school had mollified her towards Miss

Bessy; but I was surprised to learn one day that Miss Galindo
and her young friend were coming that very evening to tea at
the Hall. This information was given me by Mrs. Medlicott,
as a message from my lady, who further went on to desire that
certain little preparations should be made in her own private
sitting-room, in which the greater part of my days were spent.
From the nature of these preparations, I became quite aware
that my lady intended to do honour to her expected visitors.
Indeed, Lady Ludlow never forgave by halves, as I have
known some people do. Whoever was coming as a visitor to
my lady, peeress, or poor nameless girl, there was a certain
amount of preparation required in order to do them fitting
honour. I do not mean to say that the preparation was of the
same degree of importance in each case. I dare say, if a peeress
had come to visit us at the Hall, the covers would have been
taken off the furniture in the white drawing-room (they never
were uncovered all the time I stayed at the Hall), because my
lady would wish to offer her the ornaments and luxuries
which this grand visitor (who never came – I wish she had! I
did so want to see that furniture uncovered!) was accustomed
to at home, and to present them to her in the best order in
which my lady could. The same rule, mollified, held good
with Miss Galindo. Certain things, in which my lady knew
she took an interest, were laid out ready for her to examine on
this very day; and what was more, great books of prints were
laid out, such as I remembered my lady had brought forth to
beguile my own early days of illness – Mr. Hogarth's works,
and the like – which I was sure were put out for Miss Bessy.

No one knows how curious I was to see this mysterious
Miss Bessy – twenty times more mysterious, of course, for
want of her surname. And then again (to try and account for
my great curiosity, of which in recollection I am more than
half ashamed), I had been leading the quiet monotonous life of
a crippled invalid for many years – shut up from any sight of
new faces; and this was to be the face of one whom I had
thought about so much and so long – Oh! I think I might be
excused.

Of course they drank tea in the great hall, with the four
young gentlewomen, who, with myself, formed the small
bevy now under her ladyship's charge. Of those who were at

Hanbury when first I came, none remained; all were married, or gone once more to live at some home which could be called their own, whether the ostensible head were father or brother. I myself was not without some hopes of a similar kind. My brother Harry was now a curate in Westmoreland, and wanted me to go and live with him, as eventually I did for a time. But that is neither here nor there at present. What I am talking about is Miss Bessy.

After a reasonable time had elapsed, occupied as I well knew by the meal in the great hall – the measured, yet agreeable conversation afterwards – and a certain promenade around the hall, and through the drawing-rooms, with pauses before different pictures, the history or subject of each of which was invariably told by my lady to every new visitor – a sort of giving them the freedom of the old family seat, by describing the kind and nature of the great progenitors who had lived there before the narrator – I heard the steps approaching my lady's room, where I lay. I think I was in such a state of nervous expectation that, if I could have moved easily, I should have got up and ran away. And yet I need not have been, for Miss Galindo was not in the least altered (her nose a little redder to be sure, but then that might only have had a temporary cause in the private crying I know she would have had before coming to see her dear Lady Ludlow once again). But I could almost have pushed Miss Galindo away, as she intercepted me in my view of the mysterious Miss Bessy.

Miss Bessy was, as I knew, only about eighteen, but she looked older. Dark hair, dark eyes, a tall, firm figure, a good, sensible face, with a serene expression, not in the least disturbed by what I had been thinking must be such awful circumstances as a first introduction to my lady, who had so disapproved of her very existence: those are the clearest impressions I remember of my first interview with Miss Bessy. She seemed to observe us all, in her quiet manner, quite as much as I did her; but she spoke very little; occupied herself, indeed, as my lady had planned, with looking over the great books of engravings. I think I must have (foolishly) intended to make her feel at her ease, by my patronage; but she was seated far away from my sofa, in order to command the light, and really seemed so unconcerned at her unwonted circumst-

ances, that she did not need my countenance or kindness. One
thing I did like – her watchful look at Miss Galindo from time
to time: it showed that her thoughts and sympathy were ever
at Miss Galindo's service, as indeed they well might be. When
Miss Bessy spoke, her voice was full and clear, and what she
said, to the purpose, though there was a slight provincial
accent in her way of speaking. After a while, my lady set us
two to play at chess, a game which I had lately learnt at Mr.
Gray's suggestion. Still we did not talk much together,
though we were becoming attracted towards each other, I
fancy.

'You will play well,' said she. 'You have only learnt about
six months, have you? And yet you can nearly beat me, who
have been at it as many years.'

'I began to learn last November. I remember Mr. Gray's
bringing me "Philidor on Chess," one very foggy, dismal
day.'

What made her look up so suddenly, with bright inquiry in
her eyes? What made her silent for a moment, as if in thought,
and then go on with something, I know not what, in quite an
altered tone?

My lady and Miss Galindo went on talking, while I sat
thinking. I heard Captain James's name mentioned pretty
frequently; and at last my lady put down her work, and said,
almost with tears in her eyes –

'I could not – I cannot believe it. He must be aware she is a
schismatic; a baker's daughter; and he is a gentleman by virtue
and feeling, as well as by his profession, though his manners
may be at times a little rough. My dear Miss Galindo, what
will this world come to?'

Miss Galindo might possibly be aware of her own share in
bringing the world to the pass which now dismayed my lady –
for, of course, though all was now over and forgiven, yet Miss
Bessy's being received into a respectable maiden lady's house,
was one of the portents as to the world's future which alarmed
her ladyship; and Miss Galindo knew this – but, at any rate,
she had too lately been forgiven herself not to plead for mercy
for the next offender against my lady's delicate sense of fitness
and propriety – so she replied –

'Indeed, my lady, I have long left off trying to conjecture

what makes Jack fancy Gill, or Gill Jack. It's best to sit down quiet under the belief that marriages are made for us, somewhere out of this world, and out of the range of this world's reason and laws. I'm not so sure that I should settle it down that they were made in heaven; t'other place seems to me as likely a workshop; but at any rate, I've given up troubling my head as to why they take place. Captain James is a gentleman: I make no doubt of that ever since I saw him stop to pick up old Goody Blake (when she tumbled down on the slide last winter) and then swear at a little lad who was laughing at her, and cuff him till he tumbled down crying; but we must have bread somehow, and though I like it better baked at home in a good sweet brick oven, yet, as some folks never can get it to rise, I don't see why a man may not be a baker. You see, my lady, I look upon baking as a simple trade, and as such lawful. There is no machine comes in to take away a man's or woman's power of earning their living, like the spinning-jenny (the old busybody that she is), to knock up all our good old women's livelihood, and send them to their graves before their time. There's an invention of the enemy, if you will?'

'That's very true!' said my lady, shaking her head.

'But baking bread is wholesome, straightforward elbow work. They have not got to inventing any contrivance for that yet, thank Heaven! It does not seem to me natural, nor according to Scripture, that iron and steel (whose brows can't sweat) should be made to do man's work. And so I say, all those trades where iron and steel do the work ordained to man at the Fall, are unlawful, and I never stand up for them. But, say this baker Brooke did knead his bread, and make it rise, and then that people, who had, perhaps, no good ovens, came to him, and bought his good light bread, and in this manner he turned an honest penny and got rich: why, all I say, my lady, is this – I dare say he would have been born a Hanbury, or a lord if he could; and if he was not, it is no fault of his, that I can see, that he made good bread (being a baker by trade), and got money, and bought his land. It was his misfortune, not his fault, that he was not a person of quality by birth.'

'That's very true,' said my lady, after a moment's pause for consideration. 'But, although he was a baker, he might have been a Churchman. Even your eloquence, Miss Galindo, shan't convince me that that is not his own fault.'

'I don't see even that, begging your pardon, my lady,' said Miss Galindo, emboldened by the first success of her eloquence. 'When a Baptist is a baby, if I understand their creed aright, he is not baptized; and, consequently, he can have no godfathers and godmothers to do anything for him in his baptism; you agree to that, my lady?'

My lady would rather have known what her acquiescence would lead to, before acknowledging that she could not dissent from this first proposition; still she gave her tacit agreement by bowing her head.

'And, you know, our godfathers and godmothers are expected to promise and vow three things in our name, when we are little babies, and can do nothing but squall for ourselves. It is a great privilege, but don't let us be hard upon those who have not had the chance of godfathers and godmothers. Some people, we know, are born with silver spoons – that's to say, a godfather to give one things, and teach us our catechism, and see that we're confirmed into good church-going Christians – and others with wooden ladles in their mouths. These poor last folks must just be content to be godfatherless orphans, and Dissenters all their lives; and if they are tradespeople into the bargain, so much the worse for them; but let us be humble Christians, my dear lady, and not hold our heads too high because we were born orthodox quality.'

'You go on too fast, Miss Galindo! I can't follow you. Besides, I do believe dissent to be an invention of the Devil's– Why can't they believe as we do? It's very wrong. Besides, it's schism and heresy, and, you know, the Bible says that's as bad as witchcraft.'

My lady was not convinced, as I could see. After Miss Galindo had gone, she sent Mrs. Medlicott for certain books out of the great old library upstairs, and had them made up into a parcel under her own eye.

'If Captain James comes tomorrow, I will speak to him about these Brookes. I have not hitherto liked to speak to him, because I did not wish to hurt him, by supposing there could be any truth in the reports about his intimacy with them. But now I will try and do my duty by him and them. Surely, this great body of divinity will bring them back to be true Church.'

I could not tell, for though my lady read me over the titles, I was not any the wiser as to their contents. Besides, I was much more anxious to consult my lady as to my own change of place. I showed her the letter I had that day received from Harry; and we once more talked over the expediency of my going to live with him, and trying what entire change of air would do to re-establish my failing health. I could say anything to my lady, she was so sure to understand me rightly. For one thing, she never thought of herself, so I had no fear of hurting her by stating the truth. I told her how happy my years had been while passed under her roof; but that now I had begun to wonder whether I had not duties elsewhere, in making a home for Harry – and whether the fulfilment of these duties, quiet ones they must needs be in the case of such a cripple as myself, would not prevent my sinking into the querulous habit of thinking and talking, into which I found myself occasionally falling. Add to which, there was the prospect of benefit from the more bracing air of the north.

It was then settled that my departure from Hanbury, my happy home for so long, was to take place before many weeks had passed. And as, when one period of life is about to be shut up for ever, we are sure to look back upon it with fond regret, so I, happy enough in my future prospects, could not avoid recurring to all the days of my life in the Hall, from the time when I came to it, a shy awkward girl scarcely past childhood, to now, when a grown woman – past childhood – almost, from the very character of my illness, past youth – I was looking forward to leaving my lady's house (as a residence) for ever. As it has turned out, I never saw her or it again. Like a piece of sea-wreck, I have drifted away from those days: quiet, happy, eventless days – very happy to remember!

I thought of good, jovial Mr. Mountford, and his regrets that he might not keep a pack – 'a very small pack' – of harriers, and his merry ways, and his love of good eating; of the first coming of Mr. Gray, and my lady's attempt to quench his sermons, when they tended to enforce any duty connected with eduction. And now we had an absolute schoolhouse in the village; and, since Miss Bessy's drinking tea at the Hall, my lady had been twice inside it, to give directions about some fine yarn she was having spun for table-napery. And her ladyship had so outgrown her old custom of dispensing with sermon or discourse, that even during the temporary preaching of Mr. Crosse, she had never had recourse to it, though I believe she would have had all the congregation on her side if she had.

And Mr. Horner was dead, and Captain James reigned in his stead. Good, steady, severe, silent Mr. Horner, with his clock-like regularity, and his snuff-coloured clothes, and silver buckles! I have often wondered which one misses most when they are dead and gone – the bright creatures full of life, who are hither and thither and everywhere, so that no one can reckon upon their coming and going, with whom stillness and the long quiet of the grave, seems utterly irreconcilable, so full are they of vivid motion and passion – or the slow, serious people, whose movements, nay, whose very words, seem to go by clockwork; who never appear much to affect the course of our life while they are with us, but whose methodical ways show themselves, when they are gone, to have been inter-twined with our very roots of daily existence. I think I miss these last the most, although I may have loved the former best. Captain James never was to me what Mr. Horner was, though the latter had hardly exchanged a dozen words with me at the day of his death. Then Miss Galindo! I remember the time as if it had been only yesterday, when she was but a name – and a very odd one – to me; then she was a queer, abrupt, disagreeable, busy old maid. Now I loved her dearly, and I found out that I was almost jealous of Miss Bessy.

Mr. Gray I never thought of with love; the feeling was almost reverence with which I looked upon him. I have not wished to speak much of myself, or else I could have told you how much he had been to me during these long, weary years of illness. But he was almost as much to everyone, rich and poor, from my lady down to Miss Galindo's Sally.

The village too, had a different look about it. I am sure I could not tell you what caused the change; but there were no more lounging young men to form a group at the cross roads, at a time of day when young men ought to be at work. I don't say this was all Mr. Gray's doing, for there really was so much

to do in the fields that there was but little time for lounging
now-a-days. And the children were hushed up in school, and
better behaved out of it, too, than in the days when I used to
be able to go my lady's errands in the village. I went so little
about now that I am sure I can't tell who Miss Galindo found
to scold; and yet she looked so well and so happy that I think
she must have had her accustomed portion of that wholesome
exercise.

Before I left Hanbury, the rumour that Captain James was
going to marry Miss Brooke, Baker Brooke's eldest daughter,
who only had a sister to share his property with her, was
confirmed. He himself announced it to my lady, nay more,
with a courage, gained, I suppose, in his former profession,
where, as I have heard, he had led his ship into many a post of
danger, he asked her ladyship, the Countess Ludlow, if he
might bring his bride-elect (the Baptist baker's daughter) and
present her to my lady.

I am glad I was not present when he made this request; I
should have felt so much ashamed for him, and I could not
have helped being anxious till I heard my lady's answer, if I
had been there. Of course she acceded; but I can fancy the
grave surprise of her look. I wonder if Captain James noticed
it.

I hardly dared ask my lady, after the interview had taken
place, what she thought of the bride-elect; but I hinted my
curiosity, and she told me, that if the young person had
applied to Mrs. Medlicott for the situation of cook, and Mrs.
Medlicott had engaged her, she thought that it would have
been a very suitable arrangement. I understood from this how
little she thought a marriage with Captain James, R.N.,
suitable.

About a year after I left Hanbury, I received a letter from
Miss Galindo; I think I can find it. – Yes, this is it.

'HANBURY, *May* 4, 1811
'Dear Margaret, – You ask for news of us all. Don't you
know there is no news in Hanbury? Did you ever hear of an
event here? Now, if you have answered "Yes" in your own
mind to these questions, you have fallen into my trap, and
never were more mistaken in your life. Hanbury is full of

news, and we have more events on our hands than we know what to do with. I will take them in the order of the newspapers – births, deaths and marriages. In the matter of births, Jenny Lucas has had twins not a week ago. Sadly too much of a good thing, you'll say. Very true: but then they died; so their birth did not much signify. My cat has kittened, too; she has had three kittens, which again you may observe is too much of a good thing; and so it would be, if it were not for the next item of intelligence I shall lay down before you. Captain and Mrs. James have taken the old house next to Pearson's; and the house is overrun with mice, which is just as fortunate for me as the King of Egypt's rat-ridden kingdom was to Dick Whittington. For my cat's kittening decided me to go and call on the bride, in hopes she wanted a cat; which she did like a sensible woman, as I do believe she is, in spite of Baptism, Bakers, Bread, and Birmingham, and something worse than all, which you shall hear about, if you'll only be patient. As I had got my best bonnet on, the one I bought when poor Lord Ludlow was last at Hanbury in '99 – I thought it a great condescension in myself (always remember-ing the date of the Galindo baronetcy) to go and call on the bride; though I don't think so much of myself in my every-day clothes, as you know. But who should I find there but my Lady Ludlow! She looks as frail and delicate as ever, but is, I think, in better heart ever since that old city merchant of a Hanbury took it into his head that he was a cadet of the Hanburys of Hanbury, and left her that handsome legacy. I'll warrant you that the mortgage was paid off pretty fast; and Mr. Horner's money – or my lady's money, or Harry Gregson's money, call it which you will – is invested in his name, all right and tight; and they do talk of his being captain of his school, or Grecian, or something, and going to college after all! Harry Gregson the poacher's son! Well! to be sure, we are living in strange times!

'But I have not done with the marriages yet. Captain James's is all very well, but no one cares for it now, we are so full of Mr. Gray's. Yes, indeed, Mr. Gray is going to be married, and to nobody else but my little Bessy! I tell her she will have to nurse him half the days of her life, he is such a frail little body. But she says she does not care for that; so that his

body holds his soul, it is enough for her. She has a good spirit
and a brave heart, has my Bessy! It is a great advantage that
she won't have to mark her clothes over again; for when she
had knitted herself her last set of stockings, I told her to put G
for Galindo, if she did not choose to put it for Gibson, for she
should be my child if she was no one else's. And now you see
it stands for Gray. So there are two marriages, and what more
would you have? And she promises to take another of my
kittens.

'Now, as to deaths, old Farmer Hale is dead – poor old man,
I should think his wife thought it a good riddance, for he beat
her every day that he was drunk, and he was never sober, in
spite of Mr. Gray. I don't think (as I tell him) that Mr. Gray
would ever have found courage to speak to Bessy as long as
Farmer Hale lived, he took the old gentleman's sins so much
to heart, and seemed to think it was all his fault for not being
able to make a sinner into a saint. The parish bull is dead too. I
never was so glad in my life. But they say we are to have a
new one in his place. In the meantime I cross the common in
peace, which is very convenient just now, when I have so
often to go to Mr. Gray's to see about furnishing.

'Now you think I have told you all the Hanbury news,
don't you? Not so. The very greatest thing of all is to come. I
won't tantalise you, but just out with it, for you would never
guess it. My Lady Ludlow has given a party, just like any
plebeian amongst us. We had tea and toast in the blue
drawing-room, old John Footman waiting with Tom Diggles,
the lad that used to frighten away crows in Farmer Hale's
fields, following in my lady's livery, hair powdered and
everything. Mrs. Medlicott made tea in my lady's own room.
My lady looked like a splendid fairy queen of mature age, in
black velvet, and the old lace, which I have never seen her
wear before since my lord's death. But the company? you'll
say. Why, we had the parson of Clover, and the parson of
Headleigh, and the parson of Merribank, and the three
parsonesses; and Farmer Donkin, and two Miss Donkins; and
Mr. Gray (of course), and myself and Bessy; and Captain and
Mrs. James; yes, and Mr. and Mrs. Brooke; think of that! I am
not sure the parsons liked it; but he was there. For he has been
helping Captain James to get my lady's land into order; and

then his daughter married the agent; and Mr. Gray (who ought to know) says that, after all, Baptists are not such bad people; and he was right against them at one time as you may remember. Mrs. Brooke is a rough diamond, to be sure. People have said that of me, I know. But, being a Galindo, I learnt manners in my youth, and can take them up when I choose. But Mrs. Brooke never learnt manners, I'll be bound. When John Footman handed her the tray with the tea-cups, she looked up at him as if she were sorely puzzled by that way of going on. I was sitting next to her, so I pretended not to see her perplexity, and put her cream and sugar in for her, and was all ready to pop it into her hands – when who should come up, but that impudent lad Tom Diggles (I call him lad, for all his hair is powdered, for you know that it is not natural grey hair) with his tray full of cakes and what not, all as good as Mrs. Medlicott could make them. By this time, I should tell you all the parsonesses were looking at Mrs. Brooke, for she had shown her want of breeding before; and the parsonesses, who were just a step above her in manners, were very much inclined to smile at her doings and sayings. Well! what does she do but pull out a clean Bandana pocket-handkerchief, all red and yellow silk; spread it over her best silk gown – it was, like enough, a new one, for I had it from Sally, who had it from her cousin Molly, who is dairy-woman "at the Brookes," that the Brookes were mighty set-up with an invitation to drink tea at the Hall. There we were, Tom Diggles even on the grin (I wonder how long it is since he was own brother to a scarecrow, only not so decently dressed) and Mrs. Parsoness of Headleigh – I forget her name, and it's no matter, for she's an ill-bred creature, I hope Bessy will behave herself better – was right-down bursting with laughter, and as near a hee-haw as ever a donkey was; when what does my lady do? Ay! there's my own dear Lady Ludlow, God bless her! She takes out her own pocket-handkerchief, all snowy cambric, and lays it softly down on her velvet lap, for all the world as if she did it every day of her life, just like Mrs. Brooke, the baker's wife; and when the one got up to shake the crumbs into the fireplace, the other did just the same. But with such a grace! and such a look at us all! Tom Diggles went red all over; and Mrs. Parsoness of Headleigh scarce spoke for the rest of the evening; and the tears came into my old silly eyes; and Mr. Gray, who was before silent and awkward in a way which I tell Bessy she must cure him of, was made so happy by this pretty action of my lady's that he talked away all the rest of the evening, and was the life of the company.

'Oh, Margaret Dawson! I sometimes wonder if you're the better off for leaving us. To be sure you're with your brother, and blood is blood. But when I look at my lady and Mr. Gray, for all they're so different, I would not change places with any in England.'

Alas! alas! I never saw my dear lady again. She died in eighteen hundred and fourteen, and Mr. Gray did not long survive her. As I dare say you know, the Reverend Henry Gregson is now vicar of Hanbury, and his wife is the daughter of Mr. Gray and Miss Bessy.

As any one may guess, it had taken Mrs. Dawson several Monday evenings to narrate all this history of the days of her youth. Miss Duncan thought it would be a good exercise for me, both in memory and composition, to write out on Tuesday mornings all that I had heard the night before; and thus it came to pass that I have the manuscript of 'My Lady Ludlow' now lying by me.